THE GIRL FROM BOLOGNA

SIOBHAN DAIKO

Boldwood

First published in 2022. This edition first published in Great Britain in 2023 by Boldwood Books Ltd.

Every effort has been made to obtain the necessary permissions with reference to copyright material, both illustrative and quoted. We apologise for any omissions in this respect and will be pleased to make the appropriate acknowledgements in any future edition.

A CIP catalogue record for this book is available from the British Library.

Paperback ISBN 978-1-80549-742-4

Large Print ISBN 978-1-80549-741-7

Hardback ISBN 978-1-80549-740-0

Ebook ISBN 978-1-80549-743-1

Kindle ISBN 978-1-80549-744-8

Audio CD ISBN 978-1-80549-735-6

MP3 CD ISBN 978-1-80549-736-3

Digital audio download ISBN 978-1-80549-738-7

Boldwood Books Ltd
23 Bowerdean Street
London SW6 3TN
www.boldwoodbooks.com

For Victor

'The past is never dead. It's not even past.'

— WILLIAM FAULKNER

MAIN LOCATIONS

PROLOGUE

LEILA, 25 SEPTEMBER 1943

Keeping my head down so as not to draw attention to myself, I made my way past the German tank stationed next to the Basilica of San Petronio. I was in a hurry to get home after spending the morning at the library and didn't want to waste time having my identity documents checked. I stopped. Listened. A distant rumble followed by the ominous drone of aircraft engines echoed in my ears. The terrifying noise grew louder, and I imagined a swarm of giant angry hornets hell-bent on destruction. Dread squeezing my chest, I risked a quick glance upwards. Heavy cloud cover billowed over Bologna; there was no sign of any planes.

But my heart skittered as a ricochet of explosions reverberated from the direction of the railway marshalling yards. Plumes of thick, black smoke spiralled into the sky.

Why hadn't there been any warning sirens like there had been when the Americans bombed the railway two months ago? Not that those alarms had done much good; they'd been set off too late, just as the aircraft had come into sight. Many of the bombs had fallen not only on the station but on the historic city centre, damaging buildings and killing innocent civilians who hadn't managed to reach safety.

Oh, dear God. I'd hoped against hope that our King's armistice with the Allies would have put an end to such attacks. Except, the Wehrmacht had occupied Bologna and were using it as a transportation hub, and I feared we'd become a prime target again.

The nearest shelter was in Strada Maggiore, but my best friend Rebecca's family palazzo was even closer. The Allies' bombers were clearly visible now, flying wingtip to wingtip in a V formation, like enormous silver geese migrating across the urban skies.

I raced into Piazza del Nettuno, my feet pounding on the smooth paving stones. I tore past the fountain then headed along Rizzoli Street towards the two iconic medieval leaning towers.

Would I reach safety before a stray bomb dropped on me? Perspiration beaded my brow and my chest ached.

At the top of Zamboni Street, I arrived at a nondescript wooden door. I rang the bell and waited impatiently, hopping from one foot to the other until Giulia, the Matatias' housekeeper, let me in.

'Hurry!' she said in Bolognese dialect. She grabbed my hand and pulled me towards a metal and stained-glass gate, which opened onto a square garden. Bologna had been built around its hidden spaces, but the Matatias' was even more impressive than most.

I sprinted after Giulia, following the gravel path skirting ancient trees and shrub-filled borders. A three-storey coral-coloured palazzo stood before me. 'Everyone has gone down to the cellar,' Giulia's voice shrilled.

I found Rebecca huddled on a dilapidated sofa next to her mother. 'Ciao,' she said. 'What are you doing here?'

I explained quickly, took in her doleful expression, and gave her a hug.

Rebecca was the same age as me, nearly nineteen, and we were about to start our Italian literature studies at Alma Mater Studiorum, Bologna's prestigious university, the oldest in the world. We'd been friends since early childhood. Rebecca's family was of Jewish origin but had been baptised as Roman Catholics to avoid persecution. She was an only child, the daughter of a wealthy industrialist father and a mother who stayed at home. I loved her like I would have loved a sister if I'd had one. We could have been sisters, in fact; we were quite beautiful then, had almost identical, amber-coloured eyes, high cheekbones, bow-shaped lips and long brunette hair.

I sat next to Rebecca while Giulia joined the rest the staff – the housemaid, cook, and gardener, crouched on bales of straw beside a coal heap.

The thunderous echo of the bombardment came through the ceiling of the cellar, making my ears ring. Conversation was impossible for the awful noise, so I lost myself in thought.

I remembered hearing the shocking news that German tanks had rolled into Bologna the day after our prime minister had announced that Italy had switched sides in the war. Nazi officials hung a swastika flag from the façade of the Hotel Baglioni – the best in the city – and had commandeered part of the first floor and a large lounge to the right of the lobby, which they converted into their administrative headquarters. Not one Italian authority had turned up for a formal handover. With total political chaos there weren't any Italian authorities at hand.

Over the next several days, the Wehrmacht put their military occupation into action. Repression and intimidation began immediately with the confiscation of automobiles, limits to bicycle transport, a curfew from 11 p.m. to 4 a.m., and restrictions on gatherings of more than three people. Worst of all, the Nazis set up transit camps for deportations and slave labour, interning deserters from the Italian army – those they hadn't already loaded onto cattle trucks and transported to Germany for their nefarious needs.

It was all too horrible, I thought, snuggling against Rebecca while poor Bologna was being bombed to bits. I prayed fervently that my mother, father, and brother were safe.

Gradually, the reverberation of explosions lessened and then finally came to a halt.

'We can go upstairs,' Rebecca said in a trembly voice.

We climbed the spiral staircase to the piano nobile. 'Please may I use your phone?' I asked.

'Of course.' Signora Matatia brushed a stray dark curl from her pale forehead. 'You must be worried about your family, dear.'

With trembling fingers I picked up the receiver and dialled home.

But the lines were down, and I couldn't get through.

'I should go,' I said. 'Thank you for sheltering me.'

Rebecca saw me to the street door. 'Send a message if you can. Let us know everyone is safe.'

'I'll try.' I kissed her on both cheeks. 'Daniele will be fine. I feel it in my bones.'

Rebecca had a crush on Dani, but my brother was ten years older than the two of us. A hard-working doctor, he didn't have much time for women, and certainly not for his little sister's best friend.

'I hope Paolo is all right,' Rebecca responded. Paolo was my sweetheart, a medical student at the university.

'He'll have found shelter, I'm sure.' But I was worried. I worried about him continuously. He'd been a secret member of the Partito d'Azione clandestine political party for the past six months, attending covert anti-fascist meetings alongside his friends, and I lived in constant fear of him being arrested. My gangly boy was terribly serious about everything; I just hoped his earnest attitude wouldn't lead to his death.

I stepped outside and my heart dropped. An acrid smell stung my nostrils. A desperate, dark-haired man was clawing through the brick rubble of a bombed building. A thin woman stood next to the man, weeping, cradling a baby whose face was so white he or she was obviously dead. Other crying people had gathered around a girl of about nine or ten who'd lost an arm. She lay silently bleeding to death before me in the street, her eyes glazed open. I'd never seen anyone die before. Nausea built in my throat and hot tears streamed down my cheeks. I stepped forward to help, but a policeman turned me away.

Choking on smoke and dust, I stood rooted to the spot. Fire raged in buildings further down the road, but the two stone towers ahead appeared intact. They'd endured since the twelfth century – a time when Bologna used to resemble a medieval Manhattan – it would take more than carpet bombing to destroy them now, I hoped.

Oh, God, how I prayed Mamma, Papà, and Dani were safe. Worry spurred me into action and, sobbing, I ran home.

1

LEILA – FEBRUARY 1981

I smooth the cover of the bed in my guest room and check that everything is as it should be for the arrival tomorrow of the exchange student from the UK I've agreed to host. Rhiannon Hughes, twenty-one years old, an undergraduate at Cardiff University. I frown, hoping I've done the right thing. But, since I took early retirement from teaching last year, I've been a little lonely. If only ill health hadn't forced me to give up the job I loved. I miss spending time with young people; my favourite nephew, Gianluca, seems too busy these days for his aged aunt. When I heard that Unibo, as the Studiorum is known now, was looking for people to offer rooms for foreign students to rent, I impetuously took advantage of the opportunity. Except, now I'm not so sure I'll cope. I'm supposed to provide breakfast and dinner for the girl and help improve her Italian, but my energy levels are so depleted these days I fall asleep at the blink of an eye.

I make my way down the corridor that divides the piano nobile of our palazzo in two. Papà's legal practice used to be on the ground floor, but now it's rented out to a hairdresser. The top floor is for storage. Back in the day, it accommodated a cook and a housemaid, but no longer. I manage the cooking on my own, and a cleaner comes in twice a week.

Taking a deep breath, I step into my book-lined study. This is where I used to spend the afternoons, marking my pupils' essays, preparing lessons, and researching. When I first retired, it was wonderful to have more time to myself, to catch up on reading for pleasure, to be able to enjoy just sitting and doing nothing. But nature abhors a vacuum, and my mind, no longer occupied with work, soon began to be filled with memories – fleeting at first then increasingly tangible.

When a bomb, planted in the first-class waiting room, destroyed the west wing of Bologna station last August – an atrocity attributed to right-wing terrorists – I started to remember with ever greater clarity what happened during the German occupation four decades ago – those terrible times I've tried not to think about ever since. My declining health has led me to fear I won't live to a great old age. What purpose has my life served? Will I die without leaving a trace of who I once was?

I've attempted to write everything down but have found holding a pen for any length of time tires me. After wracking my brains, I hit upon the idea of buying a cassette tape recorder. My speaking skills have been honed by years in the classroom; it shouldn't be too difficult to dictate my memoirs. I won't publish them; I'll leave them with my papers for posterity.

Just last week, I read William Faulkner's *Requiem for a Nun* in translation. His words, 'The past is never dead. It's not even past,' resonated with me. It's true; the past is *never* past. I can no longer bury what happened; I can no longer forget. Evil has come to Bologna once more. The fascists have raised their ugly heads again. With a shudder, I remember that man with the pockmarked face, the man I've always thought of as my nemesis. I bought a Beretta pistol – I learnt how to shoot one during the war – and now I keep it fully loaded, hidden in the cupboard by my front door.

Bitter bile rises in my throat. I swallow it down and open the drawer of my desk. I began to dictate my memoirs yesterday, describing the disastrous bombing of Bologna on 25 September 1943, when the planes came without being sighted in time for any warning sirens. Over nine hundred people lost their lives in that raid, many of them caught in unprotected buildings or even out on the streets. Images of the dead baby and the young girl who died in front of me are so vivid in my head they could have occurred yesterday.

With a heavy sigh, I take out my Philips recorder, press play, and listen. My voice sounds cracked with emotion, rasping almost. I pour a glass of water from the carafe I placed on the sideboard earlier and take a sip. Then I clear my throat, pick up my microphone, and speak.

For the first week or so of the Nazi occupation, Bolognese fascists kept themselves out of political life. But when Hitler made Mussolini the puppet ruler of La Repubblica Sociale Italiana, i fascisti bolognesi became ardent members of the Duce's reformed anti-monarchist Republican Fascist Party. The repubblichini, as we scathingly called them, started working hand in glove with the crucchi, our depreciative word for the Germans.

I tried to keep a low profile and focus on my literature studies at the university, aiming to live as normal a life as possible given the circumstances. But soon it became impossible to ignore what was going on.

To thwart the invasion, a National Liberation Committee was established by antifascists in Milan. They tasked the Bologna branch with directing urban guerrilla partisan actions and taking on the role of a covert government.

Gruppi di Azione Patriotica sprang up in cities throughout the north. Born on the initiative of the clandestine Communist Party, the gappisti started attacking the Nazis and fascists openly. It didn't take long for violence to erupt. And my quiet, studious life was about to change.

The partisans had set up a secret workshop to package explosives. On 15 December, they exploded a bomb in the headquarters of a German cartographic department. Shortly afterwards another guerrilla bomb destroyed a brothel frequented by Nazi officers. Prostitutes were and still are a fixture in the seedier parts of the city. When Paolo told me what had happened, I hoped none of those women had died. My sweet boy couldn't tell me whether they had or not. But when the gappisti placed a bomb in Ristorante Diana, under a table usually reserved for the German military, it exploded and killed two innocent civilians. It was time for the partisans to alter their tactics.

Three days later, the commander of the German Security Service brought forward the curfew to 6 p.m., fined the city five hundred thousand lire, and promised a one hundred thousand lire reward to anyone who could help identify the perpetrators of the attacks. Many Bolognese, impoverished by the war, took advantage of such rewards throughout the twenty months of the German occupation to spy and report on the partisans. But still our freedom fighters were prepared to risk everything.

On the morning of 26 January 1944, I remember, Eugenio Facchini, commissioner of the Bolognese branch of the Republican Fascist Party, was shot dead by gappisti while climbing the stairs of the Casa dello Studente – the student canteen in Zamboni Street where he liked to have lunch. After the assault, the fascists established a self-styled military court which summarily tried ten antifascists who were in the prison of San Giovanni in Monte. The next day they were executed by firing squad. It was the start of a reign of terror in Bologna. I would come to look fear in the face while I lost loved ones and battled my nemesis.

And, as if that wasn't enough, we were still subjected to bombing by the Allies. The first raid of 1944 took place on 29 January. Thirty-nine American B-17s, again aiming for the railway marshalling yards, dropped tons of bombs that missed their target and fell on the city. I was at the university with Rebecca. The wail of the warning sirens sent us racing with our classmates to the nearest shelter. Afterwards, we learnt that the bombs had reduced over one hundred buildings to rubble, and that they'd killed or wounded many innocent civilians. We wept when we heard that the Archiginnasio, situated in the centre of Bologna and one of our most important university edifices dating from the sixteenth century, had also received a direct hit.

Another raid occurred on 22 March, when two hundred civilians died after the Leopardi street air raid shelter collapsed due to being struck by a stray bomb. On 7 April, the Allies managed to hit their target but explosives fell on the outskirts of the city as well. Three further raids caused little damage but, on 13 May, Bologna was attacked by over two hundred aircraft; they dropped an estimated three hundred and eighty tons of bombs on the central station and the marshalling yards. But they also struck the city, causing damage to myriad buildings, killing more than one hundred people and wounding over two hundred others. Hotel Brun, in Ugo Bassi Street, was reduced to rubble. The south-west corner of the Town Hall, near the Basilica of San Petronio, was destroyed. The Maggiore Hospital, filled with doctors and patients, received a direct hit. Many Bolognese had mistaken the raid for the daily ten o'clock air drill and had gone about their business as usual.

That was the final drop that overspilled the glass as far as my parents were concerned. Papà decided to take Mamma to Asiago in the Veneto mountains, where we had a holiday house to escape the *heat of Bologna in the summers. He tried to persuade me to go with them, but I didn't want to miss any of my university classes. Papà wasn't an authoritarian father; he let my brother and me make our own decisions once he'd considered we were old enough. Daniele promised he would keep an eye on me; he still lived at home then. Mamma wasn't happy to leave me but, like most women in the 1940s, she deferred to her husband. He insisted on their going. Mamma was suffering from her nerves, hadn't been sleeping properly for months and had lost so much weight she'd become frail and sickly. I'll never forget her distraught face as Dani and I waved her and Papà off in his Fiat 1100, the car in which I'd learnt to drive. 'The Allies will liberate us soon,' he said. 'We'll be back before you know it.*

Built-up emotion strains my throat. I push the stop button and take a sip of water. What I'll describe next hangs heavy on my heart – the inciting event that changed everything, converting me from an observer to a participant. I press record and, in a flat voice to prevent myself breaking down, I resume my story.

I went to visit Rebecca the afternoon after my parents left. I remember climbing the stairs to the piano nobile and following her into the Matatias' living room. It was such a beautiful place. Intricate glass and ironwork chandeliers hung from the centre of the coffered ceiling. Thick carpets the colour of whipped cream stretched over darkly lustrous parquet. I loved the nineteenth-century paintings – landscapes and portraits – covering the walls, and the fact that there were books, most of them re-bound, in rows behind the glass doors of huge, dark mahogany bookcases. Despite it being spring already, mammoth radiators released heat on a scale which at home Papà would have declared plain crazy – a heat redolent of a luxury hotel rather than a private dwelling, and of such intensity that, almost immediately, breaking out in a sweat, I'd had to take off my cardigan.

Giulia served us with tea on a silver tray, and we sat on leather chairs, eating home-made cupcakes while we chatted about the essay which we were due to hand in the following week. 'Let's go up to my room and listen to records,' Rebecca suggested after we'd eaten our fill.

A radiogram held pride of place by her bedroom door – a Philips as chance would have it, like the cassette recorder I'm using now. Rebecca had eclectic tastes and her collection consisted of a bit of everything: Monteverdi, Scarlatti, Bach, Mozart, Beethoven. But it was her jazz records which thrilled me most. Louis Armstrong, Duke Ellington, Fats Waller, Benny Goodman. I didn't have any records of my own in those days, and relished listening to hers.

We tapped our feet to Ellington's 'It Don't Mean a Thing (If It Ain't Got That Swing)'. I didn't speak any English – I still don't – but not even the happy-go-lucky sentiment conveyed by the music could dispel the disquiet preying on my mind, a sense of impending doom. Ever since the Germans had occupied Bologna, they'd been rounding up Jews. I'd mentioned my fear for her family to Rebecca before, but she'd assured me that her father had covered all traces of their origins.

I fixed her with a concerned look as the song came to an end. 'Did you hear that the Germans have been arresting Jews?' I reached across the space between us and held Rebecca's hand in mine. 'Shouldn't you and your parents go into hiding?'

She scoffed and squeezed my fingers. 'We're Bolognese. We haven't done anything wrong. Father's factory is manufacturing car parts. It's important work and, much as he hates it, the Nazis buy them from him and send them to Germany. We'll be fine, Leila. No need to be concerned.'

I took Rebecca at her word. What else could I do? We decided she should come to my place the next day, Sunday, so we could go for an afternoon hike along the porticoes leading to the Sanctuary of the Madonna di San Luca on a hill overlooking the city. It was our favourite passeggiata and we loved to walk under the winding vault arcades, *over six hundred of them, almost four kilometres leading from the Saragozza gate at the edge of the old part of the city.*

Rebecca saw me to the door and kissed me on both cheeks. 'See you tomorrow.' She paused and added with a blush. 'I hope to see Dani too.'

'You might well do so,' I laughed. 'I'll ask him to come along with us.'

The next day, after lunch, I waited for her. The second hand on my watch ticked on into minutes, and the minutes ticked into an hour. I knew something was terribly wrong. Daniele offered to go and see what had happened. I insisted on going with him, a sick feeling in my stomach.

'All will be well, don't worry.' My brother's words were optimistic but I could see he was concerned. He ran a shaky hand through his thick, dark brown, wavy hair.

It only took us five minutes to get there, we ran so fast. We rang the bell and Giulia answered straight away. 'They've been taken,' she said, tears rolling down her face. 'The SS came at dawn. Oh Dio,' she sobbed, twisting her hands in her apron. 'And now the Germans will move in here. I've been given a choice. To serve them or leave.' She lifted her chin. 'I will stay and look after things for my signori until the Allies get here and liberate us from those Nazi swine.'

Cavolo, I'm crying. I will have to stop recording now. Sorry, but I can't go on...'

I press the off switch and put down the microphone. Romeo, my big ginger cat, jumps up onto my lap. I stroke him and the action soothes me. My heartrate slows, my sobbing ceases and my breathing steadies. Romeo meows hungrily. 'You're a fickle lover,' I tell him with a sad smile. 'You only give me affection when you want to be fed.'

I go through to the kitchen and top up his bowl with kibble. On the table is Rhiannon's application form. I glance at the girl's photo. She's a redhead sporting a hairstyle like Lady Di's. Wide blue eyes. Very Celtic looking. Rhiannon wrote me a letter introducing herself, which I received last week. I'm looking forward to meeting her and, holding on to that realisation, I go to get ready for bed.

2

RHIANNON

Whatever possessed her to apply for a scholarship to study at Bologna University for a semester? Rhiannon has asked herself the question several times since arriving in Italy a couple of hours ago. She's never travelled on her own before. Never lived in a foreign country. Never even been to Italy, although she's been studying Italian for years. She's so nervous her legs are trembling as she steps off the airport bus.

The sight that greets her sends a shiver up her spine. She knew what to expect, but the empty space where the west wing of the railway station once stood, before it was blown up in a terrorist attack last August, makes her think of a mouth with half its teeth missing. There are cranes there now, evidence rebuilding work has started. But she read that a clock on the left-hand side of the main building has been left stopped at the time of the atrocity. She swivels her gaze until she sees it, forever frozen at ten twenty-five.

She releases a sigh. Mum tried to persuade her not to come, maintaining the terrorists could strike again. Rhiannon retorted that terrorism is everywhere these days, it seems, not least in the

UK. She told her mum she can't live her life in fear; she can't let extremists stop her from achieving her dreams. The course at Unibo's School for Foreigners is important to her. Although she gets top marks in her written work, her speaking exam results are poor. She hopes that living in Bologna and conversing with Signora Venturi will help her achieve fluency.

The driver is unloading suitcases from the belly of the bus, and Rhiannon goes to retrieve hers. She tilts it so she can pull it on its wheels towards the taxi rank. Signora Venturi wrote that her palazzo in Marsala Street is at least a twenty-minute walk from the station and Rhiannon has decided she'll splash out on a cab – trundling her suitcase with a rucksack over her shoulder and a map in her hand all the way there would be a bit of a slog.

There's a queue, but not a long one, and soon the taxi driver has placed her things in the boot and is driving her down a wide, straight avenue towards the city centre. Rhiannon stares out of the window, her heartrate soaring. She can hardly believe she's here. In Bologna. About to start the biggest adventure of her life.

The driver is friendly and tells her they are in Via dell'Indipendenza. She's tongue-tied and can only blurt, '*Interessante.*' The wide street is busy with buses, cars, bicycles, Vespa scooters and motorbikes. Continuous rows of arches front the four-storey elegant red-brick buildings on both sides. She remembers reading in the guidebook she found in a second-hand bookshop in Cardiff that Bologna is famous for its porticoes, which go on for miles and miles. She savours this nugget of information and feels a surge of excitement. She'll walk every single mile of the arcades, if possible. It will be something to write home about, and she can't wait.

The taxi turns left into a much narrower street. Rhiannon's eyes pop as they pass an ancient-looking structure with a wooden porch and living quarters built above it. It's like stepping back centuries in time. The cobbled one-way street is so narrow the taxi needs to inch forwards at a snail's pace. They come to an intersection and the road broadens momentarily into a small square fronted by a terracotta-coloured church. They crawl forwards again, a short distance, and then stop. '*Siamo arrivati*,' the taxi driver announces. We've arrived.

Rhiannon jumps out and pays him, then takes her bags. '*Grazie*.' She thanks him. She stares up at a russet-coloured three-storey terraced building. There are two windows with green louvred shutters on each of the upper floors. She steps onto the pavement under a pair of vaulted arches next to a hairdresser's and rings the bell beside an enormous oak door. It buzzes open, and she heaves her luggage up a wide stone staircase.

A tall, elderly woman stands on the landing, a woman Rhiannon can only describe as 'stunning'. Her heart-shaped face is barely wrinkled, but her dark hair is streaked with grey. Dressed elegantly in a pale grey knee-length skirt, a white blouse, and a light blue cardigan, she holds out her hand and Rhiannon takes it.

'*Buongiorno*, signora,' Rhiannon says shyly.

'*Chiamami* Leila, *ti prego*.' The older woman smiles. Call me Leila, please.

Leila ushers her indoors and leads her down a marble-floored corridor. Rhiannon gives a gasp of delight at the sight of her bedroom. The shutters have been left open to the late afternoon sun, which casts a golden glow over a double bed with a pretty multicoloured floral bedspread. The white wooden furniture – bedside tables, desk, and single wardrobe – looks freshly painted. '*Bello!*' she exclaims. *Beautiful.*

'*Il bagno è qui*.' Leila points to a bathroom on the opposite side of the corridor. She says that she'll leave Rhiannon to settle in. '*La cena è alle sette*,' she adds. Dinner is at seven.

Rhiannon sits on her bed, suddenly feeling overwhelmed. She struggled to speak Italian with her landlady. Has she bitten off more than she can chew? Get a grip, girl, she tells herself. It's only your first day. She goes over to the window. The sun has begun to set over the rooftops of the city, and the sight takes her breath. Bologna, *La Rossa*, the Red, she recalls, and it's certainly true. The skyline of roofs, broken up by church steeples and medieval towers, boasts a spectrum of colours: coral, burgundy, mahogany, rust, apricot, vermilion – she ticks off a list in her head of those she can identify, having studied Art alongside Italian and History for her A levels. Then she remembers the city is also known as *La Rossa* for another reason: it has been ruled by the communists since the end of the war.

She unpacks and, after a quick wash in the handbasin mounted in the corner of her room, she uses the bathroom and makes her way down the corridor to the sitting room Leila pointed out to her earlier. Her lips form an O of awe; the rectangular-shaped lounge is gorgeous. Solid wood furniture has been placed on an uncarpeted parquet floor under a high ceiling with faded frescoes of what look to be Roman gods and goddesses. There aren't any paintings on the walls, just remnants of more frescoes. The palazzo must be incredibly old, Rhiannon thinks. A standing lamp lightens the far corner of the room, and a dark blue velvet upholstered sofa holds pride of place between two tables piled with seemingly precious porcelain, cut glass, and silverware. Leila is sitting on a chintz-covered armchair opposite the sofa with an enormous ginger cat on her lap. She puts the cat down and says, '*La cena è pronta.*' Dinner is ready.

They eat in the kitchen, fitted with dark wooden cabinets, white appliances, laminate worktops, and a round oak table in the centre. 'Tortellini in brodo.' Leila serves the soup. She explains that the tortellini are ham-stuffed pasta morsels which she has cooked in chicken broth. Rhiannon spoons soup into her mouth and declares it to be delicious. She's hungry; she only had a sandwich for lunch on the plane.

Afterwards, Leila serves them both with plates of Parma ham and cheese accompanied by fresh green salad. They finish off with blood oranges, which are in season at this time of the year. Rhiannon is relieved that she understands everything. She wishes her speaking skills were as good as her listening. It takes her far too long to work out what she wants to say and, by the time she's worked it out, Leila has moved on to another topic. She's interested in knowing about Rhiannon's family, but Rhiannon is reticent. '*Ho una sorella.*' She tells her she has a sister. '*Si chiama* Lowri.' She gives her name. '*Ha tre anni più di me.*' Three years older. She doesn't expand that her parents have recently divorced. That her dad has moved in with a woman half his age. That her mum has joined an anti-nuclear women's peace movement and spends her time helping to organise peaceful protests to ban the bomb. The Italian for all of that is in Rhiannon's head, but not on her tongue.

Instead, she asks Leila about herself. It seems rude to enquire if she's a widow, but Rhiannon presumes that to be the case. '*Non ho figli.*' Leila says she doesn't have any children after Rhiannon enquires. She appears on the verge of adding to the statement when the sound of the front door opening and footsteps from the corridor interrupts her. '*Mio nipote,* Gianluca.' Leila explains that her nephew, Gianluca, has arrived.

Rhiannon's heart sinks. '*Abita qui?*' *Does he live here?* She didn't expect there to be a man living with them.

'No, no.' Leila goes on to say he's probably dropped in to check on her and make sure Rhiannon is a suitable lodger.

Rhiannon wants to comment that she hopes she passes his scrutiny, but she can't get the words out before a tall, good-looking young man with thick, dark brown, wavy chin-length hair steps into the kitchen.

He introduces himself and pulls out a chair. The cat winds itself around his legs. He bends, strokes it. 'Ciao, Romeo.'

What a fabulous name for a cat, Rhiannon smiles to herself.

Leila offers Gianluca a coffee, which he accepts. He inclines his head towards Rhiannon while his aunt spoons ground coffee into a Bialetti and places it on the stove. 'Tell me about yourself, Rhiannon.'

She leans away from him, annoyed that he's acting like he's interviewing her for a job. Cocky to a tee, she thinks.

'There's not much to tell,' she stumbles over the Italian. 'I'm from a village called Caerleon in the south of Wales. It's near Newport.'

'I'm interested in Roman history so I've heard of it,' he responds in good English.

'And I'm interested in the history of Bologna,' she says in her own language. 'I'm looking forward to walking along all the porticoes.' She pauses. She's on the point of asking him not to speak to her in English, that she's here to improve her Italian when Leila returns to the table with the coffee pot and three cups.

Conversation carries on in Italian. Gianluca seems genuinely fond of his aunt from the warmth of his gaze and his attentive attitude. He pours them each a coffee and passes around the sugar bowl.

'It's been great to meet you. I'd love to show you around Bologna,' he says to Rhiannon as he gets up to go a short time later.

'Thanks, but I'm not sure what my timetable at the university will be like.'

'I'll catch up with you in a day or two, then.' He smirks.

Leila collects the cups and takes them to the sink after Gianluca has left. Rhiannon gets up to help her, but she waves her away. 'You must be tired. Go and get an early night. Oh, and I'm glad you turned Gianluca down. You should stay away from him, my dear.'

Rhiannon doesn't know what to say, so she says nothing she's so surprised. But, in the quiet of her room, she wonders why Leila warned her off Gianluca. Not that she's interested in him. Far from it. She needs the complication of a man in her life like she'd need a bullet in her brain.

3

LEILA

I climb the stairs to my apartment, my chest squeezing tight; I'm out of breath as I've just hurried to buy bread at my favourite bakery behind San Petronio – a ten-minute walk there and back. I was up at dawn as usual; I'm an early-riser, always have been. I frown, hoping Rhiannon doesn't expect me to cook eggs for her breakfast. I've heard that's what the British have in the mornings but I prefer to eat them later in the day. She'll just have to fit in with my way of doing things, I decide. I unlock my front door and catch the sounds of the shower from behind the bathroom door. *She's up. Good. She's fitting in already.*

In the kitchen, I slice the thick, crusty white loaf. The sweet, yeasty aroma of freshly baked bread smells divine. I wonder if Rhiannon would prefer wholemeal. I can't stand the stuff myself – it reminds me too much of the black bread we used to get during the war. Horrible stuff, consisting mainly of chaff, and I couldn't stomach it.

Humming, I spoon coffee into the Bialetti then place it on the stove. After adding milk to a pan to heat up, I fetch the butter dish from the fridge and put it on the table next to my breadbasket and a jar of store-bought cherry jam.

The door to the kitchen swings open, and Rhiannon comes in. She gives me a sweet smile. 'Buongiorno, Leila.'

I return the greeting with warmth. Yesterday, I surprised myself when I suggested she called me by my first name. The generational gap means I should have insisted on being addressed as 'signora' and for her to use the formal '*lei*' form of 'you' instead of the familiar '*tu*'. But I felt an unexpected affinity with Rhiannon. It was almost as if I knew her already, which is odd considering we'd only exchanged a couple of letters. Perhaps my going back in time to the 1940s has made me want to drop the barriers? She's a student just like I was, although looking at what she's wearing makes me realise that life has changed beyond all recognition. I eye her tight blue jeans, which leave nothing to the imagination. At least she has a good figure and her dark pink woollen sweater is modest enough. When I attended the university, we all dressed formally, as if we were going to work in an office. The boys wore shirts and ties and the girls dresses or skirts. I hold back a sigh and tell myself not to judge.

When I ask Rhiannon if she'd have preferred eggs, she responds in halting Italian, 'I don't eat much in the mornings, so this is perfect.' She bites into her bread and jam and gives a little moan of pleasure. 'Delicious.'

I explain that it comes from the best bakery in Bologna and suggest she visits the food outlets near San Petronio. 'Perhaps you can grab something to eat from there during your lunch break?'

'Can you show me where it is on my map before I set off?' Her Italian is slow and deliberate.

I pour her a milky coffee then one for myself. She takes a sip, then says she's feeling a bit nervous about starting her course.

'You're very brave,' I tell her, 'to come all the way to Italy on your own. I'm sure, once you've met your teachers and fellow students, you'll feel fine.'

'I hope so.'

* * *

Before she leaves for her classes, Rhiannon hands me her map. I place it on the kitchen table and point out important landmarks, explaining that we live in the old section of the city, or, as we Bolognese like to call it 'inside the walls'. Just a euphemism, I clarify. Said walls no longer exist. The five-hundred-year-old battlements were demolished in the early part of this century to create the ring road, the *viali*. The urban planners at that time wanted to provide for the automobile and turn Bologna into an industrial powerhouse to rival Turin and Milan. Of the twelve original gates only nine remain, and most of these have been modified during various renovations. Such a shame...

I touch my finger to the network of large boulevards and small streets depicted on the map, warning Rhiannon that the kilometres of porticoes masking the palazzi make the roads look deceptively uniform; she could easily get lost. I explain that the arcades were built to accommodate hard-up scholars in the Middle Ages and, at night, the covered walkways were lined with the poorest students bedding down in curtained-off sections of the pavement. They still provide shelter from the sun and rain and snow, but the only people you might find asleep under the porticoes nowadays are either drunk, homeless, or on drugs. 'You'll soon get to know your way around,' I encourage. 'Each piazza is different. The city centre isn't that big and it's easy to walk from one end to the other.'

'I can't wait to explore,' she says with enthusiasm. 'I'm surprised the university doesn't appear to have a campus...'

'The majority of Unibo's buildings are in Zamboni Street. Bologna *is* the campus, in a way. The oldest structure in existence, the Archiginnasio, dates from the sixteenth century, and it's situated behind Basilica of San Petronio. But historians have traced the origins of the university back to the year 1088. The School of Engineering isn't even 'inside the walls'.' I give a shudder, remembering what went on there during the German occupation. *Don't dwell on that now.*

I show her the medieval area called 'Quadrilatero' near the Basilica. 'It's only a short distance from your school and you'll be able to buy a snack lunch in one of the bars or cafés. I'll have something more substantial for you to eat this evening.'

'*Grazie.*' She puts the map away in her rucksack. '*Molto gentile.*' She's so polite. Saying I'm very kind. I find myself liking Rhiannon more and more.

I give her a set of keys – one for the street door and one for the apartment – then see her out.

Romeo winds himself around my legs and I bend to stroke his soft fur. He meows to go outside, so I open the door onto the balcony from where he can climb down the wisteria vine to the courtyard below. It's a sunny, cloudless day and the sky above the rooftops a bright blue. But the air chills my face so I shut the door quickly.

As I rinse the breakfast dishes I think about Rhiannon. She's a pretty girl and, last night, I could see Gianluca's eyes light up at the sight of her. Why did I warn her off him? I'm not sure, to be honest. He's an investigative journalist and let slip to me after the bombing of the railway station last August that he's started investigating neo-fascists. I fear for his safety but I'm sure he wouldn't put Rhiannon at risk. No, it's more to do with him losing his fiancée, Flavia, to cancer three years ago. He maintains there'll never be anyone like her, but that hasn't stopped him from dating a series of women in recent months. 'One-night stories', I believe they are called. I wouldn't want my lodger to become a victim of my nephew's grief, and I resolve to have a word with him in private as soon as possible. Luckily, we are extremely close.

I make myself another coffee, then go through to my study. *Time to get on with recording my memoirs.* I listen to the tape I made yesterday and pick up from there.

Tears streaming down my face, I hurried home from Rebecca's with Daniele. 'We must find out where the Matatias have been taken,' I wept. 'Surely they can be rescued?'

Dani's normally swarthy face had turned pale with apparent shock. 'I will see what can be done...'

I went to my room and curled up on my bed. It's the same bedroom my lodger is sleeping in now, with a view of the courtyard below the palazzo which my cat likes to claim as his territory. God forbid that any stray feline should wander in there! He soon makes his ownership known. We didn't have any pets in the forties and I'm glad of that. The Bolognese were starving during the occupation, and dogs and cats thin on the ground. Stella, our cook, once made a dish which tasted like rabbit stew. Afterwards, I asked where she'd obtained the meat. She gave me a shamefaced look and admitted she'd cooked the cat she'd caught on the patio. Disgusted, I'd begged her not to do it again, saying that Daniele and I could survive without meat.

Anyway, I digress. Back to the arrest of Rebecca and her parents. Dani told me at supper afterwards he'd discovered they'd been incarcerated at San Giovanni in Monte, where they were being held in one of the cells of the ex-monastery which had been turned into a prison, and they would be sent to a transit camp forthwith. Someone must have informed on them to the SS. The Germans were paying substantial rewards to informers at the time, and many of our citizens were tempted into betrayal. I asked Daniele if he knew any of the urban guerrillas, the gappisti who were antagonising the Nazis and fascists.

Perhaps they might be willing to break Rebecca and her parents out of the prison. Dani put a finger to his lips and said, *'Leave it with me, little sister. I'll do everything I can.'*

The next day, I met up with my sweetheart, Paolo, in the university canteen. His mouth twisted grimly when I told him about Rebecca. *'Vile Nazi pigs,'* he hissed. *'I hope they all rot in hell.'*

'I hate them,' I said. *'I want to fight them tooth and nail.'*

He shifted in his seat and glanced away from me.

I nudged him. *'What aren't you telling me?'*

He gave an asthmatic cough. *'Nothing you need to concern yourself with, Leila.'*

'You're a partisan.' I came right out with it. *'Tell me the truth!'*

He swallowed around the prominent Adam's apple in his throat. *'Shush, my love. The walls have ears...'*

'I'll walk you back to the School of Medicine,' I said. *'I don't have any classes until later. You can tell me then.'*

We finished our lunch, then headed out. As we strolled towards the Sant'Orsola Hospital, sheltering from a shower of rain under the porticoes lining San Vitale Street, I interrogated Paolo about his activities when he wasn't with me. *'You've told me so many times that you've been busy recently, I was beginning to think you'd met someone else.'*

His face turned bright red. *'I would never do that.'* He took my hand. *'I love only you, Leila.'*

'I love you too. And I want to carry on loving you in a free Italy, not in a country ruled by fascists. After what they've allowed the SS to do to Rebecca, her parents, and other Jews, I can't stand on the sidelines any longer. I'm sure you can't either...'

Paolo lowered his voice. *'Okay, I admit that the group I joined at the university is working for the Resistance.'*

'So I guessed correctly.'

'There are two groups of Justice and Liberty partisans in the

university,' Paolo continued. 'One in the School of Arts and the other in the Department of Geography.'

'But I'm an Arts student. How come I didn't know about this?' I couldn't keep the surprise from my voice.

'It's top secret, Leila. Only members are in the know.' He coughed. 'For obvious reasons...'

I knew what he meant. Anyone discovered rebelling against the Nazi-fascists would meet with almost certain death. But the more people fought back, the sooner we'd get rid of the enemy. I was prepared to risk my life if needed. 'Please, get me an introduction to the group at my school, Paolo. There must be something I can do to help with the cause.'

He shook his head. 'It's far too dangerous. I'd be distraught if anything happened to you, my darling.'

I stopped walking and spun around. 'How about my feelings?' My voice rose. 'I mean, it's all right for you to rebel, but not all right for me. You're being hypocritical, and you know it.'

He dropped my hand and wiped his brow. 'I'm sorry. Put that way, I can see how it looks. It's just that I love you and worry about you.'

'I worry about you too. In fact, I've been worrying about you for months, ever since you started attending those clandestine Justice and Liberty political meetings.'

'I'll see what I can do.' Paolo took my hand again. 'I can't promise anything.'

'All right,' I said. 'That's fair enough.'

We'd reached Porta San Vitale, and I needed to get to my afternoon classes. I kissed Paolo on both cheeks. 'See you tomorrow,' I said.

My throat feels scratchy with dryness, and I press the off button on the Philips. My memoirs can wait for another day – I should make a few notes before my next session. In the meantime, I'll start preparing Rhiannon's evening meal. I'm looking forward to eating with her; I've been lonely since I retired. I'll make ragù alla Bolognese and home-made tagliatelle. The sauce and pasta can be made in advance – I can heat them up again when she gets home.

Smiling to myself, I go through to the kitchen and take the ingredients from my store cupboard. While I chop the onions, I think about her and wonder how she's enjoying her first day at Unibo.

4

RHIANNON

Rhiannon has been spending the morning taking assessments to ascertain her level of Italian. After a couple of hours cooped up in a small classroom, she steps out of a big double wooden door into the middle of the cobbled Piazza San Giovanni in Monte. She turns and glances up at the apricot-coloured two-storey building fronted by the ubiquitous arches of an arcade. When she went through the entrance earlier, her breath had caught. The hidden space inside, a square patio surrounded by cloisters, was so unexpected.

A sign on the wall catches her eye. She walks up to it and tries to translate the Italian words inscribed on a marble plaque commemorating the twentieth anniversary of the Resistance. The inscription recounts that on the night of 9 August 1944 twelve *gappisti* executed a cunning plan and daringly returned hundreds of patriots to life, freedom, and action. Rhiannon screws up her face in thought. She only has a sketchy knowledge of what happened in Italy during the war. Who were the *gappisti*? What was the cunning plan? She resolves to ask Leila when she gets home.

Rhiannon gives a start. A tall girl with long, almost black hair, who appears to be about her age, has come up and has started reading the words out loud. The girl's Italian is heavily accented and she pronounces the letter 'r' at the back of her throat instead of rolling it on her tongue. She shrugs and turns to Rhiannon, holding out her hand. 'Ciao, *mi chiamo* Marie,' she introduces herself. '*Sono francese.*' French. '*Come ti chiami? Di dove sei?*'

Rhiannon tells the girl her name and informs her she's from Wales in the UK.

'*Prendiamo un caffè insieme?*' Marie suggests they go for a coffee.

Rhiannon says she would like that. Marie is someone with whom she can speak Italian and she seems pleasant enough.

They leave the square, cross a road, and find themselves in Piazza Santo Stefano, where they perch on metal chairs at a round table bathed in sunshine. 'I can't believe it's warm enough to sit outside in February,' Rhiannon exclaims.

Marie removes her coat. 'Much warmer than Paris...'

They order cappuccinos and chat about their universities. Marie is studying Italian and Arabic at the Sorbonne. Her ambition is to become an interpreter at the United Nations. Rhiannon says she might take a law conversion course after she graduates in Italian, but she hasn't made up her mind yet.

She sips her frothy coffee, eyeing the beauty of the porticoed buildings hugging the piazza. Pedestrians and cyclists criss-cross the triangular space formed by the gentle widening of the narrow street. She looks up into the open windows of the elegant Renaissance palazzi of once illustrious Bolognese families, catching glimpses of colourful, frescoed ceilings. She closes her eyes and imagines the day-to-day lives of the rich silk merchants and powerful town officials who inhabited these elegant edifices, the conversations, music, laughter, and tears that filled the rooms.

'I'm hungry,' Marie interrupts her thoughts. 'I wonder if there's somewhere we can get a bite to eat nearby.'

Eagerly Rhiannon pulls the map from her bag and points out Piazza Maggiore. 'My landlady suggested the area around here. How about we give it a try?'

Marie agrees and they finish their drinks and pay at the bar before strolling up the road towards the two towers. Rhiannon remembers reading that they're called Asinelli, one hundred metres, and Garisenda – half her sister's height and leaning even more precariously than the tower of Pisa.

'I read it's possible to climb up the internal staircase of the tallest one.' The words leave Rhiannon's mouth slow and deliberately. 'Apparently, the view from the top is incredible.'

Marie glances at her watch. 'Maybe another day? We'll just have time for lunch before we need to head back for our test results. I hope you and I are put in the same class.'

Marie's speaking skills seem much better than hers, so Rhiannon doubts that will be the case. She keeps her doubts to herself, though. Instead, she consults her map and they head down a wide boulevard known as Via Rizzoli to arrive at a square with a fountain in the centre. 'Look!' Her mouth drops in amazement.

On each side of a plinth in the centre of the fountain, the statues of four sea goddesses are holding their breasts, from which squirt jets of water. Cherubs and dolphins line the next two layers below the majestic figure of Neptune, a trident in his right hand. He stands like a giant – broad, powerful, bronze shoulders capturing the warm sunlight. Head turned, he glances down, eyes following the curve of his extended left arm, stretched out in a lordly gesture, as if to placate the waves.

'How strange to have a statue of the god of the sea in the middle of a city,' Marie muses.

Rhiannon gazes at the muscular torso of the statue. 'I read the fountain was commissioned by a pope at the end of the sixteenth century. Just like Neptune was the master of the seas, the Pope was the master of Bologna and of the world.'

'Well, you're certainly a fountain of knowledge.' Marie snorts out a laugh at her own joke. She links her arm through Rhiannon's. 'I'm starving. Let's go and get something to eat.'

'Wait. What are those?' Rhiannon's attention has been drawn by wreaths decorated with tricoloured ribbons – the red, green, and white of the Italian flag – which have been set before what look to be hundreds, if not thousands, of ceramic photographs placed behind glass on the wall of the imposing russet-brick building opposite. She pulls Marie along with her to stand in front.

The images are mostly of young men, although there are several women as well. She reads one of the plaques, which again commemorates the Resistance: *14,425 Bolognese partisans of whom 2,212 were women* – Rhiannon's eyes widen – *2,059 fallen. 945 wounded. 6,543 arrested; 2,350 shot in reprisals; 829 died in Nazi concentration camps.* 'Oh, how terrible,' she wails. 'They look around our age, most of them...'

Marie shrugs. 'They were reckless.'

Rhiannon does a double-take at the French girl's lack of empathy. 'Well, I think they must have been incredibly brave.'

Marie shrugs again.

They make their way into Piazza Maggiore, and Rhiannon's spirits lift at the sight of the beautiful façade of the Basilica of San Petronio, half covered in marble. She resolves to return and visit it properly on the weekend. A group of young people, probably students, are sitting on the steps leading up to the entrance, some of whom are strumming guitars. In the middle of the square, children are chasing pigeons across a raised section built in white and pink granite, their mothers trailing behind pushing prams.

Rhiannon gasps. A familiar-looking man seated at the *caffè* on the corner of the square has come into the periphery of her vision. *It's Gianluca.* 'That's my landlady's nephew.' She points him out to Marie. 'I'd better go and say hello.'

Gianluca gets up from his seat to shake Rhiannon's hand and then Marie's. A blush heats Rhiannon's cheeks. 'We're heading over to the Quadrilatero to get something to eat,' she babbles, unaccountably flustered.

'I'll come with you,' he offers. 'Show you where to get the best *piadine.*'

'*Piadine*?' Rhiannon tilts her head. 'What's that?'

'A typical light meal in this part of Italy. Flatbread folded over and stuffed with cheese, meat, salad, whatever you like.'

'Yum.' Marie flashes him a toothy smile. 'Lead the way.'

He takes them down a narrow side street to a small snack bar, where they sit at a tiny table after they've placed their orders.

Rhiannon listens to Gianluca ask Marie about herself; his entire attention is focused on her and Rhiannon finds herself feeling like a third wheel. She bites into her mozzarella and tomato *piadina*. '*Deliziosa*,' she says.

Gianluca shoots her a surprised glance, as if he's forgotten that she's here. He tells her he's glad that she likes it before he resumes his conversation with Marie about the Sorbonne.

* * *

'Gianluca *è bello da morire*,' Marie comments as they head back to school half an hour or so later. Drop dead gorgeous.

'Oh, I hadn't noticed,' Rhiannon lies. She couldn't help noticing, of course. '*Non mi interessa*,' she adds. I'm not interested in him. Which is true. She's off men, especially men like Gianluca who, from the way he reacted to Marie, are only after one thing, an impossible 'thing' as far as Rhiannon is concerned.

'Well, I, for one, would love a fling with a handsome young Italian to improve my language skills,' Marie giggles, taking a cigarette from her bag and lighting it. 'I'd be interested in seeing him again.'

Rhiannon laughs at the French girl's candour. Marie could be angling for Rhiannon to set her up on a date with Gianluca, but Rhiannon decides she won't get involved. She nods and walks on. Shadows cross her path and sunlight plays off the mustard-gold medieval buildings leaning one against the other. Totally enchanting, she thinks.

When they arrive at the school, they discover lists have been posted on the wall of the courtyard. Rhiannon learns she and Marie are, indeed, in the same class. They are given timetables. Grammar and Italian culture lessons in the mornings. Conversation classes in the afternoons, starting tomorrow. They are also provided with letters from the university, attesting to their status pending the arrival of their photo ID student cards. Rhiannon has a wad of travellers cheques in her handbag. *Time to go and open a bank account.* She conveys the information to Marie, who responds that she has one already and will make her way back to her digs in the Bolognina district. 'It's on the other side of the railway station, so I'll take the bus.'

Rhiannon waves her goodbye, then makes her way to the bank she saw in Piazza Santo Stefano when she was having coffee earlier. She doesn't know how she feels about her new acquaintance other than a sense that she should be wary of her for some reason. Although Marie smiled a lot, her smiles seemed pasted onto her face and her eyes remained deadpan. And her angling for a date with Gianluca appeared contrived, somehow. *Really bizarre.*

After going through a load of paperwork in the bank, Rhiannon cashes enough of her cheques to pay Leila for her board and keep, then deposits the rest of them.

Outside it has turned colder as the sun has lowered in the sky. Rhiannon sets off briskly. She stops at a tobacconist's to buy postcards to send to her mother and sister before heading along Marsala Street. She unlocks the street door at Leila's, goes upstairs, and enters the apartment, eager to ask her about the *gappisti*.

'*Aiuto!*' Leila's voice calls out for help.

The voice is coming from the kitchen.

Rhiannon drops her bag and races down the corridor.

Leila is lying on the floor, her face pale. 'I've had a fall,' she says, 'and I can't get up.'

Heart thudding, Rhiannon runs to her and holds out her hand.

5

LEILA

'Are you all right?' Rhiannon asks as she helps me to my feet. She pulls out a chair and carefully sits me down. 'What happened?'

'I felt a little dizzy and my legs went from under me.' I keep to myself that high blood pressure causes these spells from time to time – especially when I forget to take my pills – although I've never fallen to the floor before.

'Is there anyone I should call?' She goes to the sink and fills a glass with water, which she hands to me.

I thank her and take a sip. 'My brother and his wife live in Vicenza. There's only my nephew in Bologna.'

I'm not keen on her spending time with Gianluca, but I'm still a little shaky and it would be good to have him here to help with supper. I don't want to bother my friends.

'I'll give Gianluca a ring.' Rhiannon heads for the telephone by the door.

After I've told her his number, she phones and I listen while she explains what happened. 'He'll be here shortly,' she says.

'How was your first day at the university?' I ask while we wait.

'It was amazing.' She goes on to recount how she's already

made a friend – French girl – and they bumped into Gianluca in Piazza Maggiore. 'He took us to a *piadine* place.'

'Wonderful!' I remind myself to establish my rules with him. I don't want Gianluca to have a one-night story with Rhiannon; I don't want her to get hurt.

She touches her hand to mine. 'If you're okay, I'll just go and freshen up.'

'I'm feeling a lot better now,' I reassure her.

She's barely left the kitchen when Gianluca arrives – he only lives five minutes away. His worried face makes me feel guilty about not taking my medication. 'Auntie, are you all right?' He lowers himself onto the chair next to mine and squeezes my fingers.

'I'll be fine once I've had a rest, dear. Would you mind helping with supper? I made the ragù and tagliatelle earlier. But the sauce should be heated up and water boiled to cook the pasta. Oh, and stay to eat with us. There's more than enough...'

'You've been overdoing things. Rushing around getting things ready for Rhiannon's arrival. Then putting yourself out to make tagliatelle from scratch. I'll get you fresh, artisan ones from a store in future.'

'*Grazie.*' I lower my voice. 'Listen, Gianluca. There's something I've been meaning to say since Rhiannon arrived. I don't want you having a one-night story with her. She's a nice girl and I feel responsible for her.'

He holds up his hands. 'I wouldn't... Besides, she's not my type.'

'I saw the way you were looking at her yesterday.'

'Only because she reminded me of a red-headed Lady Di. Anyway, you know I like dark-haired girls...'

Flavia's hair was almost black, I remember. *Her death was so tragic.*

We're interrupted by Rhiannon appearing in the doorway. 'Ciao, Gianluca.'

He greets her and goes to fill a pot of water which he places on the stove.

She stands next to him. 'Can I help?'

Before he can answer, I butt in. 'Gianluca can manage. Come and sit by me. Tell me more about your day.'

* * *

A week later, I'm in bed half-asleep, listening to the Angelus bells ringing from the nearby church of San Martino, heralding a new day. Bleary-eyed, I stare out through the windowpane. In winter and spring, I leave the shutters open to allow the dawn light to wake me. While I wait for the sky to lighten, I think about the first morning after my fall. I woke up late, staggered out of bed and hurried in a panic to the kitchen in my nightdress and dressing gown. Rhiannon would just have to be happy with supermarket bread for her breakfast, I thought. I jerked my head back in surprise as I saw Gianluca brewing coffee and slicing into a fresh loaf.

Since then, he's been coming every morning, bringing his portable typewriter to work on, and staying to keep me company until Rhiannon returns from her school. Despite my protests, he insisted on taking me to the doctor. My prescription was changed, and the new pills have brought my blood pressure right down. Yesterday, I said to Gianluca that I was feeling perfectly well and he could leave me on my own. He said he would carry on doing my grocery shopping, though, and I told him I was grateful so as not to appear ungracious. His continued contact with Rhiannon has been concerning me – even though he appears to have been a perfect gentleman. She doesn't give the impression of being the least bit attracted to him, thankfully – I can tell from her body language, the way she leans away from him and avoids meeting his gaze. A pretty girl like her is bound to have a boyfriend; I expect there's someone waiting for her in Wales. I haven't asked; she'll tell me in her own good time, I suppose.

Dawn has started pinking the sky now and I decide to get out of bed. I'm looking forward to getting back to recording my memoirs today; I was reticent about doing so with Gianluca hanging about. I'm not ready to divulge my secrets yet...

Soon after Gianluca has dropped off crusty fresh bread rolls, I wave him off to work from his own home. Rhiannon leaves after breakfast and, at last, I'm on my own. There's only so much human company I can take, it occurs to me. I've lived alone for years and have taken in a lodger only because I was missing contact with young people. I taught literature at the university, relished spending time with my students, but also loved my solitary existence in Marsala Street. Having Gianluca here during the day this past week has been nice – he's kind and considerate – but I've found his constant investigative phone calls, tapping on his typewriter and rock music on his transistor radio a little intrusive. I'm looking forward to him popping in every day, of course I am, but I'm also looking forward to some peace and quiet.

Romeo follows me into the study and jumps up onto the seat by the window to stare out at the birds. I managed to scribble some notes in the privacy of my room yesterday, and now I can't wait to carry on with my story. I open the desk drawer and extract my Philips recorder, plug in the microphone, and retrieve the notes from my pocket.

The scene in Zamboni Street during the war was completely

different to how it appears nowadays when students show their polit-ical affiliations openly by their mode of dress. Left-wingers go about in khaki military style coats; right-wingers generally wear leather jackets and Ray-Ban sunglasses. In 1944 we all dressed identically in formal clothes, hiding our allegiances while we lived in fear for our lives. One thing hasn't changed, however. Bologna's university scholars unleashed intellectual and moral tremors that shook the foundations of medieval thought when the Studiorum was first founded. They've been revolutionaries ever since.

On the hot July morning when Paolo introduced me to the gappisti at the School of Arts, I'd made my way there from home as usual, strolling past ancient ochre-coloured buildings which, in the Middle Ages, had been the domain of the rich and powerful. My heart racing in anticipation, I stepped through the big oak doors of number 38 Zamboni Street into the ubiquitous rosy-red porticoed courtyard of the inner space, then up the ivory marble staircase to the library – a long, rectangular, book-lined room on the first floor. Paolo was waiting for me by the entrance, as we'd arranged. 'Are you sure you want to do this?' he asked in Bolognese. We always spoke dialect to each other; we were proud of our roots.

'Absolutely,' I said. 'After what the Nazis have done to Rebecca and her parents, I wouldn't be able to live with myself if I did nothing.'

He took my hand and led me to a corner of the room, to a space hidden behind bookcases which had been moved to create a sectioned-off area. 'This is Leila.' He presented me to a blonde girl who was blocking the passageway. 'Remember I told you about her?'

She said she was pleased to meet me, and we followed her to stand beside a solid oak table on which had been placed a small antique-looking printing press. 'My partisan name is Carla,' she said. 'If you're going to join us, you'll need to choose an alias too.' She paused. 'To protect your family if you're caught.'

A shiver of fear went through me. Just the previous day, at daybreak, the Republican Guard – the organisation created by Mussolini in 1943 to take over from the Carabinieri police force which was loyal to the King – had executed five partisans in Piazza del Nettuno. When Daniele had told me about it I'd realised that things had become real. But I also knew that I wouldn't back down. In any case, the Allies had taken Rome a month ago and everyone said they'd liberate Bologna before Christmas.

I thought for a moment, screwing up my face as I tried to choose a name. The name hovered at the edge of my mind like the puff of a breeze and then, I had it. 'Vittoria,' I said firmly. 'I'd like to be named after the victory which will be ours.'

'I like the way you think.' A smile brushed Carla's lips.

Two fellow students were seated at the press, printing what appeared to be documents of some sort. 'This is Sebastiano, my sweetheart.' Carla introduced a handsome young man with curly brown hair. 'Not his real name, of course.'

'And I'm Matteo.' A ferocious-looking youth sporting black stubble on his chiselled jaw pierced me with electrifying blue eyes. He looked me up and down and smirked. 'So, you think you've got what it takes to be a gappista?'

I rankled at his insinuation that I wasn't up to the task. 'I'll do my best.'

'Don't be a jerk, Matteo!' Paolo bristled beside me. 'Vittoria is here to help.'

'All right, she can help by going with Carla to take the ID cards we've just printed to their recipients.'

I swallowed hard. 'Perfect.'

'It's something the boys entrust to us girls,' Carla whispered as we filled our satchels with the documents, hiding them under our books. 'The Nazi-fascists seem to think women students are harmless so they ignore us as we go about the city. The vast majority of gappisti are male, I'm sure you know.' She fixed me with a solemn look. *'I'm glad to have someone to go with me. It's scary on my own.'*

Paolo came up and bent his head to my ear. 'I'm known as Tarzan.'

I suppressed a giggle. Much as I loved him Paolo's physique was distinctly un-Tarzan-like. But perhaps his chosen name gave him the required courage to act like the lord of the jungle. Who was I to judge? I squeezed his arm. 'I'll see you later, my love.'

Carla and I left the library and headed towards the ruins of the Mercato delle Erbe in Ugo Bassi Street, the covered market recently hit by Allied bombing. We were supposed to meet gappisti there who needed the fake IDs.

We strolled nonchalantly up Zamboni Street in the direction of the two towers, then sauntered along Rizzoli. We were two students on their way home if anyone asked. We didn't expect there to be another execution in Piazza del Nettuno. Yesterday's shooting had occurred at dawn. But, when we arrived at the square, the most terrible sight greeted our eyes.

We stood frozen, paralysed with dismay.

Repubblichini were aiming their rifles at nine men – clearly partisans – they'd lined up facing the red-brick wall of Palazzo d'Accursio opposite the fountain.

The prisoners' hands had been tied behind their backs.

Cold shock gripped me like a vice.

'Viva l'Italia,' the partisans shouted with one voice.

The officer in charge of the repubblichini gave the order. 'Fire!'

The fascists' weapons barked into life. Heartlessly, they shot those poor men in the back of their necks. The partisans slumped to the ground, blood puddling around their stricken bodies.

Carla and I gasped.

Sudden tears furrowed our cheeks.

One of the repubblichini turned and stared at us. Of average height, thin, with a pockmarked face.

Carla and I held on to each other, shaking.

We could no longer pretend to be casual bystanders.

We got out of there as quickly as our trembling legs could carry us.

My heart is heavy as I switch off the recorder. Remembering what I'd seen by Neptune's fountain has made me so sad. I'll take a short break before I carry on. Romeo jumps up on my lap and I smooth his soft fur. I remember that, the day after the execution, I read the headline in the newspaper *il Resto del Carlino* 'Energetic Action Against Terrorists. Another nine outlaws shot by order of the German Command'.

How tragic that partisans were called terrorists by the authorities in those days. But we were fighting an enemy occupation of our country, unlike the terrorist cowards who bombed innocent civilians in the Bologna railway station last year, I think.

6

LEILA

I go through to the kitchen and make myself a coffee. After adding a teaspoon of sugar to the cup, I drink it down. Images from the past flood my mind and I'm eager to describe them, so I return to my study. Rain sheets against the window and wind rattles the pane of glass, but my room is warm from the central heating and I'm cosy and dry inside. Inhaling a deep breath, I press record on the Philips and resume my story.

Carla and I delivered the fake IDs to the two women partisans who were waiting for us, hidden in the rubble of the bombed-out covered market. We went our separate ways afterwards, taking the long way home through the backstreets. I opened the door to my family's palazzo, ran upstairs and lay on my bed, still shaken. What I'd witnessed in Piazza del Nettuno, the horrific execution of those men, had brought home to me how fragile and fleeting life was. I could die at any minute. But I was determined to carry on the fight; I owed it to Rebecca. How I missed her...

The next day, I met Paolo, Carla and the others and they told me that the gappisti who'd been executed had been informed upon. Since the occupation began, the Germans had been offering enormous rewards for information about the partisans; we all needed to be vigilant. Consequently, we moved the printing press down to the basement where, Carla let slip, there was also a stash of weapons. I asked her if she'd ever learnt to fire a gun and she responded that she hadn't. Did I want to take up arms? I couldn't imagine squeezing a trigger and killing anyone. The desire to do so only came later when I wanted revenge. But I'm getting ahead of myself. I need to recount my story following the order in which things happened or listeners might get confused.

One night, Dani got back from his surgery earlier than usual and slumped in a chair. I took in his dejected expression, and my heart almost beat out of my chest. 'Have you heard anything about Rebecca and her parents?'

'As far as I know, they're still in the San Giovanni in Monte prison.' He exhaled a long, slow breath. 'I'm worried about them, of course I am, but now there's something else that's concerning me.'

'Oh? What's that?'

He shook his head. 'I'd rather not say.'

He'd piqued my curiosity and he knew it. I guessed he wanted to share what was on his mind, and all that was needed was for me to give him a little push.

'You can trust me,' I said.

He opened and closed his mouth, clearly struggling to find the right words. Then he said, 'A group of Germans, who were captured and interrogated by the Allies after the fall of Rome, have let slip that the Nazis are developing a bomb which involves the use of radium. They've been systematically appropriating the material from Italian hospitals and clinics.'

'So, what does that have to do with you?'

'It has a lot to with me, Leila. My associates and I have been desperately trying to save the radium that is held for cancer treatment in the Sant'Orsola Hospital. But our efforts to persuade the director of *the oncology department to hand it over to us for safekeeping haven't met with any success.'*

My chest squeezed. From what I understood, my brother had practically admitted he was involved with the Resistance.

'Who are your associates, Dani?'

'You promise you'll keep this to yourself?'

'Of course. You know I will. I'm good at keeping secrets.'

'That you are, little sister.' He smiled sheepishly.

I nodded. 'Have you joined the partisans?'

'I have. As a non-combatant, mind you. I treat the sick and wounded...'

I gave him a hug. 'I'm proud of you, dearest brother.' I frowned. 'Is the director of the oncology department a fascist?'

'I don't think so. Apparently, he's worried about German reprisals and wants assurances about the safety of his family. We're working on a plan to keep him and his loved ones safe; we just need to convince him...'

'Maybe I can ask Paolo to help? I remember he told me a while ago that he'd spent time on the cancer wards...'

'I wouldn't want to put him in any danger.'

'He's already in danger. He's a gappista.' I took a deep breath, decided to go all in. 'And so am I.'

Daniele grabbed me by the shoulders. 'What?!'

'I couldn't stand by and do nothing after what happened to Rebecca and her parents.'

He sighed. 'Neither could I...'

'So we're both in the same boat. Ironic, isn't it?'

'Desperate times call for desperate measures.' He paused. 'I promised Mamma and Papà I'd keep an eye on you. I should scold you...'

'I'm old enough to make my own decisions.'

'I hope you won't get involved in anything dangerous, Leila.'

'I'm just a courier,' I sighed. 'I doubt I'll see any action.' I kept to myself what I'd witnessed in Piazza del Nettuno. It was too dreadful to speak about.

The next day, I took matters into my own hands and told Paolo about the radium. He immediately offered to go and see the oncology director. He'd got on well with him, he said. If he reassured him, hopefully his reassurances wouldn't fall into the abyss.

I waited in the School of Arts library, pretending to study when all I could think about was how Paolo was getting on.

An hour later, he returned with bad news. 'A couple of Germans turned up at the hospital yesterday in a car armed with a machine gun, and they requisitioned half of the oncology department's radium endowment.'

My heart sank. 'What about the other half?'

'The director has agreed to hand it over to your brother, provided he guarantees his and his family's safety. Oh, and the director wants a receipt for the radium as well.'

I kissed Paolo. 'Thank you. I'd better go to Dani's surgery and tell him.'

Two days later, after the director and his family had been spirited away to a safe house in the mountains, Daniele came home with eighty-one sheaths of platinum gold, enfolding 502 mg of radium enclosed in lead caskets in a tin box. I helped him bury it in the cellar under a heap of coal when no one was about.

'Why does it have to be you who looks after it?' I asked him afterwards. '' mean, what about your associates?'

'They're well-known gappisti. If anyone informs, it will be on them not on me as no one knows about my affiliation. We decided I'm the best person for the job.'

'It's awful there are so many informers and spies about.'

'There's a war on, dearest sister. Not only are we fighting an occupying enemy, but we're in the middle of a civil war.' He breathed out a *soulful sigh. 'Italians pitted against Italians. Fascists against anti-fascists. It's a terrible situation.'*

'I hope we'll get news of Rebecca and her parents soon. If they're still in Bologna, maybe the gappisti can rescue them?'

'I love your optimism, my darling. But I'd be a whole lot happier if you agreed to join Mamma and Papà in the Veneto. It's the summer vacation so you don't have any classes.'

'I have an exam in September to prepare for, and I want to help the Resistance.'

'If anything happens to you, it will be on my conscience.'

'It will be on my conscience if anything happens to you,' I countered.

He gave a sardonic laugh. 'Touché...'

I squeezed his hand. 'I love you, Dani.' I kissed his cheek. 'And Rebecca has a big crush on you, you know...'

'I know. It's obvious.'

'You must let her down gently when she comes home. Don't hurt her, dearest brother.'

'I would never do that,' he said. 'I've loved her for years. I was just waiting until she was old enough to know her own mind.' His big brown eyes welled with emotion. 'I mean, there's an enormous difference between a crush and true love.'

Happiness swelled in my chest and I beamed from ear to ear. 'There's nothing I'd like better than for her to be my sister-in-law one day...'

'Dearest Leila. There's something you don't know.' His voice quaked. 'The Nazis are incarcerating Jews in the most horrible camps. I fear for Rebecca and her parents' lives.'

'All the more reason for the gappisti to break into San Giovanni in Monte and set the prisoners free.'

I switch off the tape recorder and think about the incident that has become known as 'Operation Radium' in the annals of the Bolognese Resistance. Little did we know at that time that Germany was considering its use in developing nuclear weapons. Whether my brother's efforts and others like his prevented the Nazis from doing so is hard to say. Dani's actions led to consequences for him, but I'll save that story for another day.

Tiredness washes through me. I'll have a bite to eat then take a nap before Rhiannon gets home. I'm looking forward to seeing her, I realise. I enjoy my own company, but only for so long. Perhaps I was a little hasty in insisting Gianluca work from his own place? No. I like my privacy too much...

7

RHIANNON

At midday, Rhiannon steps out through the school doors into Piazza San Giovanni in Monte. She unfurls her umbrella. Today it's raining for the first time since she arrived; she almost thought it never rained in Bologna so prevalent have been the bright blue skies and warm sunshine. Thank God for the porticoes, she thought as she made her way here earlier. Rain splashed in great dollops onto the asphalt, but the only time she needed her brolly was when she crossed the roads.

Marie approaches and Rhiannon groans under her breath. The French girl clings to her like a limpet. So much so Rhiannon hasn't been able to make friends with anyone else on her course. Does she mind? She shrugs to herself. She's made the most unexpected friend in Leila; she's clicked with her despite the difference in their ages. She's satisfied with that.

'Did you ask your landlady's nephew about meeting up with us one evening?' Marie asks.

'Not yet.'

Rhiannon still feels awkward in Gianluca's presence, but at least she can now bring herself to talk to him without getting tongue-tied. Contrary to what she initially thought, he hasn't been at all arrogant. His patience while she's struggled to communicate in Italian has even made her warm to him a little.

'There're *osterias* where students hang out. Maybe he can meet us for a drink one evening?' Marie suggests.

God, she's persistent. But something about her persistence doesn't ring true.

'Maybe.' Rhiannon leaves it at that.

'Okay.' Marie nods. 'Let's have lunch at the canteen in Piazza Verdi, for a change. This weather is making me hungry for something other than *piadine*.'

'Great idea!' Rhiannon's heart leaps at the thought of mingling with the rest of Unibo's students. Up until now, she's gone with the French girl to the Quadrilatero food outlets near San Petronio along with other foreigners on her course.

She strolls with Marie up Santo Stefano Street as usual but, at the two towers, instead of turning left, they go down Zamboni Street towards the university district. Rhiannon's ears ring with the noise coming from the multitude of vehicles thronging the road. Under the portico edging the elegant municipal theatre building there's a homeless man asking for change and Rhiannon gives him some lire. The scene is chaotic and somewhat seedy, but when she peers through the open portals of the palazzi on the other side of the street, her spirits are lifted by the magnificent stairways, lush gardens, impressive sculptures, and fountains spurting streams of water. Bologna certainly is a city of contrasts, a patchwork of past and present, she thinks.

They reach Piazza Verdi and an assortment of colours, shapes and textures fill her vision. It has stopped raining and students crowd the space. Some are dressed in up-to-the-minute grunge, with piercings and magenta or orange hair. Others sport more conventional hairstyles and wear designer jeans, skirts, jackets, and boots. A motley group appear almost military in their khaki garb. Rhiannon absorbs the vibe of youth and energy, a modernity at odds with the ancient rectangular palazzi lining the square, and her spirits lift even more.

'There's the entrance.' Marie points to the door in a Renaissance building on the corner.

'Have you been here before?'

'No, but I've heard about it.'

They go through and join a line of students. A clamour of conversations, clattering dishes and kitchen noises echo, and the air is redolent with the savoury smell of the lasagne being dished up at the counter.

Marie gasps. 'I've just spotted some people I know.' She indicates towards three youths having lunch at a table by the window. 'Come. Looks as if they've finished eating and we can take their place.'

'Shouldn't we wait our turn?'

But Rhiannon is already being pulled across the room by the French girl. The men appear to be about hers and Marie's age, swarthy looking and, indeed, they've cleared their plates of food. 'Ciao, Marie,' the nearest guy smiles. 'Who's your friend?'

Marie introduces Rhiannon to Bakir, Feraz, and Roshid. 'They're in the same student digs as me,' she explains as the three of them pick up their trays and head off.

'Are they Arabs?' Rhiannon stares at their retreating backs. 'Their names aren't Italian...'

'They're Palestinian. There are several of them studying at the university.'

'Oh, I didn't know. That's interesting.'

'Italy supports Palestine. Which is good, don't you think?'

'Middle Eastern politics is a minefield.' Rhiannon picks up a salt shaker and puts it down again. She doesn't want to be drawn and, furthermore, she hasn't got the Italian skills to get into a discussion, so she changes the subject. 'Let's grab a tray. The lasagne smells delicious.'

* * *

When the afternoon conversation classes come to an end, Rhiannon heads home. She unlocks the street door and climbs the stairs to Leila's apartment. Gianluca is in the kitchen, helping his aunt make dinner. They're chatting together in the Bolognese dialect, which Rhiannon has discovered is entirely different to Italian. *Totally incomprehensible.* A wonderful aroma of simmering broth infuses the air; it steams up the windows and makes Rhiannon's mouth water despite her hearty lunch.

'*Buonasera*,' she greets Leila and Gianluca.

Leila's smile is warm. 'Ciao*, cara. La cena è alle sette.*' Dinner is at seven.

'*Grazie.*' Rhiannon thanks her, then glances at Gianluca. He says good evening and gets back to thinly slicing mortadella – the baked oval-shaped pink pork sausage which is a speciality of Bologna. Rhiannon has grown to love the intense, somewhat spicy taste. Thank God she's doing a lot of walking, she muses as she makes her way down the corridor; with the amount of good food she's eating she would otherwise put on weight.

She gets on with putting the finishing touches to an essay she's due to hand in tomorrow – her early impressions of life in Italy. It doesn't take long, so she indulges herself with a soak in the bath. Lying back in the warm water, she reflects on her experience at lunchtime with Marie. There's something slightly 'off' about the French girl. Rhiannon can't quite put her finger on it. She tells herself she's in an unfamiliar place with unfamiliar people, which is probably why she's over-thinking things. Maybe if she manages to get Gianluca to agree to meet up with Marie in an *osteria*, then the French girl will get off her back?

Rhiannon levers herself out of the bath and goes to change into a clean pair of jeans and a sweatshirt. She catches sight of herself in the mirror and pulls a face. She looks more like a ten-year-old than a young woman who's twenty-one.

Back in the kitchen, she offers to help set the table. 'I had lunch at the *mensa* in Piazza Verdi today,' she says.

'I remember it well.' Leila's eyes light up.

'Me too.' Gianluca grins.

Rhiannon knows that Leila used to teach at the university. She asks Gianluca about his degree.

'I graduated in Journalism and Communications,' he says. 'Seems like a lifetime ago, but it's only been five years.'

Leila gives him a proud look. 'He was a top reporter for *il Carlino* until he went freelance.'

'My aunt doesn't approve of my current career. But I prefer being able to work on projects of my own choosing.'

'What are you working on now?'

'This and that...'

Rhiannon deduces he doesn't want to talk about it, so she abstains from further enquiry. She remains silent during dinner, mulling over how to broach the subject of going for a drink with Marie.

After mouth-watering tortellini in brodo, followed by a plate of cold meat and salad, Rhiannon, Leila and Gianluca go through to the sitting room with their coffees.

Leila settles in an armchair by the window, Romeo curled up on her lap, and promptly falls asleep.

Gianluca gives Leila a worried look. 'My aunt phoned me this afternoon,' he whispers to Rhiannon. 'She'd taken an afternoon nap and had overslept. She was panicking about getting dinner ready on time. That's why I came to help...'

'You're so good to her.'

'She's like a second mother to me.'

'Leila told me she hasn't any children of her own.'

'She never married.' He breathes a sigh. 'She lost her sweetheart in the war.'

'Oh, how sad.' Rhiannon pauses to work out what to say next. 'I was going to ask her about the monument to the partisans. Was he one of them?'

'He was. And so was she. But don't mention the Resistance. She doesn't like to talk about it.'

'Now you've explained, of course I won't mention it. I'm so sorry for her loss.'

'It was a dark period in the history of Italy. And it's still an open wound. People don't like to remember.'

'Understood.' Rhiannon takes a sip of her coffee and puts the cup down. 'There's something I'd like to ask you,' she says. 'Do you remember the French girl you met with me last week?'

'Marie? How could I forget her?' He laughs. 'Why do you ask?'

'Well, she suggested we go for a drink with her one evening. She'd like to visit an *osteria*.'

'Sounds like a great idea. You should definitely experience an *osteria*, Rhiannon. They're a part of Bolognese life.'

'So you agree?'

'How could I say no to an evening in the company of two beautiful women?' he chuckles.

Rhiannon gulps. What has she just agreed to? She should run a mile from Gianluca. He's far too attractive and charming. Then she tells herself not to be silly. He's only agreed because he's interested in Marie. Rhiannon will be a third wheel – like she was when they had *piadine* together.

'What are you two talking about?' Leila's sleepy voice interrupts.

Gianluca explains, then says, 'I'm sorry, Auntie, but I couldn't refuse Rhiannon's invitation.'

Rhiannon feels her cheeks burn; she forgot that Leila had warned her off him. 'It was Marie, my French friend's idea,' she clarifies.

'Oh, all right then,' Leila murmurs.

'I'd better be off.' Gianluca gets to his feet. 'Let me know when you'd like to go out, Rhiannon.'

Her cheeks practically self-combust. 'Will do.'

8

LEILA

'So, how is your course coming along?' I ask Rhiannon at breakfast the next morning.

'Really well. I love the one-to-one conversation classes with native speakers in the afternoons.'

'I've noticed your speaking skills have improved.' I reach across the table and give her arm an encouraging pat.

Her smile would light the world. 'Thanks. I'm starting to feel more confident, it's true.'

'I hope you're not missing your friends at home too much.'

Her smile fades. 'I do miss my mum, my sister and my best friend, Nia. But I don't mind as it's not for ever...'

'How about your boyfriend?'

'Boyfriend?' She shakes her head. 'I don't have one.' Her tone negates any further enquiry.

'Gianluca lost his fiancée three years ago to cancer,' I tell her. 'He's still grieving.'

'Oh, how terrible.' Rhiannon clasps her hands together in her lap. 'Marie was hoping he'd ask her out.'

'Ah, well, he might do so but it won't be because he wants a relationship.'

Rhiannon turns her head towards me. 'I don't understand.'

'He's become a bit of a playboy since Flavia died.'

Rhiannon's cheeks flame. 'Is that why you warned me off him?'

'It is.'

'There wasn't any need. I'm really not interested in going out with anyone while I'm here.'

Again her tone has negated any further enquiry. She's piqued my curiosity, though. I'll need to tread carefully, but I'll get to the bottom of this. If she's more partial to women than men, that's fine by me. I'd just like to know, one way or the other...

Rhiannon glances at her watch. 'I should go, or I'll be late for school.'

She helps me clear up, then leaves me to my own devices while she heads off for San Giovanni in Monte. It's the place where I took part in my first partisan action, I remember, the jail in which Rebecca and her parents were incarcerated. The university took over the premises recently, refurbished it and housed their cultural studies department there. It's tiny compared with La Dozza, the modern prison built in the seventies beyond the city's outer ring road.

I dry my hands. *Time for me to carry on with my story.* After I top up Romeo's food bowl, I make my way to my study. It's warm in here, but not as warm as it was that sweltering summer day in 1944.

On the afternoon of 9 August, I was in the School of Arts basement with my friends and noticed that Paolo, Matteo, and Sebastiano were unable to sit still while working at the printing press. Carla nudged me, 'Something's up. And I'm going to find out what that 'something' is.'

She put her arms around Sebastiano, kissed him behind the ear, then led him away to a corner of the room.

Soon she was back, her eyes glowing with excitement. 'The guys are going to help the communists break prisoners out of San Giovanni in Monte tonight,' she whispered. 'They need a couple of drivers and I've volunteered.'

I could barely believe what I'd been hoping for – the liberation of Rebecca and her parents – might be about to happen. My stomach fluttered. 'I'd like to volunteer too.'

Paolo protested, but I told him I wanted to be with him to make sure he was safe. Matteo expressed his doubts that I was up to the task, which made me even more determined. 'I've driven a lot,' I said. 'My father taught me years ago.'

I discovered that the action to free the prisoners had been ordered by the Liberation Committee at a meeting with the communists in their Bolognina hideout. They had an insider in the jail, who'd given information about which guards would be on duty and where to find the partisans who'd been incarcerated. I hoped against hope that Rebecca and her parents would still be there. If I could help liberate the Matatias, I would take them to my parents in Asiago. They would surely be protected in the mountains, I thought.

'The gappisti might have already found drivers.' Paolo took my hand. 'But you can come along with us and wait at their headquarters if you like.'

'Thank you, my love,' I said.

We left immediately to avoid being caught out on the streets after curfew. Carla and I walked openly – as women we were practically invisible to the enemy – while Paolo, Sebastiano and Matteo darted between the ruins of bombed-out buildings as we headed across town to the working-class district on the other side of the railway station.

At the communist partisans' base, Carla and I offered our services. The gappisti said they would have driven themselves; but now we'd *offered to drive, more of them could take part in the action. We were given a bowl of watery potato soup before setting off. No one spoke much; nerves had paralysed our tongues. Carla and I put on German uniforms: calf-high black leather combat boots, olive trousers, shirt, and peaked cap, a black leather belt, and a holster with a Walther pistol. I shuddered when I thought about the person who'd last worn mine; he was probably lying dead in a ditch somewhere.*

At 9.30 p.m., Carla and I tucked our hair under our hats and climbed into the drivers' seats of two Fiat 1500s – red Nazi flags emblazoned with swastikas on each fender. I was scared – despite the heat I'd broken out in a cold sweat – but I gripped the steering wheel firmly. Paolo rode next to me, armed with a MP 40 German subma-chine gun, which we called a mitra; he was wearing a black SS uniform with a skull-and-crossbones badge. Matteo sat squashed in the back, also dressed as a German, but with three partisans in civilian clothes, who would pretend to be captured Resistance fighters. They had pistols tucked into their trouser belts under their coats.

Carla was driving Sebastiano and four others, all in fascist Black Brigades uniforms and armed with a mitra like Paolo and Matteo.

The communists had devised a cunning plan. The idea was to fool the guards into thinking they were Nazi-fascists bringing new prisoners to the jail. Paolo and Sebastiano were to disarm the sentries in front of the prison while everyone else would go inside, immobilise the repub-blichini, cut telephone wires and free the inmates. It sounded simple enough, but would it work? My heart hammered against my ribs the entire way there.

Carla and I drove slowly past the piles of rubble and bricks of the bombed-out building on the corner of Piazza San Giovanni in Monte and Farini Street, then rolled to a halt. I felt the beat of my pulse in my mouth as I watched events unfold. Waving their weapons and barking orders, my comrades in uniform made the so-called prisoners get out of our car.

Paolo and Sebastiano knocked on the big oak door. 'Let us in. We've captured a group of partisans,' they yelled.

I held my breath. Would the guards question the fact that this was a bit sudden and wonder why they hadn't been given any warning? Except, we'd learnt that the movement of detainees in and out of San Giovanni had been taking place ad hoc and there were no firm procedures in place.

With a rattle of bolts, the doors opened and the 'prisoners' were pushed inside. Paolo and Sebastiano then confronted the two repubblichini guards. 'Hand over your weapons,' Sebastiano ordered.

But, without warning, the tallest fascist fired a shot which hit Sebastiano in the thigh. He gave a yelp and dropped his gun.

Porco cane, I swore to myself.

Paolo didn't hesitate; he raised his mitra and triggered a round through the tall repubblichino's throat. The fascist crumpled to the ground, blood spurting from what was left of his neck.

The other fascist guard turned tail and fled. I caught sight of his pockmarked face as he ran out of the square and remembered seeing him at the execution of the partisans in Piazza del Nettuno.

Carla and I leapt out of our cars and dragged Sebastiano to safety. He was bleeding profusely from his leg wound and crying for his mamma. Carla stripped off her belt and we made a tourniquet. Sebastiano kept on whimpering, saying how much his leg hurt.

I left him with Carla and went to give Paolo my support. 'I'm training to be a doctor and I've just taken a life,' he groaned.

'That guard would have taken your life if you hadn't taken his, my love,' I said.

Before I could utter another word, the door to the jail burst open and a mass of people came running out. I kept my eyes peeled for Rebecca and her parents as the prison emptied and hundreds of prisoners fled through the square and onto the main road. But to no avail;

they weren't among them. My heart ached and I wanted to burst into tears.

'What are you doing hanging around, Vittoria?' Matteo came and stood next to me. 'Get back to your position and drive us away before German Command sends reinforcements.'

Back at the gappista hideout, Daniele was sent for to tend to Sebastiano's leg. His face fell when he saw me there, and I apologised to him that there hadn't been time to tell him I'd volunteered. I explained it was because I was hoping Rebecca and her parents would be liberated and he'd forgive me for keeping him in the dark.

'I still think you should join our parents,' he said gruffly. 'But you were very brave to try and free Rebecca.'

He got on with treating Sebastiano, cleaning and then suturing the wound. 'The bullet entered your upper thigh and exited just above the knee. You're lucky it missed the femoral artery,' he told him. 'You'll be out of action for the duration, I'm afraid.'

Sebastiano muttered his thanks. His face had turned pale from shock and he drifted off to sleep in Carla's arms. Part of me envied her that her sweetheart would no longer be on the front line. What I'd witnessed that night had made me realise how life could be snuffed out in the blink of an eye.

I switch off my tape recorder with trembling fingers. Reliving the past has drained me and I decide to sit for a while in my chair and rest. Romeo jumps onto my lap, purring. I think about Paolo, my sweet boy. He'd surprised me that night when he'd shot the guard. It had been so out of character; he was an academic not a soldier and had escaped being drafted into the army because he was asthmatic. I rub at my eyes, remembering his courage. I still miss him terribly even after all these years.

9

RHIANNON

Rhiannon is enjoying having Leila to herself this evening. Gianluca dropped by earlier to check on his aunt and to say that he'd like to go out with Rhiannon and Marie to an *osteria* tomorrow night. He'll call for her at eight and they'll meet the French girl by the fountain in Piazza del Nettuno.

It will be fine, Rhiannon tells herself. Marie will get whatever it is she's after and, if Gianluca behaves like a playboy towards her it will be none of Rhiannon's concern.

'Let's take our coffees through to the sitting room,' Leila suggests after supper. 'Tell me more about your family in Wales.'

They sit on the sofa, Romeo purring between them. 'My parents are divorced,' Rhiannon says in answer to Leila's question.

'I'm sorry to hear that.'

'It's for the best.' Rhiannon thinks for a moment. 'My dad wasn't about much as I was growing up. His job took him all around the country.'

And all around a series of women, she found out eventually. She used to wonder why he missed so many of hers and Lowri's birthdays. Did he love his work so much that it took precedence over his own daughters? When the latest in a string of extra-marital affairs led to him fathering another child, after a massive fight Mum kicked him out and good riddance.

'Is your mother coping all right on her own?' Leila sounds concerned.

'Oh, she's fine. She's recently joined an anti-nuclear women's peace group.'

'How interesting!'

'Yes, well. It keeps her busy.' A godsend, Rhiannon thinks, remembering the years of listening to Mum sob herself to sleep while waiting in vain for Dad to come home.

'And your sister?'

'Lowri? She works for a bank in the City of London. A career woman. It's a man's world there, but she's doing well.'

Rhiannon remembers visiting her in Islington the weekend before she left for Italy. Lowri treated her to a night out in the West End when they'd gone to a performance of the musical *Sweeney Todd*. Like Rhiannon, Lowri is single. But unlike Rhiannon, she has brief liaisons with men. Lowri simply hasn't met anyone she likes enough for commitment, she maintains.

Rhiannon sighs to herself. Her one and only attempt at a proper relationship with a man had been a complete and utter disaster and she resolved never to put herself through that misery again.

'Tell me about your friends at home,' Leila enquires. 'You must miss them...'

'My best friend, Nia, is a student like me. We met when we joined a...' Rhiannon struggles to explain her interest in potholing in Italian '...a group of people who like to explore caves and tunnels under the ground.'

A smile lights up Leila's face. 'You should visit Bologna underground while you are here.'

'Bologna underground? What's that?'

'The city was crossed by lots of canals in times past. Most of them have been covered over now, but water still flows through them.' A faraway look glows in Leila's eyes. 'When I was young, we didn't have washing machines at home. Washerwomen would collect our laundry and they would wash our sheets and the like in the Reno. There's a major road now, but the waterway is right below it.'

'Oh, I'd love to go down there.'

Excitement bubbles in Rhiannon's chest. She finds it difficult to express her love of caving in words. Lowri once quizzed her about it, and the only explanation she could give was that she felt privileged and humbled to be doing something so unique, so different to the run of the mill.

'Are you particularly close to your friend Nia?' Leila gives Rhiannon a searching look.

'She has a boyfriend, so we don't spend all our time together.'

'Ah,' Leila says enigmatically. She yawns. 'Well, it's my bedtime now. I'll see you at breakfast, Rhiannon.'

'*Buonanotte*, Leila. I've enjoyed our chat.'

'*Anch'io, cara.*' Me too, dear. '*Sogni d'oro.*' Golden dreams.

Rhiannon helps Leila to her feet and smiles when her landlady kisses her on both cheeks.

* * *

The following evening, Rhiannon steps out of Leila's palazzo into Marsala Street with Gianluca. A chilly wind whips her hair and she pushes her hands deep into her pockets. Gianluca leads her down a narrow, cobblestoned street past ancient buildings and some not so ancient to arrive at Via dell'Indipendenza. She stares at the majestic palazzo in front of her, its imposing balcony festooned with flags. 'That's a five-star hotel,' Gianluca explains. 'The Baglioni.'

They cross over to Piazza del Nettuno. A crowd throngs the area by the fountain and Rhiannon can't see Marie among the mass of people.

'What's going on?' Rhiannon asks, staring at a muscular man with long, light brown hair, dressed from head to foot in sleek black leather, who is playing his electric guitar fervently. Pounding rock music blasts from an amplifier mounted on a Harley-Davidson, reverberating off the walls of the stone palazzi.

'That's Beppe Maniglia,' Gianluca chuckles. 'See what he does next...'

Without warning, the man stops playing and picks up an empty hot water bottle. He places it to his lips and starts to blow into it.

'What's he doing?'

'*Aspetta.*' Wait.

With great puffs, Beppe Maniglia keeps blowing.

Suddenly, there's a loud bang and the hot water bottle explodes.

The throng of people erupts into an almighty cheer.

Rhiannon's mouth drops open. 'Well, that's the last thing I expected to see,' she laughs.

'It's certainly a crowd-pleaser.' Gianluca joins in her laughter. He glances around. 'I wonder where Marie has got to?'

They stand and wait in the cold for about fifteen minutes. Rhiannon shivers and wraps her arms around herself. 'She was so keen on coming out tonight. I don't understand why she isn't here.'

Gianluca huffs. 'Let's go to the *osteria*. She might catch up with us later.'

He takes Rhiannon's hand and she stiffens. 'Relax!' He gives a chuckle. 'I don't bite.'

The Osteria del Sole is in the Quadrilatero district, close to where Gianluca took her and Marie for *piadine*.

'This is one of the few remaining osterie from the Middle Ages,' he explains as they step across the threshold into a long, narrow space with an arch at the end.

'Amazing.'

'They only serve beer and wine. No cocktails or food. So people bring their own food if they want to eat.'

The *osteria* is noisy and crowded, but they find two spare chairs at a big oak table. It's like a pub at home, Rhiannon thinks. She gazes at the enormous wooden bar dominating the area under the arch. Bottles line the shelves behind, and sepia-toned photos and framed artists' sketches and paintings cover the whitewashed walls.

'Would you like a glass of San Giovese?' Gianluca raises his voice to be heard above the din of conversations and pop music blasting from speakers.

She likes the taste of the rich, red wine, having tried it at Leila's, and gladly accepts. 'I wonder what's happened to Marie?'

'I'm surprised she didn't ring you.'

'She hasn't got your aunt's phone number.'

The noise level in the *osteria* prevents further chit-chat. Rhiannon and Gianluca sip their drinks in silence.

'Let's go somewhere quieter,' Gianluca shouts above the hubbub when they've emptied their glasses. 'The night is still young, as they say.'

Rhiannon is on the point of refusing, but she doesn't want to appear rude.

'We can have a nightcap at the Baglioni. The bar area is quiet and it's on the way home.'

'I'm not dressed for a posh hotel...' Rhiannon indicates her plain black trousers and chain store bought lacy top.

He smiles. '*Sei bella come sei.*' You're lovely as you are.

She can't help the blush that warms her cheeks. 'Okay...' She shrugs on her coat.

Gianluca takes her hand, and she lets him. Strange, she thinks. *She hasn't frozen at his touch.*

Within minutes, a door attendant is ushering them through the Baglioni's entrance. Rhiannon admires the gleaming marble floors, white Doric columns and gilded antique furnishings characterising the opulent interiors.

The cocktail lounge is an entirely different kettle of fish from the *osteria* they've just visited. Here, a waiter dressed in an immaculate uniform takes their drinks order – more glasses of San Giovese – and the atmosphere of the establishment is refined.

Gianluca falls silent, his attention drawn by a middle-aged man sitting alone at a table in the far corner. Rhiannon tries not to stare at the orange-peel skin on the fellow's face; he must have suffered severe acne in his youth.

'Who's that?' she asks.

'Ugo Barzini. Right-wing newspaper proprietor.' Gianluca shakes his head, then turns his gaze back to Rhiannon. 'So, tell me, how are you getting on with your plan to walk along all the porticoes in Bologna?'

She'd mentioned it to him last week. 'Still many kilometres to go, but I'm getting there.' She pauses. 'Leila told me about the underground waterways. I'd really like to see them.'

'I can arrange for you to visit if you like, but why the interest?'

She explains about her passion for potholing. 'I'm intrigued there's so much hidden below this city. I had no idea.'

'The banks of canals that traversed Bologna under the open sky for centuries were straddled by silk and flour mills and small factories that cured skins and tobacco, made paper, dyed cloth, and worked metal. They depended on water wheels to produce the power needed to process their goods.'

'Fascinating. Such a shame the canals were all covered up.'

'I agree. But energy production changed at the same time as transportation needs.'

Gianluca knocks back the rest of his wine and she follows suit.

'I'll walk you back to my aunt's,' he offers.

'*Grazie*, but I need to use the ladies' first.'

He smiles. 'I'll wait for you out front.'

Rhiannon gets directions to the restroom from their waiter. She uses the facilities, then heads back across the lobby.

Oh my God. She stops dead in her tracks. Marie has just stepped out of the lift and is making her way towards the cocktail lounge.

Rhiannon doesn't want to be seen, so she hides behind a column. Once the French girl is out of sight, Rhiannon follows her and peers through the door.

Marie has sat herself down next to the newspaper owner and has leant forward for him to light her cigarette.

What the hell is she up to?

Rhiannon spins on her heel and makes haste to tell Gianluca about her classmate's antics.

10

LEILA

I'm alone in the kitchen, having waved a flustered Rhiannon off just minutes ago. I didn't hear her come in last night and she was non-committal when I asked her this morning about how she'd enjoyed the *osteria*. She'd overslept and was in a hurry to leave for school, so I'll probably find out more tonight.

I've got the fidgets, so I go into the sitting room to fluff up cushions, then return to the kitchen to tidy around. I'm finding it hard to settle down and record my memoirs. Even Romeo is keeping out of my way. I felt the same yesterday – the appalling human suffering caused by conflict has been preying so heavily on my mind. Sometimes I tremble as I watch the news on TV; it makes me worry for the safety of Gianluca and young people like him. As Herodotus once said, 'In peace, sons bury their fathers. In war, fathers bury their sons.' So many of my contemporaries lost their lives forty years ago. Remembering the terrible events with such clarity has made me feel sad and extremely concerned for the future. Is the world truly a jungle that will never change? I sincerely hope not.

I think about Rhiannon's mother joining an anti-nuclear peace movement, and I admire her for it. The tragic bombings of Hiroshima and Nagasaki and the consequent deaths of hundreds of thousands of innocent people must never be repeated. I can only thank God the Nazis didn't get far in developing an A-bomb. It's my firm belief that Hitler would have used it on Italy. 'Operation Radium' and others like it must surely have helped prevent such a catastrophe.

My heart aches with sadness and I ask myself if I'd known how things would turn out in the terrible autumn of 1944, would I have joined the Resistance. But, at the end of the day, I was a partisan because I couldn't just stand by and do nothing. I wanted to be involved; I wanted to help liberate my country from occupation and I wanted to live in a free and democratic society. Like so many others, I was prepared to make sacrifices for the cause.

I make a soothing cup of tea, then force myself to sit at the kitchen table and take calming breaths to lower my blood pressure.

I give a start. Romeo rubbing against my legs has reminded me of the tasks at hand. I'll feed him and then resume telling my story – I always finish what I've started and I'm not going to stop now. Reliving the past is painful but remaining silent would only support the perpetrators of evil. I hope the suffering experienced by my generation will never happen to the current generation, their children, and their grandchildren. My comrades and I paid the price for them, and those of my family who come after me need to know about that.

In the gappista Bolognina hideout, delayed reaction to the events at San Giovanni in Monte made my stomach churn and I threw up in the toilet after I'd left Sebastiano to my brother's care.

Paolo was waiting for me outside the bathroom. He wiped my mouth with gentle concern and gave me a glass of water. 'Are you all right?'

'It's only nerves. I'll be fine.'

He brushed a kiss to my forehead. 'You did well at the prison, amore mio. I'm proud of you.'

'I'm proud of you, too.' Love for him swelled in my heart. 'But I'm so disappointed Rebecca and her parents weren't there.' I sniffed back a sob.

We changed out of our German uniforms, found a quiet corner, and snuggled together, dozing until daybreak and the end of curfew. Then we walked back to the city centre. Paolo lived with his family in San Vitale; he left me at my place in Marsala Street and continued from there.

I'd just managed to have a wash and a quick lunch when the doorbell rang. Margherita, our maid, went to answer it. I wasn't concerned, thinking the caller was probably a black marketeer selling food.

But Margherita burst into the sitting room, her eyes wide and her plump fingers pleating her apron. 'Signorina, these two signori are looking for your brother.'

My heart skipped a beat. Two men were standing behind her. One, a blond German in black SS captain's attire and the other dressed in the grey-green repubblichini uniform. I peered at the fascist; his face was familiar. Pockmarked. Madonna! Would I ever escape that man? He was following me around like a bad smell.

'Where's Dottor Venturi?' he snapped.

'Gone to the Veneto,' I lied. Presumably, Dani was still at the partisans' hideout. He was due to help at a soup kitchen later – the town council had set up several of them to feed the starving populace.

'Papiere!' The German's pale eyes stared through me as though I were transparent.

I showed my ID and asked why he was there.

The repubblichino answered for him. 'We have information that your brother stole radium from the hospital.'

My blood turned to ice. 'I don't know anything about that...'

'We're here to carry out a search,' he said. 'We have men waiting outside.'

There was nothing I could do but stand by helplessly, trying to appear calm, while five militiamen turned the house upside-down.

'Take us to your basement!' the repubblichino demanded after they'd found nothing.

With quaking legs, I led them down the stone staircase at the back of the ground floor. 'It's our air-raid shelter,' I explained, pointing out the mattresses where we huddled during bombardments.

Again, I stood by powerlessly, pretending to be innocent by holding eye contact with them while they got on with their search.

The black-shirted repubblichini ransacked the cellar, ripping open sacks of flour and upturning boxes of dried beans and other staples. I kept my gaze averted from the coal heap, but, eventually, they turned their attention towards it.

'Dig!' the German barked.

One of the fascists grabbed the only spade and started to shovel lumps of coal from the enormous pile.

Fine dark grey coal dust lifted from the heap.

The German began to cough and gasp for breath. 'Genügend,' he growled.

'Enough,' the repubblichino echoed. 'Clearly, your brother has hidden the radium somewhere else, signorina. When he returns to Bologna, tell him to report to Gestapo headquarters.'

'I will,' I lied again.

Pockface brushed past me as he left the cellar, making my flesh crawl.

As soon as the coast was clear, I asked Margherita to hurry to the *soup kitchen and warn Dani. He sent word back with her that he'd decided to go to Fossoli and try and get close to the transit camp north of Modena where Rebecca and her parents had been taken. I had no idea what he planned to do there; they were almost certainly behind barbed wire. I only hoped he wouldn't put himself in any danger.*

Paolo came to see me in the evening, and I told him about the German and the repubblichini searching for the radium. 'Porco cane,' he swore, lighting his Nazionale cigarette. I wished he wouldn't smoke, it aggravated his asthma, but I didn't say anything. He maintained smoking soothed his nerves, and I couldn't argue with that.

I told Paolo I thought Dani should go into hiding when he returned from Fossoli. 'I'm scared those bastards will arrest him.'

'I wonder who informed on him?' Paolo took a drag of his cigarette.

'Could have been someone at the clinic.' I paused, changed the subject. 'Have there been any repercussions because of our raid on the prison?'

Paolo gave a sardonic laugh. 'Our spies have discovered that no one came to intervene as they thought there were forty of us not twelve. We didn't kill any Germans, so there won't be any reprisals.'

It was a victory, of sorts, and Paolo and I were young and filled with idealism. We believed there would be further victories, that things would continue to go our way. Two days after our action at the jail, we heard that Florence had been liberated. Surely it would not be long before it was Bologna's turn?

I switch off my recorder and clutch at myself as sudden tears trail down my cheeks. It was many months before my city gained its freedom, months of hardship and death. *So much death.* Better not to dwell on it now. I straighten my shoulders and wipe away my tears. I know what will cheer me up; I'll make a nice dessert for supper tonight. Zuppa inglese.

In the kitchen, I switch on my radio and turn the dial to a music station. The Bolognese singer Lucio Dalla's hit, 'La Sera dei Miracoli', comes on and I sing along while I make the pastry cream. It's the recipe I learnt from Stella, our former cook. I smack my lips; I can't wait for Rhiannon to taste it.

11

RHIANNON

Rhiannon has spent the morning with her head down, concentrating on her lessons, steeling herself to speak to Marie during their lunch break. Last night, after she'd told Gianluca about the French girl's behaviour, he said he would have a word with a contact of his at the university to discover if Marie really is who she claims to be. Rhiannon's impression there's something 'off' about the girl has resonated with him too, he added. Apparently, when he asked Marie about the Sorbonne the other day, she only answered vaguely. Not a crime, but in the light of what just happened at the Baglioni, he's more than a little suspicious. And Rhiannon is too. Why did Marie pester her to go out with Gianluca then stand him up? It doesn't make sense. Gianluca asked Rhiannon not to divulge to Marie that she's been found out. He's investigating Ugo Barzini's contacts with possible extremists, he divulged as he linked arms with Rhiannon and walked her home. If Marie is involved in something suspicious, it would be best if Rhiannon weren't to get too close to her.

Rhiannon presses her lips together while she takes notes at this morning's history of art lecture. Marie turned up late to class and Rhiannon hasn't had the chance to ask her why she didn't come to Piazza del Nettuno as arranged. She shoots her a quick look, but the French girl glances away.

Finally, their lecturer shows them the last slide, *The Visitation*, a 1550 painting by the artist Tintoretto, which can be viewed in the National Art Gallery of Bologna. Rhiannon puts her notepad away in her rucksack and hurries out of the classroom.

She finds Marie crossing the courtyard and goes up to her. 'What happened to you last night?'

'So sorry.' The French girl shrugs. 'I would have rung but I didn't have your number. My uncle came on a surprise visit from Paris and I had to meet him...'

'Oh.' Rhiannon clears her throat and matches her pace with Marie's as they step into Piazza San Giovanni in Monte. If the newspaper owner is the French girl's uncle, what's she doing staying at student digs in the Bolognina district? The family must be wealthy and could afford better accommodation for her, surely.

Marie stops mid-stride. 'There's Gianluca.' She indicates towards the other side of the square.

With a cheery wave he approaches, then kisses them both on their cheeks. 'I was in the area, so I thought I'd meet you two *belle signorine* for lunch.'

They walk to a caffè-bar in Piazza Santo Stefano and order coffees and panini. It's one of those gorgeous early spring afternoons, the sky so blue it seems to go on for ever. The sunlight is almost blinding in its intensity, and Rhiannon wishes she had a pair of dark glasses.

'I apologise about last night,' Marie has the grace to say to Gianluca. 'My uncle came to town unexpectedly, and I went to meet him.'

'Apology accepted,' Gianluca says with a smile. 'Does your uncle live in France?'

'Oh, yes. In Paris. Like me...'

'I've heard Paris is a beautiful city and would love to visit one day. Where do you live exactly?'

'Near the Sacré Coeur in Montparnasse.'

'Ah...' Gianluca says. 'Interesting.'

The waiter brings their order and, while they eat, Gianluca and Marie chat about Paris. Rhiannon feels like a third wheel again but tells herself not to be silly. Gianluca is obviously trying to find out more about the French girl.

Marie lights up one of her Gauloises cigarettes, and the burnt-rubber scent wafts towards Rhiannon. She tried smoking once when she was a teen, but it made her feel sick so she didn't try again. Even now, the smell makes her nauseous.

'And you, Gianluca,' Marie asks him. 'What is it that you do?'

'Do?'

'For a living.'

'I'm an investigative journalist.'

Marie's mouth drops open. Literally. She takes a drag of her cigarette. 'What are you investigating?'

'This and that,' he says enigmatically before drinking down the remainder of his coffee. 'Well, if you ladies will excuse me, I'd better get back to work. It was nice seeing you. Enjoy the rest of your day.' He leaves some notes and coins on the table to settle his share of the bill.

'You didn't tell me Gianluca is a journalist,' Marie mutters, linking her arm with Rhiannon's as they walk back to school.

'You didn't ask. What does it matter?'

'I don't like journalists. Always sticking their noses into other people's business.' She pauses. 'Such a shame. Gianluca is gorgeous, but I'd rather not see him again.'

Rhiannon stiffens. 'Oh, okay.' And she leaves it at that.

* * *

After class, Rhiannon is on her way home, about to step into Piazza San Martino. She does a double take. Gianluca is coming towards her.

'Ciao, Rhiannon. I'm glad I caught you. Would you like to see one of the canals that's been left open to the sky?'

'That would be great.' She lightens her step.

'It's not far. In fact, it's just up the road.' He takes her rucksack and swings it over his shoulder.

They walk together along the ancient, cobbled street leading off the square, then turn right. An old gateway, built of red brick and crumbling at the edges, occupies the periphery of Rhiannon's vision. She points towards it. 'What's that?'

'Part of the second circle of city walls which protected Bologna from the late twelfth century onwards.'

The ancient gateposts look a little lopsided, their legs stretching wide apart to straddle the road as if it were the saddle of a big horse.

After passing underneath, Rhiannon and Gianluca follow Piella Street until they come to a small, wooden, shuttered window built into a wall. Gianluca opens it. '*Ecco il Canale.*' Here's the canal.

Rhiannon peers at the narrow band of water flowing between tall houses tinted in shades of russet and gold. Washing hangs from their picturesque balconies. 'Amazing!'

'It's an extension of the Reno, which has been completely covered up where it crosses Bologna city centre. For most of its route this canal is locked between buildings which is why it's hidden from view. You can only see the waterway through windows like this one.'

Rhiannon loses herself in the scene, imagining going back in time to a Bologna crowded with medieval merchants on the busy bridges, where the smack of water against stone would have echoed in her ears instead of the clamour of cars and the revving of Vespa and moped engines. She's conscious of Gianluca standing next to her, his body aligned with hers in the small space. Unaccountably, she feels safe with him. Safe and filled with a strange sense of longing. *How odd.*

'Shall we go for a drink?' he suggests. 'There's something I'd like to tell you.'

'*Va bene.*' All right.

The sun has started to wane in the late afternoon sky. She shivers and arranges her scarf tighter around her neck.

He takes her to Bar delle Acque at the top of Oberdan Street, where they sit at a tiny table after ordering glasses of San Giovese.

'Is that the sound of rushing water I can hear?' She tilts her head.

'It's springtime and rain has been plentiful, so it's flowing in the canal right under us. Do you still want to go down there?'

'I'd love to. When?'

'I need to arrange it.' He laughs. 'You're keen.'

She joins in his laughter. 'I am...' She pauses, sips her wine. 'So, what did you want to tell me?'

'Marie said she lives near the Sacré Coeur in Montparnasse. The Sacré Coeur isn't in Montparnasse but in Montmartre...'

'Maybe she confused the two?'

'Hmm.' He rubs his chin. 'And, if she was meeting her uncle, he wasn't Ugo Barzini. Barzini lives here in Bologna, not Paris.'

'But why would she lie?'

'That's what I'd like to discover.'

'She said she doesn't want to see you again, Gianluca.'

He raises an eyebrow. 'Now that has certainly spiked my interest. She was like a bitch in heat towards me the other week.'

Rhiannon feels the burn of a blush at his racy words. 'She said she doesn't like investigative journalists.'

'Then she must have something to hide.'

'Did you learn anything about her from your contact at the university?'

'Not yet. I'll do that tomorrow.' He blows out a breath. '*Cavolo*, I was hoping Marie would be a way for me to get to Barzini. But if she won't see me...'

'I can help you,' Rhiannon offers without thinking. 'I mean, she still wants to be friends with me, I think.'

He holds up his hands. 'Absolutely not. I have no idea what, if anything, she's mixed up in. I don't want to put you at risk. Besides, my aunt would be furious if I got you involved.'

'She warned me off you.'

'She thinks I'm a playboy.'

'Are you? A playboy, I mean...'

He shakes his head. 'Did my aunt tell you about Flavia?'

'She did.'

'The past three years have been the worst of my life...'

'I'm sincerely sorry for your loss, Gianluca.' Rhiannon leans across the table and touches her hand to his.

* * *

'I was starting to be concerned about you,' Leila says as Rhiannon and Gianluca step into the kitchen.

'I should have found a pay phone and called you.' Rhiannon kisses her on both cheeks. 'Gianluca took me to view the canal from the window in Piella Street.'

'La Finestrella, we call it.' A smile lights Leila's eyes. She places a pan on the stove. 'But now it's time to eat. Gianluca, you must stay. I've made zuppa inglese for dessert and I know how much you like it.'

'Zuppa inglese?' Rhiannon translates the words in her head to their literal meaning, *English soup*.

Gianluca laughs. 'You'll see.'

And she does. After a delicious main course of tagliata di manzo – thinly sliced steak – served with sauteed potatoes and artichokes, Leila produces what Rhiannon immediately recognises as a dish of trifle. Except it doesn't taste like any trifle she's eaten before. 'It's yummy,' she enthuses. 'What kind of liqueur do you use?'

'Alchermes.'

'I've never heard of it.'

'It's very old. Dates from the fifteenth century. I believe it was a favourite of the Medici family in Florence back then,' Gianluca says.

'What's it made of?'

'A concoction of alcohol, sugar, water, cinnamon, cardamom, cloves. I can't remember what else.'

'Water of roses, raspberries and cochineal,' Leila adds. 'Would you like some more?'

'It's really good, but I couldn't manage another bite.'

'I could.' Gianluca pushes his plate forwards and Leila spoons a second helping onto it.

She beams a smile at Rhiannon. 'How was last night? You rushed off this morning before you could tell me...'

Rhiannon catches Gianluca's eye and he gives a slight nod. 'Marie, my French friend, stood us up. We went to an *osteria* but it was very noisy, so we ended up at the Baglioni.'

'Ah, yes, the Baglioni. I have such memories of that place.'

Leila visibly shudders. 'Tell me more about Marie. Why didn't she join you?'

Rhiannon catches Gianluca's eye again. A frown creases his brow. 'Oh, her uncle came on a surprise visit. She would have called but she didn't have your number.'

Leila glances from Gianluca to Rhiannon and back to Gianluca again. 'And?'

He lifts his hands. 'Don't worry, Auntie. I've been a perfect gentleman. Rhiannon and I are just friends.'

Rhiannon discerns the look of relief on Leila's face. How she wishes she wouldn't blush so easily.

12

LEILA

After Rhiannon has left for school the next morning, I head down San Vitale Street towards the archway of the Torresotto, one of the remaining gates of the Cerchia del Mille – the city walls dating from 1192. A quirky weathervane whips about in the wind at the top of the tower, and it strikes me that the vaulted opening below appears slightly askew from carrying the weight of the centuries on its back.

I walk under the arch and step into Piazza Aldrovandi, my heels making a tip-tapping sound on the pavement. My spirits lift at the familiar sight – over the years, the fruit and vegetable stands lining the porticoed pavement on the east side of the piazza have become a part of my everyday routine. I love having coffee in the friendly bars and I enjoy making purchases from the small shops selling everything from antique books to a variety of cheeses and salami. I breathe in the aroma of fresh produce and absorb the hullabaloo of myriad conversations. No one touts their wares, they don't need to, for we all have our favourite stallholders and always buy from them.

'Ciao, Vittoria,' Bruno yells from his fruit and vegetable stand. He was a partisan in 1944 and still calls me by my battle name.

'Ciao, Bruno!' He's really Giuseppe, but we went through so much together I'll never think of him as anyone else.

'I have some wonderful asparagus,' he holds out a bunch for me to examine.

'Oh, they would be perfect for a risotto tonight...'

I pay for the asparagus, then make my way to my chosen cheese vendor for pecorino, which I like to use in my pasta sauce recipes. It was only after Stella retired in 1970 that I discovered how much I love to cook. And I also enjoy shopping at the market, especially now I have more time on my hands. It gets me out of the house and my doctor said I should try and walk on a regular basis, so I'm killing two pigeons with one stone. I said as much to Gianluca this morning when he so kindly brought freshly baked bread for our breakfast. 'I'm a lot less tired now,' I told him. 'So I'll get back to buying the groceries myself.'

Walking home, I think about him and Rhiannon. Just friends, he said. He wouldn't lie to me, so I should stop worrying. It's nice for her to have a young person with whom she can speak Italian; she's probably fed up with only talking to me. The fact they went for a drink at the Baglioni made me shudder, however. Such a coincidence that I've almost come to the part of my story in which the Baglioni features. I grip the handle of my shopping trolley and make haste up Marsala Street. My tape recorder is waiting for me, and my memories too.

In early September, Daniele made a secret visit to me. He'd recently returned from Fossoli, and we shed tears of sorrow together after he'd told me he'd found out that Rebecca and her parents had been deported to a place in Poland called Auschwitz. From what he'd heard, the hateful Nazis treated the internees like slaves, using them for forced labour and making them live in dreadful conditions. 'If I could go to there and rescue Rebecca and her parents, I would.' Dani released a deep sigh.

'Rebecca is tough,' I reminded him. 'And the war will soon be over. The Matatias will be back before we know it.'

'How I hope that will be so.' He breathed another sigh. 'I wish I didn't have to go back to living in hiding, but all being well it won't be for long.'

'Stay safe,' I begged him.

'I'm a non-combatant, remember. I look after the sick and wounded.'

I pulled him in for a hug.

The next day, I met Paolo down in the School of Arts basement. 'Last night, the nazifascisti arrested the Partito d'Azione leaders,' he announced.

Dread chilled my chest. 'Oh my God, why?'

'It's because of Operation Radium.' Paolo's face reflected his concern. 'The partito has been infiltrated by spies and the nazifasciti detained two of the cancer ward nurses last week. My guess is they've talked under duress.'

I grabbed hold of Paolo's hand. 'I hope they don't find out about your involvement, amore mio.'

'Word is they're looking for the director of the oncology department. So I've decided I won't go home. And I'd better not come to the university, either. I'll go to the communists' hideout in Bolognina.'

I wrapped my arms around his waist and buried my head in his chest. 'Be careful, darling.'

'You too, Leila.' He brushed a kiss to the top of my head. 'We won't be able to see each other for a while.'

'I'll come to Bolognina when it's safe.' The words trembled in my mouth.

'God knows when that will be…'

I bade a tearful farewell to him and, for the next two weeks, performed my courier duties alongside Clara – who was still with the Resistance despite Sebastiano being out of action.

Matteo brought me news of Paolo from time to time. Matteo had become less scathing of me since the San Giovanni in Monte raid, thank God. It was Matteo who conveyed terrible information about the imprisoned Action Party leaders. They'd been tortured, then sentenced to death by firing squad, and all attempts to get their sentences commuted had fallen into the abyss. I wept when Matteo told me that one of the politicians' wives had even gone to the Baglioni, the nazi-fascisti top brass's quarters, to plead for the life of her husband. They refused to commute the sentence outright.

At 5 a.m. on 23 September, those bastards executed our party leader Messenzio Masia, whom we called Max, a man of Socratic wisdom and serenity, of superior intellect, and a brilliant politician, who'd been our mentor since the establishment of the university gappisti. Seven other politici antifascisti were shot with him. Carla and I grasped hold of each other, sobbing when Matteo gave the shocking news.

'From now onwards we shall be known as the Justice and Liberty Masia brigade,' he said. 'In honour of our brave political leader.' He paused. 'And we're moving over to the Geography department under the direction of Marroni.'

I'd met Marroni before – an intensely patriotic man, in his late twenties, who'd been one of the organisers of Operation Radium. 'I fervently hope the Allies will get here soon,' I sighed.

In fact, we'd heard on the Allies' radio station, Italia Combatte, that the morning of 21 September the Germans had withdrawn from their positions on the Rimini Line behind the Ausa River to new positions on the Marecchia. I knew the area well – it was about one hundred kilometres south of Bologna and I'd gone there with groups of friends for short breaks in the summers when I wasn't up in the Veneto mountains with my parents.

'The communists want to eliminate the nazifasciti command in retaliation for the executions. Also because it will be a lot easier without them when the time comes to rise up and take back our city,' Matteo interrupted my thoughts.

Insurrection was the word being whispered among us. Already, people were rebelling against the occupation, organising strikes and demonstrations in the small towns and villages between Bologna and the Allies' lines. 'I just pray Paolo won't be in any danger,' I said.

I went home that afternoon, my heart heavy. I missed seeing Paolo every day, and I yearned for Daniele's presence in the family palazzo.

Two days after I'd heard about Max's execution, I was missing Paolo so much, I decided to go and visit him. So, I set off well before curfew and walked for about half an hour to Bolognina. I came to a semi-dilapidated four-storey building at the corner of Piazza dell'Unità and gave the password at the door. Inside, I was surprised to discover that numbers had been depleted since the San Giovanni in Monte raid.

'Many have gone to join the partisans in the mountains,' Paolo informed me after enveloping me in a warm embrace.

'But you haven't, I'm relieved to see.'

'I'm needed here. We're about to carry out an action.'

'Can I help? I mean, do you need a driver again?'

He coughed. 'We have a driver, an older man who isn't up to fighting but wants to assist.'

'Are you going after the nazifascisti top brass?' I asked, remembering what Dani had said. My heart set up a fearful beat.

'We're planning an attack in the Baglioni tonight. I'll wear a German army officer uniform and enter the hotel for a reconnoitre. Everyone else will wait outside until I give them the all-clear. They will then rush in and do the deed before the nazifascisti know what's hit them.'

'Sounds like an excellent plan,' I said in a false bright tone.

I was worried for him and every nerve in my body ached to go with him. But what role could I play? They already had a driver, and I didn't know how to shoot a gun. A sudden idea occurred to me. 'I could dress up and act like I'm fraternising with a German.'

Paolo looked me up and down. 'I don't want to put you at risk.'

His words were like a red rag to a bull. 'I'd be the one putting myself at risk, amore. It's my life and my decision. Besides, just thinking about what might be happening to Rebecca makes me even more determined to play my part in bringing the enemy occupation to an end.'

'I couldn't bear it if anything happened to you,' Paolo said.

I turned to Bruno, the young communist who led the brigade. 'I'd like to volunteer. I could pretend to be one of those Bolognese women who, you know...'

'We have a wardrobe full of women's clothes upstairs for just such an initiative.' He smirked. 'I think your idea is a good one. It will lend authenticity to Tarzan's disguise.'

I suppressed a giggle at hearing Paolo's battle name. You shouldn't laugh, I told myself, your sweetheart has shown himself to be a great hero.

Paolo took my hand and led me to a first-floor bedroom. 'I hope you're not angry with me for volunteering,' I whispered.

'To be honest, I'm relieved you will be with me, my love.'

'I wouldn't want it any other way.' I kissed him on the lips.

The wardrobe was filled with ladies' fashion. God knew how the partisans had got hold of it and I wasn't about to ask.

'Well, I'll leave you to get changed, darling.' Paolo smiled his sweet, loving smile.

I chose a long, sleek, Grecian-style emerald-green evening gown, a fox fur wrap, and a pair of leather pumps. I pinned up my hair and applied bright red lipstick. My reflection in the mirror showed a self-assured young woman, but I felt far from certain I'd be able to pull off the deception.

Paolo met me downstairs, looking handsome yet sinister in an SS *officer service tunic with silver insignia, worn over black jodhpurs tucked into tall leather boots. A red band emblazoned with a swastika swaddled his left arm.*

He looked deep into my eyes, and I felt more confident. He was my Paolo, my gentle boy who'd grown into a strong man these past few weeks. Together, we could do this, I hoped.

We waited until shortly before midnight, occupying our time playing cards with Bruno and three others disguised in repubblichini uniforms. At the appointed hour, the fake repubblichini squashed into the back seat of one of the Fiat 1500s we'd used in the San Giovanni in Monte raid, and I sat on Paolo's lap in the front next to our elderly driver.

Within minutes, we were heading down Via dell'Indipendenza. Although I was nervous about what I'd volunteered for, I had no fear of being hauled up for being out after curfew. Our vehicle was flying German flags on the fenders and, in any case, the nazifascisti mostly went to ground at night – seemingly convinced no one would disobey their orders. Our driver rolled the car to a halt in front of Bologna's cathedral opposite the hotel, and Paolo and I went inside.

'Are you here for the dinner dance?' the doorman asked as he ushered us into the lobby.

'We are,' Paolo confirmed, coughing.

Arm in arm, we sauntered past two repubblichini guards and made our way across the gleaming marble floor. A lump of ice formed in my throat as we stopped before the open door to the restaurant and peered at the assembled company. Mostly uniformed men, although there were a few women scattered among them. Three large, round tables loaded with food and drink. An orchestra on the podium playing sultry music and couples dancing the tango in the middle of the room. I swallowed hard.

'Let's go tell the others,' Paolo murmured.

Nonchalantly, we headed back through the lobby and out the front door. The doorman gave us a puzzled look but didn't say anything. Sweat beaded my upper lip and I wiped it away with a shaky hand.

Everything happened so rapidly afterwards, I could barely keep track. Because I wasn't armed, I couldn't take part, just act as a look-out. My pulse racing, I stood by the entrance and watched.

Paolo and Bruno shot the repubblichini guards before they could react. Ragged wounds bloomed red in their chests and they crumpled to the floor, dead.

Between them, two of our gappisti carried a crate loaded with ninety kilos of TNT and quickly placed it in the centre of the lobby.

The other gappista had a cannister of petrol, which he doused liberally all over the carpeted grand central staircase.

Paolo and Bruno, joined by the men who'd carried the crate, started firing indiscriminately at the Nazi-fascists in the restaurant.

Ra-ta-ta-ta-ta, their submachine guns went, the noise so loud it rang in my ears and almost drowned out the sound of the screams coming from the dining area.

The partisan who'd drenched the carpet in petrol lit a fuse to the crate of explosive.

Bruno barked the order to leave and we all ran out of the hotel, leaving the enemy in chaos and confusion.

It was only when we'd piled into the car and were racing up Via dell'Indipendenza that we realised, in our haste, no one had set fire to the petrol. Porca miseria!

We listened for the boom of the expected explosion.

Nothing.

Cavolo, the fuse to the crate must have gone out.

Returning to the hotel to relight it wasn't an option. We'd been lucky to have got away without any of us being killed.

Back at the communist headquarters, we changed out of our disguises and had a glass of wine. None of us felt like celebrating, *however; we hadn't achieved our objective. 'We'll have to make a second attempt,' Bruno muttered.*

It would need a different approach, I realised, and I knew I wouldn't be able to take part. The realisation that Paolo could be injured, or worse, and I wouldn't be there to help him, made me choke on a sob as he held me tight. 'What's wrong, love?' he asked.

'Just a reaction to what we did,' I mumbled into his chest. 'Keep holding me, my darling. I'll be fine.'

I switch off my microphone and lean back in my chair, my chest aching terribly. Little did I know then how short a time Paolo and I had left. Only a couple of months, as it turned out. My vision blurs as I'm blinded by my tears. I sniff and wipe at my nose. *So many lives lost...*

13

RHIANNON

It's Saturday morning and Rhiannon's second weekend in Bologna. She stretches out in her comfortable bed, enjoying a short lie-in. Excitement tingles in her tummy; she's meeting Gianluca at eleven. Today, he's organised for someone to take them down to the Aposa, the stream which flows directly under Piazza San Martino. He called in briefly last night after supper to tell her about the arrangement. Rhiannon wanted to hug him in gratitude; but she didn't, of course. She simply thanked him and said, 'This will definitely be something for me to write home about.'

He chuckled. 'It will be a bit smelly, I'm warning you. Unfortunately, some sewage still empties into the channel. The council are supposed to be diverting it but haven't got round to installing the right equipment yet.'

'Ah.' she suppressed a shudder. She hadn't thought of that aspect. 'I won't let it put me off.' And she gave him what she hoped was a convincing smile.

'How was school today?' he asked.

'Good. Marie wasn't there.' She lowered her voice. 'Did you find out anything about her?'

'I did,' he whispered. 'I'll tell you tomorrow.'

'What are you two whispering about?' Leila asked from her armchair, where she was sitting watching a musical programme on TV.

'I'm taking Rhiannon down to explore the Aposa in the morning.' Gianluca smiled. 'We'll grab a bite to eat together afterwards.'

'Take clothes pegs for your noses.' Leila laughed uproariously. 'And watch out for rats,' she added with a twinkle in her eye.

Whatever have I let myself in for, Rhiannon thinks now as she swivels her legs and gets out of bed.

She takes a shower, then dresses in jeans and a jumper before going to the kitchen for some breakfast. The enticing aroma of freshly brewed coffee wafts in the air. She pushes the door open.

'*Buongiorno*,' Leila regards her. 'Did you sleep well?'

'Like a dormouse.' Rhiannon pulls out a chair.

They chat about Bologna's canals while they drink their cappuccinos.

'The system of waterways linked the city to the Po River and the Adriatic Sea during the Middle Ages.' Leila takes a sip of coffee. 'It also had important political ramifications for Bologna and its relationships with Ferrara and Venezia.' A faraway expression spreads across her face. 'If we'd lived in those times, we could have begun an ocean voyage to the exotic Orient from here.'

'Wonderful.' Rhiannon smiles. 'When did they start covering over the canals?'

'About three hundred years ago. But the Aposa, which was completely uncovered in the Roman period, began to be covered up during the late fifteenth century. By the end of the nineteenth century, only a third of the stream was open to the skies. Now, just a small section is visible from above, the part where it flows into the Moline canal, which you saw with Gianluca the other day. The last waterway to be concealed was the Reno in the fifties.'

'Intriguing.' Rhiannon drinks down the rest of her coffee, then takes hers and Leila's cup to the sink. 'I'll just go and get my coat.' She inclines her head towards Leila. '*Cosa fai di bello oggi?*' What are you doing today sounds so much nicer in Italian, she thinks. What beautiful thing are you doing today?

Leila pushes herself to her feet. 'I'm recording my memoirs of when I fought with the Resistance.'

Rhiannon's breath catches. 'That's so brave of you...'

'Well, the past is never past. I believe that our history is still haunting us and it's important for people to know about it.'

'I almost wish I hadn't arranged to meet Gianluca. I'd love to hear about the partisans in Bologna.'

Leila gives Rhiannon's arm a pat. 'You go, dear. I'll tell you some of my story when you get back.'

They kiss each other on both cheeks and it occurs to Rhiannon how comfortable she feels with Leila. It's as if she's known her for years. Strange to have developed such a connection with someone she only met a couple of weeks ago. There's no accounting for it, but Rhiannon can't help lightening her step as she leaves the apartment.

Cars, bicycles and buses crowd Piazza San Martino, a stone's throw from Leila's palazzo. Gianluca gives Rhiannon a cheery wave. 'We have to wear these.' He takes a helmet and rubber gloves from his backpack and hands them to her. 'I've been down there before and, believe me, you'll need them.'

A young man with curly, brown hair approaches. 'This is Angelo,' Gianluca introduces him.

'*Piacere*.' Rhiannon says she's pleased to meet him.

Angelo attaches a cord with a small box on the end to a socket next to what Rhiannon thought was a cordoned-off parking space. He presses a button on the box, and the metal plate covering the space lifts to reveal a cast-iron staircase.

'We're going down to a depth of eight metres,' Angelo informs them. 'I'll switch on the lights.'

The rotten egg smell almost makes Rhiannon gag and she wishes she'd followed Leila's joking advice to pinch her nose with a clothes peg. Surreptitiously, she lifts her scarf to cover her mouth.

She widens her eyes. The stream has been mostly covered over with cement, but there's a channel with stinking, brackish water flowing. A narrow stone bank is visible on both sides, just wide enough to walk single file.

Angelo takes the lead and Rhiannon and Gianluca follow. She tries not to touch the dirty, red brickwork, even though she's wearing protection on her hands.

'That's part of the first city wall.' Giancarlo indicates ancient stones piled on top of each other at the side of the tunnel. 'Dates back to the fourth century. We're close to the foundations of the two towers at this point.'

Rhiannon points to a stone archway, supported by Acrow props. 'What's that?'

'A Roman bridge. The lower part was built more than one hundred years before Christ.'

'Only yesterday, then.' She laughs.

He chuckles. 'It was restored in the first and fourth centuries AD. A road, the Via Emilia, passed over it and led to Rome.'

'Amazing.'

'How does this compare to caving?'

'The exploration aspect is similar. Also the sounds of splashing water.' She pauses. 'But not the smell.' She catches sight of a rodent darting up ahead. 'Nor the rats.'

'Are you regretting coming?'

'Not at all. It's so interesting.'

The names of the roads above them have been attached to the walls. Via Rizzoli. Via Clavature. They're under the Quadrilatero, she realises.

As they walk on, she notices several wooden doors built into the sides of the tunnel, presumably leading to people's basements. Soon, they come to a second cast-iron staircase and Angelo heads up the steps.

Rhiannon climbs behind him.

Suddenly, her feet slip from beneath her and she yelps, finding herself falling into the void.

Strong arms grasp hold of her.

'It's all right. I've got you.' Gianluca settles her back on the step. 'Your shoes must have picked up something slimy down below.'

'*Grazie*,' she breathes. She's shaking like a leaf. 'You saved me.'

'All part of the service,' he quips.

Angelo presses a switch on the wall at the top of the staircase. Another metal plate covering a cordoned-off fake parking space lifts to reveal the light of day.

'Where are we?' she stares around a small square, relieved to be breathing the fresher air. She takes off her helmet and gloves.

Gianluca does likewise. 'Piazza Minghetti. We aren't far from your school.' He puts their helmets and gloves in his backpack. 'Don't know about you, but I could do with a drink. How about you, Angelo?'

Rhiannon and Angelo both respond that they would, indeed,

appreciate an aperitivo, so they go to have a glass of wine in Piazza Santo Stefano. Angelo then heads off, after explaining that his wife is expecting him home for lunch. Gianluca and Rhiannon thank him for showing them the Aposa.

'He's a good man,' Gianluca says when Angelo has left. 'He has a job with the city council in the public works department.'

Rhiannon smiles. 'It was kind of him to take the trouble to show us the underground canal.'

'He'd like to organise visits for tourists. But, first, that sewage needs to be diverted.'

'It was rather smelly,' she giggles.

'I hope it hasn't taken away your appetite.' He points across the square. 'My favourite restaurant is just over there, and I was hoping to introduce you to their signature dish.'

'*Grazie*, I'd like that.' It's not a date, she tells herself. *Gianluca is your friend and he's just being friendly.* Besides, she wants to hear what he's found out about Marie.

The restaurant is old-style, the décor reminiscent of a bygone era with starched white tablecloths and waiters in formal attire – black bow ties and waistcoats. Gianluca is greeted warmly – he's clearly a regular – and the ambiance is welcoming; the other tables are filled with families enjoying a meal out.

'What's that dish you mentioned?' Rhiannon asks, picking up the menu.

'Tortellini alla panna.' Pasta parcels with a cream sauce.

'Sounds delicious, but fattening. It's a good thing we did a lot of walking earlier.'

'I'm starving.' He grins. 'I'm going to have *cotoletta alla bolognese* for my main course.'

'What's that?'

'Fried veal, covered with prosciutto and smothered with melted Parmesan.'

'A bit rich for me.' She glances at the menu again. 'I'll have the *petto di tachinella con funghi* porcini.' Turkey breast with porcini mushrooms.

'Bologna is not only La Rossa, for its bricks and its politics.' *The Red.* 'And La Dotta, for the university.' *The learned.* 'But also, La Grassa, for its food.' *The fat.* 'Our meat-heavy cuisine can be rather... heavy.'

'I love the true Bolognese sauce. It's nothing like what we call spag Bol at home.'

He laughs. 'The way it's prepared abroad makes us squirm. For a start Bolognese ragu is served with tagliatelle not spaghetti.'

'So I've noticed.'

Their waiter approaches and takes their order. Gianluca requests sparkling mineral water and, after consulting with Rhiannon, asks for a bottle of Lambrusco red wine.

They chat about their families while they wait for their food to arrive. Rhiannon learns that Gianluca has a brother, Lorenzo, who's thirty-three, seven years older than him, and a sister, Claudia, who's four years older. Both are married with kids and they live in Vicenza, where Gianluca's parents moved after the war. 'I was born there but studied at Unibo and decided to stay on in Bologna after I graduated.'

'Leila must be glad you did so. She must miss her family.'

'My aunt was busy with her teaching until recently. Her doctor advised her to seek early retirement due to her blood pressure problems.'

'She told me she's recording her memoirs of the war.'

'What?!' Gianluca exclaims.

'I know. It's such a brave thing for her to do.'

'I'm surprised, to be honest. Neither Auntie Leila nor my parents ever talk about what happened during those terrible times.'

'She said it's because she thinks the past is never past.'

He taps his chin. 'Mysterious.'

'I'm sure she'll tell you everything.'

'You and she have become close, haven't you?'

'I feel an affinity with Leila. It's as if she gets me...'

'She's a wonderful woman.'

Their first course arrives and they dive in. 'This is delicious.' Rhiannon licks her lips. 'But it *is* a little heavy.'

'Bologna La Grassa, remember?' Gianluca winks.

He finishes his helping, but Rhiannon can only manage half of hers. She takes a sip of wine. 'You were going to tell me what you discovered about Marie.'

'Ah, yes. Marie. She's a conundrum, for sure. My contact at the university told me she isn't French but Lebanese.'

Rhiannon drops her fork in surprise. 'Why would she say she's French if she isn't?'

He shrugs. 'It's her association with Ugo Barzini that concerns me.'

'Oh? Why's that?'

'He's a friend of the financier Licio Gelli, who once was closely involved with the fascists. My guess is that he still is. Barzini's newspaper *Avanzare* is so far to the right it's off the charts.'

'I thought fascism finished with the Second World War.'

'If only,' he says. 'Remember I told you Bologna is also known as La Rossa?' *The red.*

She nods.

'There's nothing the Italian right wing would like better than to pin what happened at the station last year onto the ultra-left. You've heard of the Red Brigades?'

'Didn't they kidnap and murder Aldo Moro, your former prime minister?'

'Yes. Three years ago. They're a far-left terrorist group who claim to model themselves on the partisans.' Gianluca grimaces. 'They're not like them at all...'

Their waiter arrives to clear their plates and serve the main course. Rhiannon declares her turkey to be excellent, but again, she can't manage to finish the enormous portion. Instead, she sips her wine and listens to Gianluca expound on Italian politics. 'Since the war, our government has been in the hands of Democrazia Cristiana, a broad-based Christian political party, with the opposition led by the Italian Communist Party,' he explains. 'Italian communism doesn't have much in common with Soviet communism these days,' he further clarifies. 'Lately, the party has transitioned from rigid Marxist ideology to a more democratic form of socialism.'

'I'm not normally that interested in politics.' Rhiannon takes another sip of Lambrusco. 'But what you've told me is fascinating.' She hopes she hasn't sounded too gushing; the wine has loosened her tongue. She puts her hand over her glass when Gianluca offers her a refill. 'I'd better not, thanks.'

After they've drunk their post-lunch coffees, Rhiannon offers to split the bill. Gianluca won't hear of it. 'You can treat me another time,' he says, pulling a credit card from his wallet.

They stroll arm in arm up Via Santo Stefano, and soon they are back in Marsala Street. 'I'll go in with you,' Gianluca offers. 'I'd like to say hello to my aunt and ask if I can listen to what she's recorded of her memoirs.'

A sudden thought occurs to Rhiannon. Perhaps she shouldn't have said anything? But Leila didn't ask her not to tell anyone; it will be fine.

'*Va bene.*' Rhiannon unlocks the front door. 'I expect Leila would like to hear about our excursion down the Aposa.'

At the top of the steps, she turns and faces him. 'Thanks for today, Gianluca. I really enjoyed myself.'

'I did too.' He hesitates momentarily, then bends and kisses her on the cheek.

She touches her hand to where his lips were, unable to deny the fluttery feeling in her chest.

14

LEILA

I'm sitting on the sofa in my living room, waiting for Rhiannon and Gianluca to get back. Today, despite my best intentions, I couldn't face narrating what comes next in my memoirs. I just wasn't feeling strong enough. So, I decided to take a break and now I'm catching up with some reading instead. I stare down at the book on my lap, *The Far Pavilions*, a saga set in the time of the British rule in India, translated into Italian. The clash between East and West appears to be the central theme of the novel, which also deals with divided loyalties and friendship that endures until death.

The murmur of voices in the corridor makes me glance up. 'How was the Aposa?' I ask Rhiannon as she steps into the room.

'Amazing. Especially the Roman bridge.' A smile gleams in her eyes. 'But you were right about the smell.'

'Rhiannon didn't complain once,' Gianluca says. 'I was proud of her.'

She sits next to me on the sofa. 'Did you manage to get on with recording your memoirs?'

'I wasn't in the mood...'

Gianluca perches on the other side of me. 'Rhiannon told me what you are doing, Auntie. I'm surprised...'

'It was the bombing of the railway station last year that prompted me. And the supposed involvement of neo-fascists.'

'Ha, the government tried to pin it on the Red Brigades. But what happened last August wasn't their modus operandi. The ultra-left doesn't bomb innocent civilians setting off on their summer holidays...'

'No one should bomb innocent civilians,' Rhiannon chips in. 'It's despicable.' She stares at the cover of my book. '*Padiglioni Lontani*,' she reads the title. 'I've read it and loved it.'

'So, when are you going to let me listen to your memoirs, dearest Aunt?' Gianluca interrupts.

I chuckle to myself. *Gianluca persisting with his line of enquiry like the good journalist that he is.*

'Perhaps in a week or two, *caro*. When I've got to the end of narrating my story.'

* * *

It's Monday morning, and Rhiannon has gone to her classes. I can't stop smiling; yesterday Gianluca took us both for a drive in his Lancia and I had a wonderful time. I close my eyes, lost in thought, remembering meandering through the picturesque hills to the south of the city, as the road undulated between green slopes and flowering fields past churches, chapels, and ancient water mills, until we arrived at the small town of Savigno. There, we had lunch in a trattoria famous for its truffle-centred dishes – the fungi grow abundantly in the woods around here and there's even a local breed of dog, the *Lagotto Romagnolo*, trained to hunt for them.

I love the fact that almost all the ingredients on the restaurant's menu are locally sourced: eggs from the hen house out back; vegetables and fruits from their own garden; and meat and game from the surrounding fields and forests. The proud owner boasted to us that they roll their pasta dough by hand and the flour for the organic bread comes from a nearby eighteenth-century gristmill.

The dishes we chose were simple and flavourful, using only two or three fresh seasonal ingredients – nutty-tasting artichokes, tender new potatoes, and sweet fennel. It reminded me so much of when Stella used to cook for my family and I felt nostalgic. While Gianluca and Rhiannon were arguing about who would pay the bill, I excused myself, said I needed the bathroom, and went to pay for our meal myself. Their protests fell on my deaf ears; I told them it had been my pleasure, and it had. Spending the day with them had made me so very happy.

After Gianluca had dropped us home, I fulfilled my promise to Rhiannon and told her a little about my involvement with the partisans. But not everything. I said I would let her listen to the cassettes sometime soon. And now I must carry on, even though it pains me to do so.

I go through to my study, open the drawer, take out my cassette recorder, and unfurl the notes I made earlier. Romeo jumps up onto my lap and I press record.

By the start of October, the Liberation Committee had prepared an insurrection plan. The Gappista Brigades, strengthened by partisans arriving from the mountains and from nearby towns on the plain, were setting up new bases and arms deposits in the heart of Bologna and the immediate outskirts, ready to rise up as soon as the British and Americans approached.

The devastating air raids went on relentlessly, however. On 11 October, over a hundred Martin B-26 Marauder bombers of the Twelfth Air Force dropped around seven hundred bombs on a German ammu-

nition depot located inside the city, hitting both their objective and, tragically, the historic centre itself. They struck thirty-seven buildings, killing twenty-one citizens, and wounding twenty-three others. It was bad, but worse was to come.

The following day, 12 October, Bologna suffered an even more terrible bombardment, known as 'Operation Pancake'. Over six hundred B-17, B-24 and B-26 bombers of the Twelfth and Fifteenth Air Force took off from the Foggia airfields in the south of Italy and released more than a thousand tons of bombs (the heaviest bomb tonnage dropped on an Italian city in a single raid during the entire war). They hit German fuel and ammunition dumps, arms depots, troop concentrations, the Borgo Panigale airfield, bridges over the Reno and the Ducati plant (which was engaged in munitions production at that time and was completely knocked out by the raid).

The Americans' purpose was to weaken German forces in Bologna and its surrounding area to support the advance by the Fifth Army, whom we all thought would liberate us before Christmas. Once again, many of the bombs fell on the city centre; over four hundred buildings reduced to complete ruin and more than eight hundred partially destroyed. Estimates of civilian losses varied between three and six hundred. It was horrible and I can only thank God no one I knew was killed or injured then.

Following this dreadful attack, tens of thousands of bolognesi fled to the surrounding countryside or to nearby villages in the Apennines. I went out on the streets not long afterwards, and Bologna appeared like a ghost town. The absence of people and noise made me think of the scenes in a science fiction novel after an alien invasion – H.G. Wells' War of the Worlds sprang to mind.

Unable to bear the oppressive silence on my own, I went to the comfort of Paolo's arms at the communist safe house. We spent a couple of hours together before I had to leave, avoiding talking about what was foremost in our minds: the upcoming battle to liberate

Bologna. I was terrified for him but couldn't say so – it would have been unpatriotic. And he kept repeating how much he loved me and longed for the time when our lives would get back to normal. 'This is why I'm fighting,' he said. 'For our future as well as the future of Italy.' We hugged for ages as we said goodbye; we didn't know when we'd see each other again.

In mid-October, advanced parties of the US Fifth Army came to a stop on the outskirts of the town of Pianoro only fifteen miles away, but the partisan command didn't order the demobilisation of its bases, because it was believed to be only a temporary halt. It was a major mistake on the part of the Liberation Committee, as it turned out. While we waited in vain for the Allies to approach, the partisan hide-outs, one by one, began to be discovered by the Nazi-fascists.

Early in the afternoon of 20 October, I was in the Geography department library with my comrades, discussing the success, two days beforehand, of the second action against the Baglioni. We had just learnt that, at 1 a.m. Paolo, Bruno and four other gappisti, dressed as Nazis and repubblichini, had snuck into the hotel lobby and had managed to carry a crate containing thirty kilos of dynamite inside. They succeeded in lighting the fuse correctly and then made it back to their stolen German car in time before the bomb went off, causing massive damage.

Afterwards, we found out that the central section of the building had collapsed into a pile of rubble. The transition from being fast asleep to spiralling into the nothingness of death for many of the enemy must have been instantaneous, but the Carlino newspaper only reported the incident as 'a very big explosion brusquely interrupted the quiet of the night'.

Perhaps my comrades and I had been lulled into a false sense of security by the lack of immediate reprisals. We had no presentiment of what was about to occur. We'd just had lunch and were busy printing fake IDs and chatting about the recent bad weather, the constant rain, and the floods in the countryside. I'd known the group only for a few months, but I loved them to the depths of my soul. Matteo, whose sarcastic exterior hid an inner shyness I discovered when he'd let down his guard. Edoardo, who always had his nose in a book. Vito, the weapons expert due to his love of game hunting with his father. Salvo, the joker who often made us laugh hysterically with his imitations of Hitler and Mussolini. Aldo, the quiet one who kept himself to himself, and Marroni, our political leader, whom I've mentioned already.

Carla and I were about to leave, our satchels filled with the documents we'd take across the city to one of the gappista hideouts, when a shout came from the courtyard outside. Marroni peered through the shutters. 'Porco cane, fascisti,' he yelled. 'Seems to be hundreds of them. Arm yourselves, partigiani. We're easy targets here, so we'll take our escape route.'

Cold fear gripped me. The designated escape route was also our way to the air raid shelter tunnels via the Chemistry department; it entailed a quick run between the buildings lining the courtyard. I was rooted to the spot, every nerve in my body quaking.

The men snatched up their handguns and made haste to follow Marroni. Carla grabbed hold of me and dragged me with her.

But it was too late.

The repubblichini had set up machine gun nests and were firing indiscriminately at the windows of the Geography department library.

I flinched at the din of explosions and the reverberation of shattering glass.

'We can't get out,' Matteo muttered. 'Even if we made a dash for it, the maledetti, goddamned fascists would mow us down.'

Marroni returned to the library. 'Vittoria, Carla, run to the office and hide with the admin staff. You must pretend to be secretaries.'

We did as he'd asked. What else could we do? The men had already begun to fire from the windows and throw the grenades they'd stockpiled. We hurried to the back of the school and begged the three middle-aged women who carried out administrative tasks to let us join them. I felt ashamed and sick to the stomach for not staying and fighting. But I didn't know how to shoot a weapon and would surely have been more of a hindrance than a help.

Carla and I flattened our backs to the wall in the corner of the room, listening intently to the echoes of the raging battle. The ra-ta-ta-ta-ta of the machine guns and the ear-splitting explosions of the grenades. The women in the office began to whimper and pray out loud to the Madonna.

The saliva in my mouth had turned to sand. All I could think about was my dear, brave comrades and how much danger they were in. They were so vastly outnumbered it would take a miracle for them to defeat the enemy. Marroni could have escaped, but he'd come back to help them, and I admired him for it.

Eventually, the battle sounds transformed into shouts.

My heart set up a frantic rhythm.

The door crashed open and three repubblichini erupted into the room. They waved their guns at us. 'Line up,' they ordered. 'We're arresting you.'

The admin staff launched into a chorus of wails. 'Join in,' Carla whispered, 'or they'll think we aren't who we're pretending to be.'

So, Carla and I added our voices to the lamenting ladies, cowering with them while the fascists herded us downstairs and out onto the courtyard. There, they corralled us into a space opposite the Aula Magna lecture theatre.

Shock wheeled through me. Marroni, Matteo, Edoardo, Vito, Salvo, and Aldo had been lined up with their faces pressed against the wall. The wretched Republican guards, dressed in their field-grey uniforms, had started hitting them with the butts of their rifles and jeering at them.

Cowards, I thought. It had taken a couple of hundred fascists to bring down six brave partisans. How I wanted to run to my comrades *and help them. But there was nothing I could do except stand and watch, my heart thumping. I knew something was about to happen, something so awful it was unthinkable.*

Pockface – him again – had assumed control of the militiamen. 'Squad,' he barked. 'Take aim.' He drew himself upright. 'Fire!'

And they shot my dear friends in their upper bodies and legs. One by one, they crumpled to the ground, moaning and bleeding onto the flagstones.

I took a step forwards, ready to go to them, but Carla held me back.

Pockface shouted another order, and a group of men went up to Marroni, Matteo, Edoardo, Vito, Salvo, and Aldo. Without hesitation, they finished them off at point-blank range, firing bullets in the back of their necks.

The women around me stopped wailing they were so shocked.

Bile rose in my throat and I wanted to be sick. My legs threatened to give way and tears ran down my cheeks.

Pockface approached and said, 'We're awaiting our commandanti. Then you'll be taken to the San Giovanni in Monte prison.'

More whimpering from the admin staff. Carla nudged me. 'Join in!'

I did as she suggested and gave way to my shock and sorrow, crying the hot, salty tears of grief.

A vile ritual then ensued. The sun had gone down, so the repubblichini lit torches and paraded around the courtyard singing 'Giovinezza', the fascists' anthem.

> *The poets and the artisans,*
> *The lords and the countrymen,*
> *With Italian pride*
> *Swear fealty to Mussolini*

We watched in disgust until, finally, their commanding officers arrived and their men herded us in the direction of a lorry waiting in Zamboni Street.

I was just about to climb into the vehicle behind Carla and the others when I felt a hand land on my shoulder.

My skin prickled and I turned around.

It was Pockface.

'I know you,' he hissed. 'You're not a secretary. You're a student.' He roved his cold eyes over me. 'The sister of Daniele Venturi who is wanted for subversion. I bet you're a partisan whore...'

'I'm just a student,' I stuttered. 'In the wrong place at the wrong time.'

'We'll soon find out.' He smirked.

And my veins became shards of ice.

15

LEILA

I switch off the recorder. The back of my throat aches and tears streak my face. Telling this part of my story has been harrowing, to say the least. The cruel death of my comrades is something I'll never forget. I found out later that their bodies were left in the courtyard, lying in pools of blood, for the entire night and half the next day. The *Carlino* newspaper published an article entitled, 'Capture of an organised group of dangerous outlaws'. Barely a mention of the executions and they omitted to reveal that the action had taken place at the university. Not a word, either, of the fact that the militiamen had gone on a rampage afterwards, vandalising the Geography department's maps and papers, looting the rooms accommodating university staff and their families, stealing food, clothing, and personal property. It was appalling.

Never a year goes by when I don't make a pilgrimage to the memorial plaque on the Aula Magna's wall, the exact place where Matteo and the others met their untimely fate. I lay flowers there and say a prayer for their brave souls. My heart still bleeds for them...

Romeo winds himself around my legs, meowing to be fed. I go through to the kitchen and top up his bowl before making myself a *panino* for my lunch. After I've eaten, I return to my study with a cup of coffee. I need to narrate what occurred next in case my courage deserts me. But can I bear to give all the details? I must, I decide. Future generations of my family should know the truth about how evil invaded Italy with the Germans during those dreadful months at the end of the war. I vehemently hope nothing like that will ever take place again. Except, the past is never past, is it?

The repubblichini locked us up in a cell, the five of us. They gave us water to drink and coarse black bread. We talked among ourselves, bewailing what had happened at the university and expressing our hope against hope we would soon be freed.

I stretched out on a bench next to Carla and slipped into a fearful, tense sleep, not resting, feeling threatened by forces beyond my control.

In the morning, two dark-haired republican guards brought more bread and water. Then they took the women, one by one, to be interrogated. Carla and I waited, whispering our worry that one of the admin staff might expose us in exchange for being released. As it turned out, our concerns were well founded.

The guards came for Carla first. She went calmly although the two men, the silver insignia on their black collar patches shining, made a show of asserting their dominance, prodding her with the barrels of their pistols and tying her hands behind her back.

I waited over two hours for her to be returned to the cell. And, as the time passed, I grew more and more concerned. What were those bastards doing to her? My stomach rolled with unease.

Finally, the guards returned with Carla, their arms slung around her shoulders to half lift half carry her. I raised my hands to my mouth to stop from crying out loud. She was unconscious, naked, her face horribly swollen, her inner thighs streaked with blood and what looked like semen. Oh, good God!

I launched myself at the guard and raked my nails down his cheek.

'Bitch!' He threw me to the floor, pounded me with his fists, and crashed his foot into my stomach. Pain sliced through me, but I struggled to my feet.

The other guard grabbed me, pinned my arms behind me, and tied them with a cord. 'It's your turn now,' he leered. 'I can't wait to sink my cock into you.'

'Don't you dare,' I screamed.

'Ha,' the man laughed. 'Captain Barzini gives me my orders, not you.'

They pushed and shoved me in the direction of a room at the back of the prison. It was then that I learnt the name of my nemesis. 'Captain Ugo Barzini,' he introduced himself, coming right up to me, his foul-smelling breath in the air between us. 'I know who you are. No need to give me your battle name. One of the Geography department secretaries confirmed that you are Leila Venturi, the sister of Daniele. If you tell us where he is, we'll release you.' He paused, roved his cold, cruel eyes up and down my body. 'If you don't, we'll make you talk.'

There wasn't much saliva in my mouth, but what there was I spat in his face.

He slapped me hard. 'Strip her,' he barked at his men.

They tore the clothes off me, my blouse, my bra, my skirt, and my underpants. All that were left were my socks and shoes.

'Bend her over the desk,' Barzini growled.

I tried to squirm from their grasp, but to no avail. They were strong, and I was like a sparrow being held by a couple of hawks.

Fingers probed me from behind, prodding my most intimate parts. 'Tell me where your brother is hiding, and I'll release you,' my nemesis repeated.

'I don't know where he is,' I lied.

'Turn her around,' he commanded his men. 'Place the gas mask on her.'

Porco cane, I'd heard about that despicable torture. Could I resist? No question, I had to resist. I wouldn't reveal Dani's whereabouts.

Black rubber enveloped my head and claustrophobia overwhelmed me. Blind fear held me in a vice. I knew what would happen next, and it did. 'Close off the air filter,' Barzini gave the order.

I gasped to breathe and began to choke.

Just when I thought I would lose consciousness, they opened the filter.

'Tell me where your brother is!'

'I already said I don't know where he is.'

Black rubber enveloped my head again. I was suffocating but I wouldn't talk. If I had to die for the cause, then so be it. But Barzini didn't want me dead. He barked another order and his flunkies removed the mask.

Pockface entwined his fingers in my hair and pulled my head backwards. My scalp stung as if thousands of needles had been jabbed into it and I couldn't help the scream of pain. Tears fell, impossible to stop them.

He stared at me, watched the tears rolling down my face.

'Talk,' he snarled. 'Tell me what I want to know!'

'Never!'

Slaps landed on my face and punches to my belly. Barzini repeated the same question again and again. I shook my head and screwed my eyes shut to contain the tears. Rage and hatred boiled within me. If only I were strong enough, I'd grab him around the neck and throttle him, hang the consequences.

'Talk, whore!'

I remained silent.

'Hold her,' he ordered his men.

They stood, one on each side, and pinned my arms down.

Merda.

Barzini was staring at me, lust in his eyes.

'Don't touch me!'

He laughed.

'Please,' I begged. 'Leave me alone!'

He slid between my legs and unbuttoned his trousers.

I screamed.

Suddenly, the wail of an air raid siren echoed.

'Take her back to the cell,' Barzini bellowed, buttoning up his flies. 'We'll finish this later.'

And he turned on his heel and hurried out of the room.

The guards marched me along the corridor, prodding me with their pistols. In the cell, Carla had regained consciousness and was attempting to wipe the blood and semen from her thighs with an old rag dipped in a pail of water someone had provided. 'My poor darling,' I exclaimed, taking the rag from her as she swayed with the effort.

I helped her as much as I could – I was in pain from the blows I'd received – and when the repubblichini returned our clothes, I dressed her then dressed myself. We sat side by side on the bench and, with gasping breaths, told each other about our ordeals. She'd been raped, brutally, by all three men. 'But I didn't talk,' she said, weeping.

'I'm proud of you.' I held her while she sobbed. 'If ever we get out of here, I want to learn to fire a weapon. I want vengeance. After what they did to Matteo and the others, and to you, I want to kill every one of them.'

'Me too,' she muttered. 'I'll become a partigiana combattente.'

The bombardment went on for hours, it seemed, and we pressed our fingers to our ears. The air around us vibrated with the detonations and the floor of our cell literally shook. We'd been left callously to our fate. But at least no one came to take me back for further interrogation. The day wore on and darkness fell. After the barrage came to an end, a different guard brought us bread and water.

I was about to drift off into an uneasy sleep when the cell door crashed open. 'Get to your feet,' a gun waving guard yelled. 'We're transferring you to the prison in the School of Engineering. The SS want to question you there.'

Carla and I shot each other terrified looks. We'd heard about the terrible torture inflicted there.

Cold night air wrapped around us like a shroud as we were led across the piazza to a waiting car. Our hands had been tied behind our backs, and we were bundled into the rear seat.

The vehicle headed towards Porta Saragossa, and I stared out at the silent streets of the city. Would I ever see Paolo again? We'd never made love, having agreed to wait until we could be married. I couldn't bear the thought that it might be Barzini or even a German who'd take my virginity. I'd be sullied and unable to give Paolo what I'd always considered most precious.

Without warning, the bang of an explosion echoed in my ears. My breath stuttered. Had the Americans come back to bomb us again?

With a screech of tyres, the car abruptly swerved and stopped. Carla and I yelped. It looked as if small bombs, or was it hand grenades, were landing on the road up ahead.

Dark figures emerged from under the gateway. I squinted into the smoke billowing from where the devices had landed. Men were coming towards us, brandishing sub-machine guns. 'Carla, Vittoria, get out of the car,' a voice shouted.

A voice I knew.

My heart sang.

Paolo!

Before the guards had time to react, he wrapped his loving arms around me and pulled me to safety.

I turned and looked behind me for Carla. She was all right, thank God. Bruno was leading her away from the scene while the rest of his men took care of the repubblichini, shooting them dead.

16

RHIANNON

Monday morning's last class comes to an end. Myriad examples of when to use the subjunctive mood in Italian, like when you talk about hopes, fears, doubts, and other unreal vagaries. It's practically died out in English, Rhiannon ponders as she gets on with grammar exercises. Not many people say, 'I wish I were rich' – which is grammatically correct – but use the more common, 'I wish I was...' instead.

'Is there much subjunctive in French?' she asks Marie as they head towards Piazza Santo Stefano to grab a *panino* for lunch.

'Oh, yes. It's like Italian,' Marie takes a packet of Gauloises from her handbag, extracts a cigarette and lights it.

The burnt rubber smell tickles Rhiannon's nostrils. 'Did you have a nice day off on Friday?' she enquires.

Marie squints into the sunshine. 'I went to Rimini for a long weekend with my uncle. We stayed in the Grand Hotel, which is a favourite of Fellini's, apparently.'

Rhiannon remembers seeing his famous film, *La Dolce Vita*. 'I don't suppose he was there, was he?'

Marie giggles. '*Magari*.' If only.

The so-called French girl doesn't ask Rhiannon about her weekend, and Rhiannon doesn't volunteer to tell her. She takes a bite of her ham *panino*. 'Is your uncle staying in Italy for long?'

Marie pushes her dark hair back from her forehead. 'What do you mean?'

'You said he lives in Paris...'

'Only part of the time.' She gives Rhiannon a quick glance. 'Why the interest in my uncle?'

Rhiannon reaches across the table and places her hand on Marie's. 'I'm just being friendly, that's all.'

'I only call him my uncle for appearances as he's so much older than me.'

Rhiannon's breath hitches. 'You mean – you and he?'

'We're in a relationship.' Marie smirks. 'And I don't want to talk about it.'

'That's fine by me.' Rhiannon drinks down her coffee. She checks her watch. 'Time for our afternoon classes.'

Walking back to San Giovanni in Monte, she can barely contain her excitement at the smidgen of information she'll be able to give Gianluca.

Except, he said he didn't want her to help him in his enquiries, didn't he?

She sighs to herself.

* * *

After school, Rhiannon heads straight home. She drops her bag in her room and goes through to the kitchen to find out if she can help Leila prepare supper.

Her landlady is chopping onions, tears running down her face.

'I'll do that for you,' Rhiannon offers.

Leila sniffs. '*Grazie.*'

Rhiannon takes over, but Leila has started crying great heaving sobs, so she puts down the knife and wraps her arm around her. 'What's wrong?'

Another sniff. 'I've just finished recording something very sad. And now I can't get it out of my head.'

Rhiannon pulls out a chair and sits Leila down. 'I'll make us both a cup of tea. My mum believes there isn't much that can't be fixed with a...' Rhiannon screws up her face, trying to work out how to convey the meaning of 'cuppa' in Italian.

A gentle smile curves Leila's lips. 'Some tea would be nice.'

Rhiannon boils the kettle, then steeps tea bags in hot water. Leila likes hers black with a slice of lemon, but Rhiannon adds a dash of milk to her own cup.

She sits next to Leila. 'Maybe you should take a break from recording your memoirs if they're so painful for you?'

'I think you're right, dear. I'll do that.' She takes a sip of tea. 'Tell me, how was your day at the university?'

'It was good. But I'm still not as fluent as I'd like to be.'

'You've come on a lot. *Pazienza.*' Be patient.

Rhiannon goes back to chopping onions and Leila teaches her how to make the sugo, amatriciana pasta sauce. 'It's easy,' she says. 'Cubes of cured pork cheek, pecorino cheese, tomatoes and chopped onion.'

While they work together, Leila mentions how much she enjoyed the outing to the hills yesterday. 'I gave up driving years ago when I sold my car. Living in a city, I didn't see a need for one.'

'It was kind of Gianluca to take us both.' Rhiannon pauses to gather her thoughts. 'He's a nice guy.'

'He is. I'm glad he's found a friend in you. He's been lonely since Flavia passed away.'

'What was she like? Flavia, I mean.'

'Beautiful. Clever. Charming. You'd have liked her.'

'So sad she died young.'

'Breast cancer is a terrible disease. Once it was discovered, there was nothing the doctors could do to save her. Gianluca was distraught, as was everyone who knew her.'

'I wish I could have met her.'

'She'd have enjoyed meeting you, I'm sure.'

Leila fries the onions in olive oil, then adds the rest of the ingredients while Rhiannon watches.

'The *sugo* needs to cook slowly to bring out all the flavours. You go and get on with your homework, *cara. La cena è alle sette.*'

Rhiannon is about to head out of the kitchen, when her eye is caught by the headline of an article in the newspaper which Leila has left on the table. '*Due giornalisti italiani scomparsi in Libano.*' Two Italian journalists missing in Lebanon.

She goes to her room to tackle an essay, but she can't stop thinking about Marie being Lebanese. It could be just a coincidence, but she needs to tell Gianluca what she learnt at lunchtime, she decides. Marie has lied about being French, and she lied about her uncle. What else has she lied about?

* * *

Next day, when Rhiannon gets home from her classes, she finds Gianluca in the kitchen with Leila. 'Can we go for a drink after dinner?' Rhiannon whispers when her landlady's attention is distracted.

'Are you asking me out on a date?' He winks.

Her cheeks burn. 'There's something I need to tell you.'

'Mysterious.' He laughs. '*Va bene.*'

The evening follows a by-now-established routine. Rhiannon

goes to her room to do her homework, she eats with Leila and Gianluca, then helps with the washing-up. But, instead of leaving her to watch television with his aunt, Gianluca takes her to an *osteria* around the corner from Piazza San Martino. The pub's atmosphere is cosy and it's crowded with students. They find seats at a wooden table by the bar.

After they've ordered glasses of San Giovese, Gianluca leans in. 'What did you want to tell me, Rhiannon?'

She gives him the information she discovered at lunchtime yesterday. That Marie admitted to being in a relationship with Ugo Barzini.

Gianluca draws his brows together. 'I thought I'd told you not to try and help me?'

'I didn't ask her anything. She came right out with it.'

He takes Rhiannon's hand, squeezes her fingers. 'Be careful. There's a much bigger picture here than a young woman involved with an older man. Barzini has a hidden agenda and Marie has lied about being French.'

'I saw the headline about those journalists going missing in Lebanon...'

'They disappeared in Beirut last year and there's been no sign of them since.'

'Why were they there?'

'Investigating arms trafficking and PLO training camps. I heard from a reporter friend who knows them that they discovered the involvement of the Italian Secret Services.'

'Sounds a bit James Bondish,' Rhiannon swirls her wine. 'Call me naive, but I didn't even know Italy had a secret service.'

'Most countries have a secret service, ours is known as Sismi – Servizio per le Informazioni e la Sicurezza Militare – and they operate in that grey area between black and white which is tinged with nefariousness.'

'What's their involvement with the Palestinians?' Rhiannon asks, suddenly remembering meeting Marie's friends in the university canteen.

'Not many people know this but, since 1970, our government has allowed the PLO to carry out undercover paramilitary activities in Italy, offering our country, in exchange, their promise never to perpetrate terrorist attacks here.'

'Wow. *Sono sbalordita.*' I'm flabbergasted.

'As was I when I found out. The arrangement was made by Aldo Moro.'

'The former prime minister who was kidnapped and murdered by the Red Brigades?'

'Yes.'

She tells Gianluca about meeting the Palestinian students with Marie.

'All the more reason for you to stay away from her,' Gianluca says.

'We're classmates. It would seem odd if I unaccountably started avoiding her.'

'Agreed. But she could be involved in something highly dangerous. I would hate it if you came to any harm.'

'What harm could I come to? I only go for lunch with her. In full view of everyone. Don't worry.'

They finish their drinks and walk back to Leila's, arms slung around each other's waist.

At the door to Leila's palazzo, Gianluca pulls Rhiannon in for a hug. '*Buonanotte, cara. Sogni d'oro.*' Golden dreams.

Without thinking, she lifts her face.

Her gaze meets his, and she gives a little nod.

He eases her into the kiss, pressing his mouth down, waiting for her to open for him. When she does, their tongues roll together in a slow dance.

Warning bells ring, and she pulls back with a gasp.

'What's wrong?'

'We can't do this.'

'Why not?'

'We're friends. I don't want to spoil our friendship.'

'We were just kissing, Rhiannon. Didn't you enjoy it?'

'That's not the point. Leila would be furious if she knew.'

'Ah, yes. My aunt. She thinks I'm a playboy...'

'She was upset when I got home from school yesterday, said it was because of her memoirs. I don't want to do anything that would upset her further.'

'Poor Aunt Leila.' Gianluca's eyes fill with sadness. 'She's suffered so much...'

17

LEILA

'How are you this morning, Auntie?' Gianluca enquires, stepping into the kitchen. His concern for me this past week, since Rhiannon told him my memoirs had been upsetting me, has touched me to the core.

'I'm ready to get back to recording today, *caro*. And thank you again for yesterday.'

It was Sunday, and he took Rhiannon and me to visit Ferrara, the beautiful Renaissance city less than an hour's drive on the motorway from Bologna. It was wonderful. We wandered through the streets, soaking up the medieval charm before we visited the castle in the centre. With a moat, three drawbridges, and four massive towers, the red brick stronghold dates from the sixteenth century; Rhiannon declared it to be beautiful, and it certainly is so. Afterwards, we had lunch in a simple restaurant overlooking the River Po.

'Are you sure you're emotionally strong enough to remember the past again?' Gianluca asks now.

His words make me stiffen but I take a breath. 'I've never forgotten, dear. It's always been at the back of my mind. What my comrades, I and so many others went through for the freedom of Italy should never be forgotten, never be denied.' I exhale a long, slow breath. 'I fear a future where it could happen again. A future with the *fascisti* back in government, spreading division and hate.'

'I hope that won't ever happen, Auntie. But I'd really like to listen to your cassettes. I'd like to transcribe them, and maybe find a publisher. Those who prefer to deny the past won't have a valid reason to do so if they hear the truth told by someone who lived through it.'

'Oh, no, my darling. The recording is only for our family, for future generations. I don't want to call attention to myself.' I touch my hand to his arm.

He nods. 'Okay, but please indulge me and let me listen...'

I can't refuse him; he's Daniele's son and so like his father. 'Come through to my study and I'll give you what I've narrated thus far.'

* * *

After I've waved Gianluca off, I make myself a cup of coffee and carry it to my desk. Today is spring-like, so I open the window. Romeo immediately jumps up on the sill to watch the birds. He's too old and too chubby to chase after them, thankfully. But that doesn't stop him from chattering at them, wide eyed, his ears tilted forwards. Smiling at his antics, I take my Philips from the drawer.

The aftermath of the ambush passed in a flash. Paolo and the communists had kept the German car with Nazi flags on the fenders. They bundled Carla and me into it and sped to the Bolognina base. There, Daniele checked me and Carla over and prescribed a sedative to get us through the night. 'I was so worried about you when I heard you'd been arrested, little sister,' he said, holding me close. 'Thank

God the gappisti rescued you before… you know what,' he lowered his voice.

Diego, our burly, black mustachioed cook, fed us a late supper of watery leek and potato soup. His wife, Mafalda, a motherly woman who helped in the kitchen, took Carla and me under her wing. After we'd eaten, she led us upstairs to a spare bedroom and gave us freshly laundered nightclothes. We washed at the wall-mounted basin and stretched out on the big double bed. Carla began to sob. 'I still feel dirty. After what those men did to me, I'll never feel clean again.'

I hugged her, tried to soothe her. 'Cry out your pain, my darling.'

And she did, sobbing until she finally fell into a restless sleep.

The next day, I sat with Paolo having breakfast in the dining room at the side of the safe house. 'I won't be able to go home until the war is over.' I gave a heavy sigh. 'Barzini knows where I live.'

'In a way, I'm glad of that. It means you'll be staying here with me.'

I looked him in the eye. 'Please, would you teach me how to shoot. I want to be a partigiana combattente.'

'No,' he snapped. 'You'll get yourself killed.'

'If you won't teach me I'll ask someone else.' I squeezed his hand. 'And I'd much rather it be you.'

He laughed wryly. 'You're impossible. But I'm proud of you all the same, my brave girl.'

'Not that brave, darling. When the front passes, I'm scared the Allies will smash everything in their way until they're certain they won't meet up with a German face.'

'Which is why we need to get rid of the enemy first.' Paolo dunked bread in his barley coffee, to make a kind of soup in which a spoon could stand straight up.

I leaned into him, and it occurred to me how much I relied on him; he truly was my rock.

'I want to take part in the liberation battle, Paolo, please.'

'All right.' He gave an exasperated laugh. 'I'll teach you after we've finished our breakfast.'

Commander Bruno arrived to give the orders for the day; he changed the guard, assigning posts to everyone except me, Paolo, Carla, and Sebastiano – who'd come to assist as a non-combatant. We were to rest, Bruno ordered.

Dear Carla, earlier this morning she hadn't wanted to see her sweetheart, she was so traumatised by what those vile men had done to her. But Sebastiano had come straight to her when he'd heard what had happened, and she fell into his arms, sobbing.

I smiled at her sitting next to me with her fiancé – she'd told me a while ago that they were engaged – and I gave her a thumbs-up. 'Be of good courage,' I said.

Bruno came and sat opposite us. He was smiling as if he knew something we didn't know. 'I am here as representative of the free government,' he announced.

'You are,' Paolo agreed.

'In every brigade there is a commander who has the duty to die in action, if necessary.' Bruno's eyes twinkled. 'But also the authority to celebrate a wedding.'

'A wedding?' I stuttered. What was he going on about?

'I'm a happily married man. If I died in battle, I'd take the love I share with my wife to the grave. Then, I'd wait for her in Heaven, for I know that's where I'd be headed.'

'And?' Carla stared at him.

'What are you suggesting?' Sebastiano asked.

'I'm suggesting that I marry you. Tarzan and Vittoria. Carla and Sebastiano.'

Our mouths dropped open.

'But Tarzan hasn't proposed to me,' I blurted, not knowing what else to say.

Without hesitation, Paolo got down on his knees in front of me. 'I love you. Will you do me the honour of becoming my wife, amore?'

I'll never forget his face as he smiled up at me. Nor the tears of joy that wet my cheeks. 'Yes. Oh, yes. This is completely crazy, but of course. I love you so much.'

Bruno grinned with obvious happiness. 'Good, I'll perform the ceremony tonight.'

And he left us staring at each other in amazement.

'What shall we wear?' Carla asked as we took the breakfast dishes to the kitchen.

I told her about the wardrobe of clothes upstairs. 'I'm sure we'll be able to find something suitable, but first Tarzan is going to teach me how to shoot.'

'Can you ask him if he'll teach me too? Maybe not today, though.' She shuddered. 'I'm still a little sore.'

I brushed a quick kiss to her cheek. 'You've been so strong, my dearest. I dread to think how I'd have felt if those pigs had done to me what they did to you.'

'I'll carry it with me for ever...'

Carla shared more with me at that point, but I won't mention it here.

Not many brides can have spent part of their wedding day learning how to fire a weapon, I thought as I went down to the basement with Paolo half an hour later.

I stood in the centre of the long, narrow, underground room, which was also our air-raid shelter.

Paolo coughed and pulled a Beretta 7.65 semi-automatic pistol from his belt.

'Always treat a firearm as if it were loaded.' He pointed it at the ground.

'Is it loaded?' My heart hammered.

'Of course.' He grinned. 'Remember to keep your finger off the

*trigger and outside the guard until you have made a conscious deci-
sion to shoot.'*

*I nodded, breathing out a long slow breath. It twinged in my
stomach where I'd been kicked, but I gritted my teeth.*

*Paolo took my right hand and placed the Beretta in it. 'This is your
gun hand, darling.'*

*Next, he took my left hand and wrapped all four fingers under the
trigger guard with the index finger pressed hard underneath. 'Like
that,' he told me. 'This is your support-hand.'*

Again, I nodded, so filled with anticipation I couldn't speak.

*'Now stand with your feet and hips shoulder width apart. Bend
your knees slightly. It will allow you to shoot the weapon with stability
and mobility. You won't feel much recoil. Raise the firearm, point at
your target.' He indicated towards a sack of beans at the back of the
basement. 'Line up the sight at the front with the indent at the back,
yes?'*

I brought the gun up to eye level, my hand shaking a little.

*'Now bring your finger gently to the trigger and take a breath in.
Holding your breath will you allow you to be still and to focus. When
the sights are aligned, squeeze the trigger gently.'*

*I did as he'd asked, and all that was left for me to do was to
shoot.*

'Ready?'

I nodded.

'Just press on the trigger.'

*The backward movement as the bullet discharged took me by
surprise, but Paolo had prepared me well and I kept hold of the gun.*

'Bang on target,' he whooped.

*I couldn't believe I'd actually hit the sack of beans, but when I went
up to it, sure enough, I'd blasted a hole in its centre.*

*After a dozen or more shots, I was getting quicker at aiming, at
breathing in, squeezing the trigger, and the sack of beans was no*

more. 'You're a natural,' Paolo patted me on the back. 'But are you absolutely sure you want to be a *partigiana combattente*?'

'I am. After what that bastard Barzini did to Matteo and the others, and then to Carla, I hope to come across him in battle and take him down.'

'You've heard the saying 'revenge is a dish best served cold'?'

'I have, but what does it mean?'

'It means that vengeance is more satisfying when exacted some time after the harm has been done. I hope we'll get to the end of the war and see him tried as a criminal.'

'Hmm. I think I'd rather see him be taken down by one of us and suffer in agony.' I paused. 'Hopefully by me...'

We went back to the dining room. The *gappista* known as Giant had returned from guard duty. Over two metres tall at age twenty-three, he weighed around one hundred and twenty kilos, which was a lot for someone in those times. Usually two partisans were placed on guard, but when it was Giant's turn he went on his own; he was so big and strong that he counted double.

Giant finished eating the chunk of bread in his hand. 'Oh, *regaz*, *avete una paglia*?' he asked Paolo for a cigarette. 'I'll pay you back tomorrow...'

I left the two men smoking and set off to find Carla.

She was in the kitchen, peeling potatoes. 'Can I borrow Carla for a minute?' I asked Diego.

'Of course.' He winked. 'The brides-to-be shouldn't need to work on their wedding day, anyway.'

'It's all a bit strange.' I breathed a sigh as I flicked through the clothes in the upstairs wardrobe. 'I mean, I never thought I'd be getting married in these circumstances.'

'I'm glad about it. What happened to our comrades at the university, and what Bruno said about his wife, made me realise we need to live every day as if it's our last.'

'And hope that it isn't,' I added.

'I was raped yesterday and I'm getting married today. Life has taken a turn I never expected.' She smiled a sad smile. 'But I want to make Sebastiano happy and put the past behind me.'

We each chose a dress. Mine was pale blue with puffed sleeves and a thin belt. Carla selected a jade green outfit which skimmed her trim waist.

There were more tears and much hugging as we readied ourselves. Tears of sorrow and tears of joy mixed together were the strangest thing, it occurred to me.

Downstairs, Paolo told me how beautiful I looked. 'I love you so much, Leila. I wish we could be married in better surroundings, but I couldn't be prouder than I am right now.'

'I feel the same, my darling.' I couldn't stop grinning, I was so in love.

The meal was ready: not great in quality, but enough in quantity. Roasted potatoes and chestnuts had become our staple diet. We partisans were easily satisfied and didn't split hairs. Besides, no one ever suffered an upset stomach or complained about feeling liverish after eating the food Diego cooked for us. We devoured it ravenously, without a word spoken. Hunger in the brigade was a foe to combat in silence. Only when satiated, or almost, could we speak.

'I'm sorry this wedding party is rather miserable,' Bruno apologised. 'But a bottle for the brides and grooms can be found. You can dig one up, can't you, Diego?'

'Of course,' our cook chuckled. He scurried to the kitchen and returned with a big flagon of San Giovese, which was enough for a communal toast.

Bruno appeared to be in a good mood and his exuberance spread through the group; everyone laughed and joked as they knocked back the wine.

'Get into a circle, men,' Bruno commanded when the bottle was empty, his voice solemn. 'You are observers to this happy event.'

They did as he'd ordered, encircling me, Paolo, Carla, and Sebastiano.

'Do you, men whom we call Tarzan and Sebastiano, want to marry these women known as Vittoria and Carla?' Bruno intoned.

'Yes,' Paolo and Sebastiano answered, loudly.

'And do you, women whom we call Vittoria and Carla, want to marry these men known as Tarzan and Sebastiano?'

'Yes,' we affirmed just as loudly.

'As representative of the free Italian government, I declare you united in matrimony.' Bruno cleared his throat. 'In due course, the documents will be filed.'

He turned to the intense faces surrounding us. 'You are witnesses to their vows.' And then to us, the brides, and grooms, 'You may kiss. I've finished.'

Blushing, Carla and I went with our new husbands to our marital beds in the rooms prepared for us earlier by Mafalda.

I press stop on the cassette recorder, lost in thought. Both Paolo and I were virgins. We'd never gone further than him kissing the tops of my breasts. He hadn't even touched me below the waist, and I hadn't touched myself either. I'd experienced a sheltered upbringing and didn't know about such things.

That night, I gasped at the sight of his engorged penis and looked away in embarrassment. He made several fumbling attempts before he managed to penetrate me. I'd heard it would hurt, and it did. But it was over so quickly I barely registered the pain.

He held me afterwards, apologising. Then he kissed the bruises on my belly, swearing vengeance against the *repubblichini*.

After a short rest, I gave him permission to make love to me again, and it was so different the second time. Incredible, in fact. We kissed and kissed until I felt a throbbing need for him. My thighs fell open and he rocked into me slowly, building up a tingling pleasure that took my breath. I felt myself on the brink of something extraordinary and, when my release came, the force took me by surprise.

I cried tears of happiness afterwards in Paolo's arms. Just thinking about it now makes me weep. Except it's not happiness I feel, but intense sorrow and regret for what might have been a wonderful future with the man I loved. I cover my face with my hands and sob until my tears run dry.

18

RHIANNON

Rhiannon is carrying out a role-play in her conversation class this afternoon. Her tutor, Giana, has teamed up with Marie's tutor, Chloe, to help Rhiannon and Marie prepare to argue the question, 'Can money buy happiness?' Marie is debating 'for' and Rhiannon 'against'.

Rhiannon focuses her efforts; it's not an easy subject and requires extensive use of the subjunctive.

Sunlight filters through the window, falling on Marie's olive-skinned face and luminating her shiny long, dark hair. It strikes Rhiannon that the Lebanese girl's heart doesn't seem to be in the debate; her points lack conviction and she appears distracted.

The lesson comes to an end, and their teachers diplomatically declare them both to be winners.

Marie grabs her books and, without a word, makes a beeline for the door.

Rhiannon shrugs on her coat and trails behind Marie towards the exit of the building. She stops at the threshold and takes a step back.

Outside, in the piazza, Marie and Ugo Barzini are deep in

conversation. He spits a spate of words at her and she rattles back a response. Her gestures speak of frustration, impatience. She places her hands on her hips.

Barzini resignedly reaches into his jacket and produces his wallet. He hands her two, three, four banknotes.

Marie says something, and he gives her another two, or three, then opens his wallet wide and waves it in front of her as if to show it is empty.

The Lebanese girl unclasps her brown, leather handbag and tucks the notes into a white envelope.

Rhiannon frowns. Barzini gave the money to Marie in full view of students, spilling out of the school building and onto the piazza in their droves. *How bizarre!*

The pair go their separate ways. Barzini turns left into an alleyway leading out of the square, and Marie heads to Farini Street.

Without hesitation, Rhiannon starts to follow her; she'll be careful not to be seen.

Head down, the Lebanese girl strides up Santo Stefano. She seems intent on where she's going, and oblivious to the fact that she's being tailed. At the two towers, she turns into Rizzoli Street before heading up Via dell'Indipendenza.

Will she go into the Baglioni? But no, she keeps up a brisk walk, and Rhiannon carries on tailing her, darting between the columns of porticoes lining the street.

After about fifteen minutes, the colonnades come to an abrupt halt before the road opens out into a wide piazza. *It's too exposed here, damn it.* Rhiannon grudgingly slows her pace.

The Lebanese girl strides past the Porta Galliera gate and the last remaining section of the old city walls, then makes her way in the direction of the bridge crossing the railway tracks.

It's clear that Marie is heading towards the Bolognina district.

Maybe she wasn't fibbing about where she lives? Rhiannon glances around uneasily. Should she take a risk and keep following the girl? *Better not.* She turns on her heel and reluctantly goes home.

* * *

'Did you record any more of your memoirs today?' Rhiannon asks her landlady later, after they've had dinner and are sitting sipping herbal tea in the living room.

A solitary tear runs down Leila's cheek. 'I did...'

Rhiannon jumps up from the armchair and gives her a hug. 'I'm sorry, I hope I didn't make you sad.'

'You didn't. I'm feeling emotional because earlier I narrated a poignant part of my story.'

Slowly, stopping every now and then to collect her thoughts, Leila tells Rhiannon about the battle for the university, the execution of her comrades, her own arrest and torture by the fascists. 'My sweetheart rescued me, along with his fellow partisans. We got married afterwards.'

Rhiannon's heart weeps for her. 'I thought you were single...'

'Yes. Well, the marriage documents were never filed.' Leila breathes in a deep breath and lets it out again. 'Paolo was killed before that could happen.'

'Oh, no,' Rhiannon can't help wailing. 'How tragic. I'm so sorry...'

'I still miss him.' Leila sniffs back another tear. 'If there's an afterlife, I hope we'll find each other again.'

'You must have loved him very much.'

'I did. And I still do.' Her voice rasps. 'We were soulmates then and will always be, even though we've been cruelly separated by his death.'

Rhiannon wants to ask Leila how Paolo died, but she doesn't want to upset her further. 'I've never been in love,' she says by way of distraction.

'You're very young. There's time.'

'I doubt it will ever happen.' Rhiannon sighs. 'There's something blocking me.'

'Oh, my dear. Would you like to talk about it?'

'I had a boyfriend once. But when we tried to be intimate...' Heat creeps up Rhiannon's neck and flames her cheeks. 'It wasn't possible. My body wouldn't let him in.'

It's Leila's turn to pull Rhiannon in for a hug. 'You shouldn't worry too much about that. When you meet the right person, all will be well.'

'I'm not sure,' Rhiannon says. The memory of those excruciating times when Owen and she tried to make love will always be with her. They gave up trying in the end and he dropped her for another girl. 'I think I'm better off on my own.'

'Ah, you say that now, but you'll meet someone one day who'll change your mind.' A soft smile brushes Leila's mouth. 'Let's have a glass of limoncello,' she suggests. 'I have a bottle a friend gave me last Christmas.' She gets to her feet and goes over to the sideboard where she retrieves the liqueur and two small glasses.

The intense, sweet, citrus concoction slips down Rhiannon's throat. 'Yum.' She licks her lips.

Leila chuckles. 'I'm glad you like it.'

'Very refreshing.' Rhiannon yawns, suddenly sleepy. 'I'll go to bed now if you don't mind. School was tiring today.' *Not to mention her walk across the city.*

Leila pats her on the arm. '*Buonanotte, cara.*' Goodnight, dear. 'I hope you feel better for sharing your worries with me. As the proverb says, *mal comune mezzo gaudio.*' A trouble shared is a trouble halved.

'It has helped, *grazie*.' Rhiannon pecks Leila on the cheek. '*Sogni d'oro*.' Golden dreams.

In her room, as Rhiannon brushes her teeth, she thinks about Gianluca kissing her last week. It was silly of her to kiss him back, especially with her hang-ups. She can't believe she told Leila about them. Her landlady must think she's such an idiot.

She gets into bed and falls into a troubled sleep. In the early hours she wakes from a horrible nightmare. Her heart hammering, she blinks her eyes open. She screws up her face, trying to remember. The dream comes back to her in vivid images. She was underground by the Aposa. Barzini brandished a gun and pointed it at Gianluca. In a flash, Leila stepped between them and took a bullet in the stomach. Rhiannon screamed silently as Leila fell into the stream. Gianluca jumped in and Rhiannon followed him to help save Leila. The Aposa had become a raging river and Rhiannon found herself swimming for her life, gasping for breath. The struggle woke her and now she can't stop shaking.

Cold sweat coats her chest and there's a sick feeling in her stomach. She goes to the kitchen, drinks down a glass of water, and returns to her room. But sleep eludes her for the rest of the night. Every time she closes her eyes, she sees Barzini's pockmarked face, and his cold eyes boring into her.

Next morning, Leila glances at Rhiannon as she steps into the kitchen. 'You look terrible, *mia cara*.' My dear.

'I'll be fine,' Rhiannon breathes. 'Just had a bit of a sleepless night.'

'Go back to your room,' Leila practically pushes her through the door. 'Skip school today.'

'You think it will be all right for me to do that?'

'Of course. Everyone has the right to feel unwell from time to time.'

Having returned to her bedroom, Rhiannon takes off her jeans and jumper, then gets into bed. She falls asleep almost immediately, a deep, dreamless sleep.

The pealing of the midday church bells wakes her. She stretches, yawns, then goes to the bathroom. Bleary-eyed, she stares at her reflection in the mirror. *Urgh, what a mess.*

A sudden shout comes from the sitting room, 'Who's there?'

Her heart hammers. *Bloody hell, it's Gianluca.*

'Just me,' she calls out.

She dashes back to her room, throws on her clothes, and goes through to the lounge.

Gianluca is sitting in an armchair, flipping through a magazine. 'My aunt isn't here,' he says. 'I dropped by to talk to her about her memoirs, but she must have gone to the shops.' He gives Rhiannon a concerned look. 'Are you ill? I mean, you're not at school.'

'I didn't sleep well and Leila insisted I went back to bed.' She averts her gaze. 'I feel a bit guilty, to be honest. I should have struggled in.'

'How are you feeling now?'

'Much improved.' She smiles. 'Maybe I should go to my afternoon class?'

'I've got a better idea. Let's have lunch together and then I'll show you a bit more of Bologna before I return to work. We can leave a note for my aunt.'

Rhiannon's tummy gurgles with hunger. 'That would be great, but you must let me pay my share of the bill.'

He laughs. 'You're so funny. First time I've ever taken a girl out who doesn't want me to buy her a meal.'

'That's just it. We're not going out with each other, Gianluca. Aren't we just friends?'

'You have an answer for everything.' He laughs again.

She goes back to her room to put on some lip gloss while he scribbles the note for Leila.

* * *

Gianluca takes Rhiannon to Ristorante Diana, one of the oldest in Bologna. 'It was a favourite place for the Germans to hang out during the war,' he tells her while they wait to be served.

'How are you getting on with listening to Leila's memoirs?' She picks up a grissini breadstick and takes a bite.

'They're fascinating. I was hoping she'd recorded some more, which is why I dropped by to see her just now.'

'She told me last night about the battle at the university. Her friends were executed. Such a tragic thing to happen.' Rhiannon is silent for a moment. 'Did you know that Leila was arrested and tortured?'

'*Porca* Madonna!' Gianluca snaps his breadstick in half. 'I had no idea.'

'Her sweetheart and some other partisans rescued her, apparently. His name was Paolo and they got married afterwards, but he died before the papers could be filed.'

'Wow! No wonder she's finding narrating her story so upsetting. It's immensely courageous of her.'

'She's the bravest person I've ever met.'

Have I said too much? Rhiannon frowns. *Maybe Leila would prefer the revelation to come directly from her?*

Their food arrives, the Diana's signature dish of bollito, slowly simmered beef served with mostarda, a condiment made of stewed fresh and candied fruit mixed with mustard-flavoured syrup.

Rhiannon tucks in hungrily and declares the dish to be yummy. 'I'll miss Italian food when I go home.'

'Is that all you'll miss?' He meets her gaze.

'I'll miss Leila terribly. And you too, of course. You've become a good friend.'

His face assumes a serious expression. 'I was hoping we could be more than that...'

A fluttery feeling spreads through her. 'We can't. I mean, I'm only here for another couple of months. And, besides, you're still mourning Flavia.'

'If you're worried I'd treat you like the women I've dated since Flavia passed away, hand on heart, I swear I'm over that now. I'm ready to move on. Flavia would have wanted me to...'

'And you want to, as you call it 'move on'—' Rhiannon makes quote marks with her fingers '—with me?' She discerns the panic in her voice.

'I'm sorry. I should have said that I'm developing feelings for you. I'm an idiot, Rhiannon. I didn't explain myself properly.' He looks deep into her eyes. 'Dare I hope you feel the same way?'

She leans away from him, fighting the urge to get up and run. *Breathe, Rhiannon, Just Breathe.* 'I don't know.' She frowns. 'This is so sudden.'

'I love that about you. You're not at all presumptive.'

Her thoughts have turned fuzzy; she doesn't know what to think. She opts to tell him about seeing Barzini in Piazza San Michele in Monte, about watching him hand over the money to Marie and about her decision to follow the Lebanese girl. It might distract him from pursuing the subject of his burgeoning feelings for her, and it does.

'*Minchia,*' he swears. 'Were you out of your mind?!'

'No need for that tone, Gianluca. I did what I thought was right. And I was careful.'

'I don't want you getting involved.'

Rhiannon reaches into her handbag and extracts a twenty-thousand lire banknote. 'Here's my share of the bill. You don't want me getting involved, and I don't want to involve myself with someone as overbearing as you.'

She pushes back her chair and leaves him staring after her, open-mouthed.

Outside, on the pavement, she stops dead in her tracks. *Oh, God, what have I done?* She let her hang-ups get the better of her, that's what. And now she's made a fool of herself.

She turns to go back into the restaurant, but Gianluca is already coming through the doors. 'I'm sorry,' she says. 'I didn't mean to be such a cow.'

He wraps his arms around her, holds her close. 'And I apologise for being overbearing. I'm just concerned for your safety, Rhiannon. I didn't make that clear.'

'I know,' she murmurs into his chest. 'I like you. Really like you. But there are things I need to tell you. And you'll probably decide I'm not worth the bother when you've heard them.'

'Ha, that I doubt.'

She lifts her face and he kisses her. Soft, lingering. Her knees wobble, and she loops her arms around his neck. He deepens the kiss and her heart pounds so loudly she's sure he can hear it.

19

LEILA

'I've listened to your memoirs and they are incredible, Auntie,' Gianluca says the following morning. We're having coffee together in Piazza Aldrovandi before I do some shopping and he goes to interview a contact about something he won't reveal. 'Rhiannon told me you were upset again.' He takes my hand, gives it a squeeze. 'I'd like to listen to the next cassette, but perhaps you wouldn't mind telling me what made you so unhappy?'

I wonder if Rhiannon has shared with him what I blurted to her. When I got home from the market yesterday and found the note from Gianluca that they'd gone for lunch together, I surmised she might reveal my secrets. And from Gianluca's concerned expression, I think my guess is correct. Not that I mind – he'd have discovered the truth when he heard my story in any case. And so, I tell him, tell him about my being arrested and tortured, and about my partisan wedding. There were many such happy events during the war, I found out later. Some with joyful outcomes, and some ending in grief like mine.

'You must have loved Paolo very much.' Gianluca lifts my

hand and kisses it. 'And I'm sorry about what those bastards did to you.'

'War is terrible. And our civil war particularly so. Italians fighting Italians...'

'My generation needs to know what their parents went through.' He squeezes my fingers. 'If you'll reconsider and let me find a publisher, Auntie, I believe your story will raise awareness.'

I release a breath. 'People prefer to forget. Or at least, not to rake up the past. I'm sure some of your friends had parents who were ardent fascists. And others whose parents were partisans like your father and me. Having extreme opposing factions in society is extremely divisive.'

'Which is why people need to remember. So it doesn't happen again.'

'Don't forget we weren't just fighting between ourselves, but also an occupying army. The Germans were taking everything from us. Rounding up men and using them as slave labour. Stealing our food and equipment to transport to Germany. It was because the Nazis were in Bologna that the Allies bombed us so mercilessly. Your father and I were caught in the middle. We couldn't stand by and do nothing. We fervently believed that fighting back was the only way.'

'If only world leaders would learn from history that they can't just go in and occupy another country against the will of its citizens. It tends to end in failure, sooner or later. But it's always the innocent civilians who suffer most.'

'You're right, Gianluca. As I've said before, the past is never past much as people would like it to be.' I drink the last of my coffee. 'Well, I must go and buy some strawberries before Bruno runs out.' I get to my feet. 'Come for supper tonight, dear, and I'll give you my latest cassettes.'

'*Grazie*, Auntie.' He picks up the tab. '*Perfetto*.'

Back home an hour later, I put away the groceries I purchased, feed Romeo and make myself a quick lunch of spaghetti with fresh tomato *sugo*. After tidying up the kitchen, I square my shoulders and step into the study. I bought myself some new cassettes when I was out shopping earlier. I insert one into the recorder, plug in the microphone, and settle into my chair.

After our wedding, Paolo and I hung about with our comrades, bored by the lack of action while we waited for the call from the Liberation Committee that the Allies were about to arrive. The Anglo-Americans had been delayed by the recent bad weather, by all accounts. The ground between their front and Bologna had been turned into a quagmire by the seemingly endless rain. So, we passed our time playing never-ending card games, our daily routine only alleviated by guard duty and training sessions with Bruno.

One morning in early November, Bruno bustled into the dining room where we were having breakfast. 'The committee want us to join the brigade quartered in the old municipal slaughterhouse in Azzo Gardino Street,' he announced.

'I thought that building was in ruins,' I said, dunking bread in my barley coffee.

'Only partially. Which makes it a good hideout as no one suspects it's occupied. There are about sixty gappisti there, and I'm to take charge of them as their previous commander is ill. Given the strategic position near Porta Lame, we'll be used as backup to the Allies when they enter Bologna.'

'Not many men for such a task.' Paolo coughed asthmatically.

'There are about two hundred gappisti in the ruins of the former

Ospedale Maggiore in nearby Riva di Reno,' Bruno went on to say. 'Plus myriad others dotted all around the city. The battle is at hand, comrades. Our patience has borne fruit.'

We packed our meagre belongings into rucksacks and set off in small groups under cover of darkness. By then we knew how to cheat the curfew. On arrival at the abattoir, we were greeted warmly by those who were there. Bruno did a stock take of the weapons situation. Like us, most of the partisans were armed with a Beretta 7.65. They had a few sub-machine guns and a plethora of hand grenades, stolen in previous actions. The gappisti in the abandoned hospital down the road had better weapons than us, having 'requisitioned' a long-range machine gun that they'd dismounted from a German armoured car.

For the next week, we spent our time playing the waiting game. Paolo and I laughed wryly at the setting for our 'honeymoon'. In the Bolognina base we had some privacy, but not so in the slaughter-house. We slept in a room on the first floor with Carla, Sebastiano, Daniele, Bruno, and Giant, huddled together on bales of straw like the cows who once met their fate in the abattoir below. At least it was warm and we had plenty of food, thanks to the generosity of local producers and farmers from the surrounding area who gave us bread, some meat, jars of jam and other essentials.

The commander of the Liberation Committee, a wiry man with a hook nose, visited us on the morning of 6 November. At Bruno's request, we formed a circle around the man and listened to his words. 'The Allies have announced a new offensive and soon we will go into action to liberate the city from within,' he said before congratulating us on the efficiency of our organisation and on our high morale. 'The Germans are in retreat along their entire front and the time for insurrection is fast approaching.' He added that it was difficult to establish exactly when that would be. Everything depended on the movement of the Allies, who didn't seem to be in much of a rush.

Next morning, Paolo and I went out on patrol at five thirty. It was still dark and the weather had turned cold. We strode briskly and had just reached Riva di Reno when we came to an abrupt halt by the canal. Voices and the stomping of boots echoed a short distance away. Paolo put his finger to his lips and we flattened our backs to the chilly wall of the tall red-brick building behind us.

A big group of Black Brigades militia were going from house to house, taking men too old to be conscripted away from their families, and herding them into lorries which we knew would transport them to slave labour camps. Uniformed officers of the German Feldendarmerie and the fascist Police Assault Department appeared to be in charge.

Stealthily, we hurried back to base to warn our comrades.

Everyone was up already, having breakfast.

'Nazis and fascists,' Paolo yelled. 'Heading this way.'

Mafalda dropped her tray with a yelp and ran to Diego in the kitchen.

Bruno calmly told the brigade to get into defensive positions at the windows of the first and second floors. 'They might not come here, but we must be prepared.'

I stood next to Paolo at our assigned place overlooking the Cavaticcio Canal.

Two young Wehrmacht soldiers were approaching along the path below. My heart set up a fearful beat.

Almost as if they were children playing a game, the Germans tried to enter the slaughterhouse through a hole blasted in a prior air raid, blocked by fallen wooden beams.

Bruno and Giant went downstairs to meet them and take them down, but things didn't go according to plan. With shouts of, 'Kamaraden!', the soldiers came running out of the abattoir.

My training sessions with Bruno took over and I raised my pistol to take aim.

Paolo and I fired a quick burst.

The Germans screamed and toppled into the canal, where they floated face down.

Bitter bile rose in my throat. I'd killed a man. Admittedly, it might have been Paolo's bullets that had done it, but I had been a willing participant.

I didn't have time for remorse. The nazifascisti had turned up, after hearing the soldiers' shouts. Bruno barked orders to open fire.

Shooting with small arms at an enemy armed with long-range weapons might have seemed a task doomed to failure, but we had high morale on our side and a fierce determination not to give in.

The Nazi-fascists tried several times to occupy the building, with assaults as furious as they were fruitless.

The battle wore on, hot and intense, but our courage and resolve stayed firm.

We lobbed grenades and inflicted many casualties.

A German captain crumpled to the ground, nothing left of his face except blood, bone, and sinew.

But the enemy attack intensified at around ten o'clock, when our scout came to tell us that the Nazis had set up an 88 mm gun and two-barrel heavy machine guns on nests in Azzo Gardino Street.

We braced ourselves and my hands turned clammy on the grip of my gun. Shells arched through the air and exploded against the exterior wall of the abattoir, sending bits of brick flying.

An almighty explosion made me flinch. The entire building shook and the men who'd been on the second floor burst into the room where Paolo and I had taken up position. 'The roof has caved in,' Giant roared. 'Rubble, stone and tiles everywhere.'

My pulse raced, but I carried on shooting. The Germans were demolishing our refuge, blasting enormous holes in it, and I feared for my life.

A sudden shout came from Giant. Porco cane! He'd fallen to his knees, clutching at his throat.

Daniele went to him; there was nothing he could do.

Giant bled quickly to death from his carotid artery in front of our shocked eyes, while Carla and I held him, whispering what words of comfort we could summon. Numbness overcame me. How could this brave, strong man have been taken? The brigade wouldn't be the same without his solid, reassuring presence.

The first floor had started to collapse now and it would have been impossible to defend the building from the ground.

'Head for the annex next door!' Bruno commanded.

Icy terror clawed at me. We'd have to cross a courtyard exposed to long-range machine-gun fire.

Bruno grabbed his rucksack. We all kept them with us for just such a circumstance. 'Everyone must leave. No one should be taken prisoner,' he cried out, leading the charge.

We snatched up our bags and hurried down the stairs, leaving poor Giant to be buried with the building.

Bruno stepped into the patio, yelling for us to follow.

With a mighty bang, a grenade landed and exploded in front of him, spinning him upwards.

He collapsed to the floor, clutching at his left arm.

Oh Dio mio!

Without thinking I ran to him, Paolo and Daniele hot at my heels.

Between them, they helped him to his feet, and the three of us managed to get him into the annex.

Sebastiano came through the door carrying Carla. I gave a gasp. She'd taken a bullet in the shoulder and was bleeding profusely. Daniel patched up the torn flesh and splintered bone, but she was out cold, her face pale and her breathing shallow. Sebastiano burst into tears and, my heart aching, I comforted him as best as I could.

'You're in command now,' Bruno told Paolo. He indicated his shrapnel lacerated left arm. 'I'm in no fit state.'

I was torn between staying with Carla and fighting with Paolo, but my husband took first place and I stuck by his side.

Again, we repelled the enemy's attempts to take the building. We kept firing at them and they returned our fire without getting anywhere.

'Make smoke bombs.' Paolo gave the order to a group of men. 'We might need them if we run out of ammo.'

At around 5 p.m., another of our scouts rushed in. 'A Panzer Tiger tank has rolled into Don Minzoni Street,' he exclaimed in a panic-stricken voice.

Dread rippled through me. Its long-range cannon would make short work of demolishing the annex.

Shelling from the tank started in earnest, and Paolo gave the order to abandon the base. He divided us into three groups. The first and third were armed, the second, non-combatants including Diego, Mafalda, Daniele, and Sebastiano, supported the wounded, carrying them on their shoulders.

We grabbed the smoke bombs, lit them, and threw them onto the road. Then we made our way down to the Cavaticcio canal.

The incendiary devices made the night-time darkness even more impenetrable. We crept in a single line along the ledge used by washerwomen, heading upstream.

The fascists were on the banks high above us. We could barely see them in the murkiness, but we heard their shouts. Would they realise we were below them? I held my breath.

With every moment that passed my spirits lightened. It seemed we'd managed to escape. We followed Fratelli Rosselli Street until we arrived at Piazza Umberto Primo (now known as Piazza Martiri, named after the martyred partisans).

My chest tightened.

We'd come across a fascist checkpoint.

Four men, apparently asleep at their posts.

Thankfully, Paolo had suggested we carried grenades in our bags. 'Throw a hand bomb, Leila,' he whispered.

I reached into my rucksack. Heart pounding, I pushed the string loop, with its small button attachment, into my mouth, gripped the thin cord with my teeth, and pulled hard. Not even attempting to aim, I hurled it in the direction of the fascisti.

All hell broke loose as the militiamen screamed and reached for their weapons. But my comrades got there first and eliminated them, the exploding grenades making sure of their demise.

Our group of seventy-five was now seventy, having lost Giant and four others in the battle. Paolo gave the order for everyone to return to their old bases and for the wounded to be taken by Daniele and Sebastiano, in the lorry parked at the fascist checkpoint, to the secret partisan infirmary in Andrea Costa Street beyond the ring road.

I made my weary way to the Bolognina safe house with Paolo and the others. It felt strange to be there without Bruno, Giant, Carla, Dani, and Sebastiano. We held an improvised memorial service for our fallen comrades and said prayers for Bruno and Carla's recovery.

Diego and Mafalda found some supplies and prepared a plate of pasta, which I ate without tasting, so exhausted and emotionally drained did I feel. Upstairs, in the room I shared with Paolo, I washed and got into bed. He joined me, and I wept as he held me and soothed me until I fell into a fretful sleep.

Next morning, a representative from the Liberation Committee arrived to tell us that almost at the same time as we'd descended to the canal, the partisans occupying the ruins of the Ospedale Maggiore had come out into the open and attacked the Nazi-fascist deployment from the rear to allow us, the comrades they believed were still surrounded in the former slaughterhouse, to escape.

The nazifascisti disbanded and, when the partigiani entered our semi-demolished premises, they found them empty. Deciding not to hang around in case the enemy returned in force, they too left the area and went back to their former bases.

I switch off the tape recorder, exhausted. Porta Lame has gone down in history as one of the largest pitched battles fought in Europe by partisans in the heart of a city. I'm proud to have played a small part in it but reliving the events has tired me. I sit for a while, Romeo on my lap. My eyes prickle with tears and my heart aches as I think about my old comrades.

20

RHIANNON

Rhiannon strolls past the Nettuno fountain, hand in hand with Gianluca. He came round to Leila's for supper earlier and, after they'd eaten, suggested he and Rhiannon went for a drink while his aunt watched *Colombo*, dubbed in Italian, on television.

Beppe Maniglia, the muscular man with the hot water bottle, is performing to the crowd like he was the last time she came here. Loud rock music blasts, amplified by the electronic device mounted on his Harley-Davidson.

They go over to the wall with the ceramic photos of the martyred partisans. 'It's so sad to think that Leila's husband was one of them.' Rhiannon breathes a sigh. 'I wonder which one is him?'

'Auntie didn't mention his surname.' Gianluca peers at the faces. 'There are several with the first name, Paolo.'

'There's a plaque at my school mentioning the Resistance. Are there any monuments elsewhere in Bologna?'

'All over the city. For example, there are a couple of bronze sculptures in the Montagnola Park. They were made in 1946 from a melted down statue of Mussolini.'

'Sounds appropriate.' Rhiannon grins ruefully.

Gianluca takes her to Bar Vittorio Emanuele in Piazza Maggiore. It's too chilly to sit outside, so they go indoors.

They're greeted with a wall of noise and there aren't any free tables.

'Let's go to my place instead,' Gianluca suggests.

'Or we could back to Leila's.' Rhiannon pastes a smile to her lips.

'Don't worry. I only want to talk.'

Heat suffuses her cheeks. Gianluca must think her such an idiot. She doesn't know why she blurted yesterday, after their disastrous lunch at the Diana Restaurant, that she needed to tell him things about herself. Of course he's curious. Why wouldn't he be? And now she's going to have to explain what she meant.

They head down Rizzoli Street and turn right at the two towers. In Zamboni Street, they come to an unremarkable wooden door. Gianluca unlocks it and leads Rhiannon towards a metal and stained-glass gate which opens onto a garden. It's the entrance to one of those amazing palazzi she peered into on the way to the university canteen, she realises, gazing around her in awe.

They follow a gravel path lit by lamplights until they come to a three-storey coral-coloured building.

Inside, a staircase wraps around a glass lift. Gianluca presses a button and the doors slide open. They ride past the main floor right to the top of the palazzo. 'This is my apartment,' Gianluca waves his hand at the open-plan warehouse-style living space.

'It's stunning,' she says, and it's true. A huge sofa faces an open fire set within a bare red-brick wall, logs slotted inside a rusted-iron holder sculpted like a wave. At the far end of the room, a wooden staircase curves up to what she presumes is the loft space.

Gianluca leads her down three steps into the sitting area and takes her coat. Through the tall windows, the bulk of the spot-lit Basilica of San Petronio towers like a fortress above the roofs of the city.

'A glass of San Giovese?' Gianluca offers.

'Lovely. *Grazie*.'

She lowers herself onto the sofa while he goes to a cabinet in the corner and extracts a bottle of wine.

He hands her a glass and clinks *his* glass with hers. 'Salute!'

'Salute,' she returns the toast to good health. 'So, what did you want to discuss?'

'I'd like to know why you're so often like a rabbit caught in the headlights when you're with me. It's a conundrum. I mean, you seem fearless of Marie and her shenanigans. You didn't complain about the smell or rats in the Aposa. I just don't get it...'

'Oh, Gianluca, it's not you. It's me.' She releases a heavy sigh, then sighs inwardly at the cliché.

'What do you mean?'

'I mean, well... I'm hopeless where men are concerned.'

He gives a little laugh. 'I like it that you're shy. I think it's charming.'

She straightens her back. 'I'm embarrassed to talk about it.'

He quirks a brow. 'Tell me. Please?'

'I'm just no good at...'

'*Non capisco*.' I don't understand.

She lowers her gaze. 'I'm...I'm frigid.' *There, she's said it. Told him the mortifying truth.*

'I didn't get that impression when we kissed yesterday.' He looks deep into her eyes. 'Your response was warm, womanly, dare I say.'

A tingling feeling sweeps across her chest and prickles her face. 'You're a good kisser.' She blushes like a fool.

'Can I kiss you again?'

She closes her eyes and he touches his mouth to hers, his tongue seeking entrance. And she can't help herself, she gives it to him.

She clings to him, breathless, and tangles her fingers in his hair.

Before she knows it, she's lying back on the sofa and he's covering her with his body.

She freezes.

Oh God.

He rolls off her. 'I'm so sorry. I got carried away.'

'It's not you, Gianluca. I told you already, it's me.' A stupid tear rolls down her cheek.

'Did something happen to make you this way?' he asks, brushing the tear away.

His directness floors her momentarily. Then she says, 'No. Nothing. I'm just hopeless at intimacy.' She clears her throat and decides to go all in and tell him about Owen, her ex.

Gianluca listens without interrupting. He's a good listener, it occurs to her. But he would be, wouldn't he? It's required in his line of work.

'Hmm.' He taps his chin when she gets to the end of her sorry tale. 'Owen might not have been your Mr Right...'

'And you think you could be?' She can't believe she's saying this. 'Gianluca, we barely know each other.'

'I know enough to know that I'm falling for you.'

'Leila would be furious if she found out.'

'I'll come clean with her. Explain how I feel. But only if you agree.'

'Okay...' Her pulse races. 'I do like you, Gianluca. More than like you, I think. But I'm only here for a few months. If I let myself fall for you and my idiotic frigidness didn't put you off, how would I cope when I went back to Wales? I'd miss you and be unhappy without you.'

A smile crinkles the corners of his dark eyes. 'You're putting obstacles in our path before we've even started our journey.' He enfolds her in a warm embrace and whispers, '*Volere è potere...*' Where there's a will there's a way.

21

LEILA

I blink my bleary eyes open. *Cavolo, I must have fallen asleep.* Detective Colombo has solved the murder without me knowing who did it, and now the *telegiornale* has come on. I watched the news earlier, so pick up the remote control and switch off the TV.

The sound of voices echoes from the corridor. 'Ciao.' Gianluca steps into my living room. 'How was the programme?'

'I slept through it,' I laugh. 'Did you have a nice time in Piazza Maggiore?'

'It was crowded and noisy.' Rhiannon sits herself on the sofa. 'So we went to Gianluca's place.' A wistful expression crosses her face. 'What an amazing apartment!'

Gianluca and Rhiannon glance at each other. She gives a little nod, and he clears his throat. 'Auntie... well, not quite sure how to say this so I'll spit it out.' A smile glimmers in his eyes. 'I want to tell you something.'

'Oh?' I tilt my head.

Rhiannon leans towards me. 'Gianluca wants for him and me to be more than 'just friends'.'

I send him a look, and he holds up his hands. 'I'm behaving myself...'

'You mean you're no longer a playboy?' I twist my mouth ruefully. 'That's good to know.'

'You're not upset, I hope,' Rhiannon says.

I glance from her to Gianluca and back to her again. 'The fact that you've been honest warms my heart.'

Gianluca throws his arms around me and gives me a hug. 'I won't do anything to hurt Rhiannon, you have my word.'

'Good.'

I chew my lip, not wanting to spoil their party by pointing out the pitfalls. I wonder about Rhiannon's intimacy problems and how she'll cope with being separated from Gianluca in a few months' time.

'Be kind to each other, my darlings,' I say. 'You have my blessing.' And they do. Life is short. *Carpe diem.* They should seize the day.

'*Grazie*,' Rhiannon blushes. *She's so sweet I could eat her.* How I'd love to welcome her into the family. But that's unlikely, I sigh to myself. She'll go home to Wales and Gianluca will stay on in Bologna. She risks heartbreak, and I hope she knows what she's getting herself into.

'Could I borrow your latest cassettes, Auntie?' Gianluca interrupts my conflicted thoughts.

'Certainly. I'll go and fetch them for you.'

* * *

Back in my study the following morning, I take a deep breath. Today is the day I've been dreading since I started recording my memoirs. But I owe it to Paolo's memory to carry on and, although it will pain me, I must hold back my tears.

Romeo sits on my desk and fixes me with a green-eyed stare while I open the drawer to retrieve my tape recorder. Steeling myself, I plug in the microphone and pull up my chair.

The fascists reported they'd lost eighteen men in the Porta Lame battle of 7 November, plus one who died of his injuries the next day. The partisans killed fifteen Germans and wounded twenty, by all accounts, but the underground Resistance newspapers – for propaganda reasons – maintained that we'd slain over two hundred, a fabrication to boost morale. We lost twelve brave comrades that day, including Giant, and my heart still weeps for him and for them.

Dani and Sebastiano stayed with Bruno, Carla and the thirteen others who'd been wounded. An Austrian doctor, secretly anti-fascist, oversaw the clandestine infirmary beyond the ring road. As soon as Bruno and Carla were better they would rejoin us in the Bolognina base, Daniele had promised, and I couldn't wait to see them again.

Paolo and I, together with eighteen of our fellow freedom fighters, spent our time playing the ubiquitous waiting game. On 13 November, we were sitting listening to the radio station Italia Combatte when a proclamation, addressed to the Italian Resistance on behalf of General Harold Alexander, Supreme Commander of the Allied Forces in Italy, came over the airwaves.

'The summer campaign, which began on the eleventh of May and has been conducted without interruption, is over. The winter campaign will now begin. This means ceasing large-scale operations and preparing yourselves for a new phase of struggle to face a new enemy, the winter itself.'

I grabbed hold of Paolo's hand. 'I don't understand.'

A frown creased his brow. 'The Allies have halted their advance and left us to manage on our own.'

Paolo didn't meet my eye, didn't say what we were all thinking. Alexander had, for all intents and purposes, thrown us to the nazi-fascisti like the Romans had thrown the Christians to the lions.

'The Allies only want us to stop taking part in 'large-scale operations'. We'll carry on as we've been doing, battling the enemy with everything we've got.' Paolo gave an asthmatic cough.

I gazed at him, traced a finger down his cheek. 'You're so brave, my darling, fighting like you do despite your asthma. I'm incredibly proud of you and I love you so much.' I kissed him on the lips.

Tigre, the youngest of us at barely eighteen years of age, fresh-faced and blue-eyed, picked up his guitar and strummed the introduction to a patriotic song we'd recently learnt to sing. With melancholic voices, we all joined in.

> One fine morning I woke up
> Bella ciao, bella ciao, bella ciao, ciao, ciao
> One fine morning I woke up
> And I found the invader at my door
> Oh, partigiano, please take me with you
> Bella ciao, bella ciao, bella ciao, ciao, ciao
> Oh, partigiano, please take me with you
> Because I feel like I'm going to die.

'Viva l'Italia!' we cried out in unison, and the refrain helped assuage the bitter disappointment in our souls.

That night in bed, Paolo held me close and loved me, and I gave myself to him, loving him heart, body, and spirit. We spoke of dreams, our dreams for the future. 'I can't wait to get back to studying medicine again,' he sighed. 'I want to save lives instead of taking them.'

I snuggled into his chest. 'You'll be a wonderful doctor, my love.'

'And you, a wonderful teacher.' He brushed a kiss to the top of my head.

Two days later, on the morning of 15 November, we were having breakfast when the ominous sound of heavy vehicles reverberated from Piazza dell'Unità.

My chest froze.

Before I could say anything, Tigre, who'd been on guard duty, burst into the room. 'Tanks and armoured cars, masses of Germans and fascist soldiers. Out on the square,' he yelled.

We leapt to our feet, clutching our weapons.

'Wait, everyone,' Paolo barked. 'The nazifasciti could just be carrying out one of their usual roundups of men for the forced labour camps.' He paused. 'They might not have come for us.'

At first, it seemed Paolo was right. We grouped together behind a barred door and listened out for the sounds of the enemy coming up the stairs.

The morning wore on, and no one approached. 'What time is it?' I asked Paolo.

'Past midday,' he coughed.

Guttural voices lifted from the square, shouts of 'Achtung!'

Surely there were no able-bodied men left for the Nazis to send to their godforsaken lagers. They'd been bleeding Bologna dry for over a year…

Suddenly the thump of footfalls on wooden boards and the murmur of men speaking Italian echoed from the stairwell.

Porca Madonna, the fascisti were in the building.

I held my Beretta so tightly my knuckles blanched.

The door rattled but held.

The fascists began to smash their way in.

'Take aim, comrades!' Paolo gave the order.

We moved off to one side, took our aim just as the wood of the door splintered and five men in the green National Republican Guard uniform burst into the room.

I gave a gasp.

Captain Barzini was leading the charge.

His cold eyes landed on me. Or rather my gun, aimed at his chest.

I pulled the trigger.

Just like that.

He fell in a crumpled heap.

Paolo, Tigre, and the others made short work of the rest of Barzini's men. We hurried out of the room, blocking the door behind us, leaving them for dead.

'Head upstairs, *partigiani*,' Paolo commanded. 'Everyone except Vittoria and Tigre.'

My mouth dropped open. 'What?!'

'I want you to get out through the rear of the building,' Paolo clarified. 'Make your way to the fruit and vegetable market in Fioravanti Street.' He wiped sweat from his forehead. 'In the meantime, the rest of us will shoot from the upstairs windows.'

'I'm not leaving you,' I wailed.

'You will obey my order,' he countered.

I stared down at my hands and shifted my weight from one foot to the other.

He pulled me into a rough embrace. 'Do as you're told, my love. We'll be together again, I promise. Wait for me in the market square. I won't be long.'

I kissed him and he kissed me back, a desperate kiss, our lips bathed by the salt of our tears.

'Go!' He pushed me away from him.

Oh, how I wanted to disobey. But I couldn't. I had to show him the respect of a soldier towards her commander.

I hurried down the back stairs with Tigre.

We reached the rear garden, the crack of gunshots ripping the air above us.

'Run, Vittoria,' Tigre called out. 'I'll cover you from behind.'

A rush of adrenaline burned through me, and I ran as fast as I could.

Tigre had begun shooting, and the ra-ta-ta-ta-ta of his sub-machine gun sent fear slicing through my chest. Who was he firing at? I didn't dare look.

Without warning, I tripped and my feet slipped from under me. I cried out as I fell into a flower bed.

I landed with a thud. My Beretta had broken my fall, but its barrel was packed with earth. *Porco cane,* I swore to myself.

The shooting had stopped so I scrambled to my feet.

I shot a quick glance behind for Tigre, but he was nowhere to be seen.

What should I do?

Paolo and my comrades were still drawing fire, I could tell from the noise.

I realised that I mustn't let them down, that I had to get away or their sacrifice – for that was what it was – would have been for nothing.

Slowly, the thumping of my heart eased and the gasping of my breaths lessened. I hid my gun under a rose bush, wiped my hands down my skirt, and walked nonchalantly into the road.

'*Alt!*' Two Repubblican guards stopped me. 'Where are you going?' *Cavolo.*

I fluttered my eyelashes at them, pretending to be a helpless woman. 'I live up there—' I indicated the adjacent building '—but I was scared by the shooting so I'm going to my sister's place in Tibaldi Street.'

'Show me your ID,' the taller of the two men demanded.

I retrieved my fake document from the pocket of my jacket.

The *repubblichino* gave it a cursory glance. 'Be on your way, signorina. It isn't safe for you out here.'

'*Grazie, signore.*' I gritted my teeth to stop myself from spitting in his face.

Gunshots were still cracking from the upper floor of our base. I hoped against hope Paolo and the others wouldn't delay in making good their escape. Clinging to that hope I made my way to the market square.

There, I wandered shakily from stall to stall, trying to give the impression I was shopping for groceries. The scant selection of goods available – only potatoes, chestnuts, and a few worm-eaten apples – made it difficult to act like a discerning shopper. All I could think about was Paolo. I bit my nails to their quicks as I paced, praying desperately that he and my comrades would soon arrive.

All of a sudden the boom of explosions ricocheted, sending up coils of black smoke from the direction of Piazza dell'Unità.

Oh, God. What now?

Tigre ran into the square. 'The Germans are firing at our base with tank guns,' he informed me, wide-eyed.

My stomach twisted into knots. Paolo, my Paolo. How I feared for him. 'We must go back there,' I said to Tigre. 'Our comrades need us.'

'What can we do? If we return, we'll be killed.' Tigre shook his head. 'Better we wait here like Tarzan ordered.'

And so, we waited. I tried to take calming breaths. But every second that passed was like a living nightmare I was so worried. I pulled at my hair and wished I hadn't obeyed Paolo's order.

An elderly stallholder gave us a cup of barley coffee and pulled out chairs. 'I know who you are,' he said. 'I've taken supplies to Diego this past week. I hope he, Mafalda and the others manage to escape.'

Almost as soon as he'd spoken those words, our black mustachioed cook and his kind wife appeared before us, white-faced, their bodies shaking. 'The Nazis have reduced the building to rubble,' Diego's voice trembled. 'We got out just in time.'

'And Tarzan? Did he and the rest of the brigade make it?' The question quivered on my lips.

'Mi dspiase, cóca mì, I'm sorry, my dear,' Mafalda said in Bolognese dialect as she took my hand. 'The palazzo collapsed with them still in it.'

Nausea squeezed my belly. 'We must go to them. Dig them out.' I jumped to my feet and began to run.

Tigre ran faster and blocked my way. 'Tarzan asked me to look after you if anything happened to him. I can't let you put yourself in danger.'

'I have to go to my husband,' I pleaded.

'Let's wait until nightfall,' Tigre said. 'We can return to our base after curfew starts and see if there's anything to be done.'

I knew he was talking sense, knew that Paolo would be furious if I deliberately put myself at risk, but the hours that followed, while I waited with Tigre, Diego, and Mafalda, were the longest of my life. I alternated between clinging to hope and total despair. What if Paolo and the others were still alive? We needed to rescue them and get them to the infirmary as soon as possible.

Finally, darkness fell and the four of us crept back to Piazza dell'Unità.

My breath hitched. A contingent of nazifascisti were digging in the debris. They must have been searching for the Repubblican guards whom we'd left for dead.

'We'll have to wait until they've gone,' Tigre whispered.

We hid under a partially collapsed portico and watched in horror as they dug man after man from the wreckage. I bit back a sob. There was Paolo, his dear face unscathed but ghostly white, his poor body twisted and broken.

I set off to run to him, but Mafalda grabbed hold of me, and I cried silent tears against her motherly shoulder.

Then, before my horrified eyes, the repubblichini pulled Ugo Barzini out from under a fallen beam. 'He's alive,' one of them shouted gleefully.

I stared in disbelief as they bundled him onto a stretcher and carried him away from the scene.

Eventually, we were alone in the square and could go to our martyred companions. I rushed forwards and threw myself over Paolo's *body, sobbing. 'I love you so much, my darling. There will never be anyone else for me.'*

The others left me to my grieving while they checked the rubble to see if any of our comrades had survived.

But they hadn't.

How could that bastard Barzini have made it when everyone else had been taken?

Fate had dealt me such a cruel blow…

I can't record any more, I'm crying so much. I press the off button and wrap my arms around myself, rocking my body.

The click of the front door opening startles me. Only Gianluca and Rhiannon have keys to the apartment. She's at school, so it must be him.

'Ciao.' He smiles, coming into my study, then stops dead in his tracks. 'Oh my God, Auntie, what's wrong?' He helps me to my feet and holds me close.

I hiccough on a sob. 'I've just narrated the part in my story where Paolo died. Life can be so unfair. I thought I'd killed the man who was my nemesis. But, somehow, he survived my shooting him. He even survived the collapse of a bombed-out building.'

'Are you talking about Ugo Barzini?'

'Yes,' I say through gritted teeth.

'I just listened to your recording about him torturing and then attempting to rape you. What a bastard! I came right over to tell you that I'm investigating him. Such a coincidence…'

Shock wheels through me. 'You should stay away from him,' I warn, horrified. 'He's as slippery as an eel and crueller than the Devil himself.'

'Too late for that, I'm afraid,' Gianluca says.

22

LEILA

I dry my tears and offer to make us both a coffee. The fact that Gianluca is digging into Barzini's background has distracted me from my grief. I must find out what my nephew is up to, then repeat my warning.

In the kitchen, Gianluca places the Bialetti on the stove. 'Sit yourself down and relax, Auntie.'

'How can I relax? You've just dropped a massive bombshell on me.'

'I'm sorry to have done it when you were so upset...'

'Yes, well. You weren't to know.' I sniff. 'But you do owe me an explanation.'

He folds his arms. 'I'm looking into Barzini's connections with Licio Gelli.'

'The financier?'

Gianluca nods. 'Did you know Gelli was implicated in the failed Golpe Borghese?'

I remember reading about that botched right-wing coup. Neo-fascist militants had tried to seize power in December 1970. But Borghese – wartime commander of the 10th Assault Vehicle

Flotilla and a hero in the eyes of many post-war fascists – subsequently aborted his secret operation when he'd learnt the government had found out about it. Borghese fled the country shortly afterwards and died in Spain four years later.

'I didn't realise Gelli was implicated.' I flare my nostrils. 'Do you believe Barzini was also involved?'

'Highly likely. He and Gelli are close friends. Have been since they met when they went into self-imposed exile in Argentina back in 1946.'

'They're both fervent anti-communists,' I sigh, recalling how one of the fascists' prime doctrines was to fight the 'red peril' and how Barzini delighted in torturing the partisans he captured during the war, many of whom were reds.

Steam rises from the Bialetti. Gianluca pours the espresso into two cups and sets them on the table.

'So, dear nephew, what led you into this investigation?' I take a sip of coffee, willing myself to appear calm.

'There are loads of unanswered questions floating around about the bombing of the railway station last year.'

'I thought that had been attributed to the neo-fascists?' I lift my chin. 'Everyone thinks they did it. An ultra-right attack on left-wing Bologna la Rossa. We're the Italian Communist Party's showcase city council at a time when the Cold War prevents it from getting into national government.'

'Doubts have arisen about the perpetrators of the terrorist atrocity. So many false trails. I would really like to attribute the misconceptions to Gelli. I'm worried he's trying to mislead the investigation.'

'How far have you got with your enquiries?'

Gianluca stirs sugar into his espresso. 'Rhiannon's fellow student, Marie, isn't who she says she is. She's in cahoots with

Barzini. I believe if I can find out what the two of them are up to, I might be able to get more info on Gelli.'

My body tenses. 'Have you said anything to the authorities yet?'

'I've told Sergio. He's supporting the judicial investigations here in Bologna.'

The fact that Gianluca has mentioned his inquiry to the policeman son of Carla and Sebastiano, has me closing my eyes in relief. Sergio has been a good friend to Gianluca since they were students at the university. I know he'll do all he can to cover Gianluca's back.

Even so, nothing is guaranteed...

I draw my brows together. 'Be careful, Gianluca.'

'I will.'

'I don't want you involving Rhiannon in anything dangerous, either.'

'What?! No way. I've pleaded with her not to get too close to Marie. She's Lebanese, incidentally. Not French.'

I give a little gasp. 'Please don't end up like those two Italian journalists who went missing in Beirut.'

Gianluca shakes his head vigorously. 'No chance of that.'

'Hmm. I hope not.' Time to change the subject, I think. Gianluca has blocked all my attempts to put him off. 'Would you like to come round for supper this evening?' I ask.

'Why don't I take you and Rhiannon out for dinner, instead? We could go to Cesarina's...'

'Oh, yes, good idea. I haven't been there in ages.' I reach across the table and pat Gianluca's hand. 'It will give me something to look forward to after I've finished recording my memoirs.'

'So, you're almost at the end?' Gianluca lifts a brow.

'I am.'

* * *

After Gianluca leaves, I make a salad for lunch, feed Romeo, and return to my study. I left the tape recorder on my desk earlier, so all I need to do is pick up where I left off.

Mafalda, Tigre, and Diego prised me from Paolo's battered body and walked me to Mafalda's sister's house in Lavoro Street. She took us all in and mothered me, holding me against her ample bosom while I wept hot tears of grief. For days after the Bolognina battle, as the action against us came to be called, I alternated between living in state of numb disbelief and one of abject misery.

When I managed to fall asleep, my nightmares woke me up again. Before dropping off, I tried to think about the happy times with Paolo before the war, the fun we had at the seaside in Milano Marittima, the sweet smile that lit up his eyes whenever he saw me, even his endearing asthmatic cough.

I held on to the memory of his handsome face as sleep claimed me. But strange visions of him dead yet still alive – stumbling through the rubble, his beautiful body twisted, his arms distorted, his legs broken – plagued my dreams. Then, Paolo would transform into Barzini, rising from the flames of the burning building like a malevolent phoenix, and I'd wake up screaming.

Time passed, but I was still a shell of my former self. I felt so empty without my gangly, earnest boy who'd grown into a man in the harrowing times we'd gone through. One night, I snuck back to my family's palazzo in Marsala Street. Stella greeted me and we wept together after I'd told her about Paolo. 'I've come to get the photo of him that I used to keep by my bed,' I said. 'Then I'll have to leave or I'll put you in danger.'

In early December, Daniele and Sebastiano turned up with Bruno and Carla, who'd recovered from their injuries. The Anglo-American front had stalled fifteen kilometres away and their planes no longer bombed us so mercilessly. The Bolognese who'd fled to the hills last summer, now returned to the city in their droves, their numbers augmented by the inhabitants of the nearby villages. Within weeks, Bologna's population doubled from three hundred to six hundred thousand. Farmers arrived with their livestock, and the city began to resemble a massive Noah's ark. People took over the bombed-out buildings, constructed shelters in the ruins, in the basements of the palazzi, and even under the San Luca porticoes. Cows, chickens, pigs, goats, sheep, and other animals lodged with them, and the air was redolent with the odour of manure mixed with the fumes of myriad campfires and makeshift cooking stoves.

My heart wasn't in fighting any more, so I spent my time helping in the soup kitchens. Dani went back to practising medicine, Carla and Sebastiano focused on courier duties, Bruno and Tigre rejoined the partigiani.

A new command had been set up, grouping all the partisan forces of the Bolognese territory into a single battalion, called the 'Bologna Division of the Volunteer Corps of Freedom'. They established their headquarters in Piazza Aldrovandi, and decided that, if the allied offensive were not successful, they would go out into the countryside and carry out guerrilla actions on the enemy there.

Reprisals continued against us, perpetrated by the fascists as they intensified their hunt for partisans. Stool pigeons would stroll through the city centre, accompanied by fascisti in civilian clothing. They would go into bars and meeting places and point out members of the Resistance with a simple nod. How it pained me that the informers often informed on their ex-comrades in return for monetary rewards.

The partisans, while maintaining anonymity and their secret bases, concentrated on combatting the evil represented by infiltrators. Urban guerrilla warfare continued as the gappisti hunted down fascist spies. It was a hard winter filled with hatred.

On a wet, chilly February evening, Daniele returned from his rounds, his face ashen. 'Take a seat, Leila. There's something I need to tell you,' he said.

I did as he'd asked, my chest squeezing with dread. 'Has... has something happened to Mamma and Papà?'

'No. Not them.'

And I knew, I just knew Dani was about to tell me something awful about my best friend. I could read it in his eyes.

He lowered himself to the chair opposite.

'Remember Rebecca was taken with her parents to a place called Auschwitz in Poland?'

I nodded.

'I don't know how to say this without breaking down, little sister, but I'll try.' He took in a deep breath and let it out slowly. 'The camp was liberated by the Russians last month. They were appalled at what they found. There were gas chambers and crematoria. Most of the prisoners had been murdered.' Daniel's voice sounded strangled. 'I'm afraid for her. So terribly afraid...' Tears of anguish ran down his cheeks.

I leapt up from my chair, crossed the space between us, and wrapped my arms around him. 'Did any of the inmates survive?'

'I believe a few did.'

'Rebecca is a survivor.' I tried to inject a note of optimism into my voice.

'I'm praying that is the case.'

But I could see in Dani's forlorn expression that he didn't hold out much hope.

'What can we do?' I asked with a sudden sob.

'Nothing yet. But as soon as the Germans are defeated, I'll go to Poland. I believe the survivors are being looked after in transit camps.'

'We can only pray the war will end quickly,' I wept.

Before long, a series of events made me believe that the winds of change were finally blowing. On 3 March, the women of Bologna took to the streets, about a thousand of them, to demonstrate against the lack of salt in their rations. A week later, another group managed to infiltrate the local government headquarters in protest at the scarcity of food. A silent demonstration took place on 26 March when several women started walking behind a vehicle taking the bodies of two martyred partisans to the cemetery, even though funeral processions broke the law. Those brave women threw red flowers on the coffins and waved small green, white, and red flags, Tigre told me after he'd followed at a safe distance.

That same night, we heard that the Germans were bracing themselves along the Genghis Khan defensive line to the south-east of Bologna to counter the now imminent Allied offensive. It didn't stop the fascists from continuing to hunt down the gappisti, though. It seemed that the Nazis had left them to their own devices, and it was apparent their only role was one of capturing partisans, torturing and then executing them. Their cruelty knew no bounds.

On the morning of 16 April, groups of women gathered in Piazza Umberto Primo (now known as Piazza dei Martiri). Carla and I joined them, how could we not? We waved placards with the words, 'Enough with the War!', 'Surrender, repubblichini!', 'Germans, get out of Italy!' and 'Give us back our men!'

Then we marched to the Garibaldi statue in Piazza Otto Agosto, a symbol of freedom dating from the Italian uprising against the Austrian occupation in 1848. As we passed, women came out of the side streets and from the front doors of their homes to swell our numbers. Just as we were crossing Via dell'Indipendenza, we came across a column of Wehrmacht lorries. We kept on marching, and I heaved a sigh of relief as the Nazis let us pass without incident.

When we reached the piazza, a German car approached with two officers in the back. My heart nearly beat out of my chest, but the automobile simply slowed down and the Nazis took photographs of us waving our banners and tricolour flags.

We made speeches exhorting the fascists to join the liberation movement for the sake of peace. They didn't, of course, but carried on with their reprisals until they could see the game was up. Finally, on 18 April, the higher-ranking repubblichini and Black Brigade militia began to leave Bologna. Not for the first time, I wondered what had happened to Barzini. I'd heard nothing of him since the Bolognina battle and hoped he'd died of his injuries.

The Germans, in the meantime, were demobilising. On 20 April, we watched them march shamefaced out of the city. At dawn the next day, the first Allied units started to arrive. They didn't need to fire a shot – the Resistance had already taken possession of the police stations, the town council, prisons, barracks, and had seized control of the main arteries of Bologna.

'Come,' Carla said, grabbing my hand when we heard the news. 'We must go out and celebrate.'

I didn't feel much like celebrating, but I also didn't want to let the occasion pass without at least trying to honour my beloved Paolo. I took the photo of him I kept by my bed; he would be with me in spirit.

And it seemed I wasn't the only one. Carla and I joined a throng of women heading in the direction of Piazza del Nettuno. My gaze widened. The women were laying flowers and posting photographs on the external wall of Palazzo d'Accursio, the town hall. The pictures were of their loved ones who'd been killed by the nazifascisti. I added my precious photo of Paolo; he deserved to be honoured in the place where so many of his fellow-partisans had been executed by repubblichini firing squads.

I bumped into Signora Monari, Paolo's mamma, whom I hadn't seen since before Operation Radium. We held on to each other, weeping, and I told her how heroic her son had been in his final hours.

With a heavy heart, I went with Carla to the main square, which had filled with citizens, partisans, allied soldiers, and armoured vehicles on which had climbed girls bearing flowers and waving tricolour flags. The jubilation around me barely registered, I was missing Paolo so much.

The days that followed were characterised by bloody reprisals, carried out by the partisans against those *fascisti* who hadn't fled north. The *partigiani* caught and executed many *repubblichini*, actions which were tolerated by the Allies until 8 May, when the war in Europe officially ended. On 10 May the *gappisti* handed over most of their weapons to the American military government. Nevertheless, skirmishes between the partisans and fascists continued, on and off, for weeks.

Mamma and Papà came home from Asiago soon afterwards but didn't stay long. Bologna had been reduced to heaps of rubble and they'd made a new life in the Veneto, where they still live now, both in their late nineties.

In August, Dani set off across Europe to try and find Rebecca. I got letters from him as he went from transit camp to transit camp, searching for her.

In the meantime, Paolo's family were able to retrieve his body from the communal grave beyond the city walls – where hundreds of patriots had been buried – and lay him to rest in the Certosa cemetery. I visit him there regularly.

Then, not long before Christmas, I was in the kitchen with Stella learning how to make tortellini when the door to the apartment crashed open and in strode Daniele, hand in hand with Rebecca. It was the most joyful occasion, but it was also bitter-sweet. On arrival in Auschwitz, she'd been separated from her parents and kept in inhumane conditions while forced to work in a factory. When Soviet troops approached the camp in January 1945, the SS had made her walk with other survivors in what came to be known as a death march. She'd had to struggle more than fifty-five kilometres with snow up to her knees to Gliwice, joined by prisoners from subcamps in East Upper Silesia. Those who couldn't walk were shot. There they were herded *onto cattle trucks and taken to Bergen-Belsen, which was subsequently liberated by British forces and turned into a displaced persons camp. Rebecca was so ill and weak that she was unable to return home straight away. It was only thanks to Dani arriving to take care of her and help her travel that she was able to make it.*

Dani and Rebecca were married in 1946. After Rebecca graduated from Unibo, they decided to move to Vicenza, where Daniele practises medicine and Rebecca has raised three children. Her parents' beautiful palazzo in Zamboni Street was restored to her after the war. Gianluca lives in the apartment on the top floor now, and the lower floors are rented to the university.

What happened to the fascists who perpetrated such vile acts between the autumn of 1943 and the spring of 1945 in Bologna? The highest ranking fascisti, Barzini included – I found out later – went into hiding. Bitter disappointment shrunk my heart when I learnt, in June 1946, soon after the birth of the Italian Republic, that an amnesty had been granted to them. They either reintegrated themselves into society, many without giving up their ideals, or emigrated en masse to countries like Argentina.

The period after the war has seen many ups and downs in my country. It was a time of social and political tension, but also a time of renewal. Cities and citizens had to be completely rebuilt, physically and socially. The indomitable spirit of the Italian people, which almost foundered in the darkest period of our history, has been reborn. But our new democracy is fragile, and we must do everything we can to protect it.

I switch off my recorder with a sigh. Something is missing, it occurs to me. My story is incomplete. I can't stop thinking about what Gianluca told me regarding Barzini. I knew he was back in Bologna, having given Argentina a try and apparently deciding it wasn't for him. His right-wing newspaper is sold openly in the newsstands, and I guess it was Gelli who financed him.

What is Barzini up to with the Lebanese girl?

I frown. Over the years, I've maintained contact not just with Bruno, but also with Tigre, Carla, Sebastiano, and other ex-partisans. They keep an eye on the *fascisti*, I know for a fact. I must tell them what Gianluca has revealed. He's an intellectual, not a fighter like them. He might try to take a bigger step than the length of his leg would allow.

I go through to the living room and look up Bruno's number. I'll organise a meeting with him and the others, I decide.

23

LEILA

'You should keep well away from the Lebanese girl.' I repeat my warning to Rhiannon as we're sipping our after-dinner coffees in the restaurant, after Gianluca has told her about my connection to Barzini. 'She's almost certainly involved in something suspicious. And Barzini is a cruel man who wouldn't think twice about hurting you.'

'Don't worry.' A reassuring smile brushes Rhiannon's lips. 'I won't go anywhere near him.'

'Good. I'd never forgive myself if anything happened to you.'

'And neither would I,' Gianluca adds.

I gaze at the two of them. They've barely taken their eyes off each other throughout dinner. It warms my heart that Gianluca has developed feelings for Rhiannon, but I can't help the quiver of unease in my stomach. I just hope my nephew can contain his desire and not rush her or she'll bolt like a frightened filly at the first fence.

Gianluca goes to settle the bill, he insists, and Rhiannon and I slip on our coats. 'That was a lovely meal,' she says. 'The pumpkin ravioli was delicious.'

'It was,' I agree.

Outside, the air has turned heavy and a rumble of thunder echoes. Raindrops splatter the cobbles in Santo Stefano Street, but the arcades keep us dry. We walk, arms linked, my nephew between Rhiannon and me, and soon we arrive at the top of Zamboni Street.

I wonder if Gianluca would like to spend time with Rhiannon, the two of them on their own, but he pecks us both on the cheeks. 'See you tomorrow,' he says. 'I'll meet you after school and we can go for a drink, if you like, Rhiannon.'

She blushes delightfully. 'I'd like that a lot.'

We go our separate ways and, back in my apartment, I make Rhiannon and myself a cup of herbal tea. Now I've got her on her own, I decide I need to find out more about the Lebanese girl. 'Where does Marie live?' I enquire once Rhiannon and I have sat ourselves down in the living room.

'Student digs in the Bolognina district.' Rhiannon takes a sip of her drink. 'But I think she's in a relationship with Barzini.'

'Isn't she a little young for him?'

'That's what I thought.' Rhiannon makes a face. 'She also hangs around with three Palestinian guys. I met them once in the student canteen.'

I swallow the sudden lump of dread in my throat. 'Please, keep your distance from them, dear.'

'I will,' Rhiannon promises. 'But what do you think could be going on?'

'I have no idea.' I don't give voice to my thoughts. There were rumours that Palestinian terrorists could have been involved in the bombing of the railway station last summer. Except, the PLO doesn't support the neo-fascists, from what I've read. Apparently they supply arms to the far left.

Rhiannon yawns. 'I'll go to bed now if that's all right.'

'Of course. Off you go. Sleep well.'

'*Grazie, Sogni d'oro.*' Sweet dreams.

Next morning, after Rhiannon has left for school, I let Romeo out onto the balcony, then stand and breathe in the rain-scented air. Before me, an undulating wave of terracotta rooftops sweeps towards the two towers, russet-damp tiles glowing beneath a sheen of steam. The sun has broken through the clouds, I notice, and it will be a beautiful day.

Shortly before twelve, I lock up and make my way to Piazza Aldrovandi. Bruno returned my call yesterday afternoon within the hour to say he'd set up a meeting with our ex-comrades. Looking forward to seeing them, I step under the tall red-brick columns of the Torresotto archway. A peal of church bells rings across the city. I smile to myself at the cacophony of sound, which I always think of as a joyful celebration of everyday life.

'Ciao, Vittoria, you're a little early,' Bruno says as I approach his stall. 'Why don't you go straight to the pizzeria opposite. I'll be there with the others shortly.'

I do as he proposes, order myself a coffee then take a seat at a square table at the back of the small room. I'm looking forward to seeing Carla; I've been neglectful of her since Rhiannon arrived. My old comrade's real name is Rita, but I've never called her that. She, in turn, always refers to me as Vittoria. Sebastiano was baptised Arturo, except he still prefers to be known as Sebastiano. Tigre, on the other hand, has gone back to his baptismal name of Roberto.

I close my eyes and think about Rebecca, how ill she was when Daniele brought her home from Germany. She suffered from stomach complaints and psychological distress but was determined to finish her studies. Recurring illness prevented her from going out to work, so she stayed at home after she and Dani were married. It was the terrible memories of her parents' deaths, triggered by living in the Zamboni palazzo, that made Daniele suggest she and he move to Vicenza. The Matatias were killed in the gas chambers of Auschwitz almost as soon as they'd been separated from their daughter. Such unimaginable horror, and Rebecca will never get over it. She's a wonderful mother and grandmother, though, and I love her as much as I did when we were younger. I try to get on a train to Vicenza as often as possible but, having committed myself to looking after Rhiannon, I'll have to wait until the summer before I can make my next visit.

Familiar voices echo from the entrance to the pizzeria and there, in front of me, are my dear friends. I jump to my feet, and we hug and kiss each other before pulling out chairs.

A waitress takes our orders and Carla talks proudly about her boys while we wait for our food to arrive. Her youngest, Angelo, is employed in the public works department – in fact it was he who showed Gianluca and Rhiannon the underground Aposa. And Sergio, the *carabiniere* son, is doing brilliantly. The years have been kind to Sebastiano and Carla. After they graduated from the university, they set up their own successful real estate business; they're semi-retired these days.

Our pizzas arrive and, while we eat, Bruno tells everyone what I've found out about Gianluca's investigation into Barzini's connection to Licio Gelli, and about the Lebanese girl.

'Rhiannon said that Marie is friendly with some Palestinians who live in student accommodation in Bolognina,' I add the latest information I received last night.

'Do you know if Sergio is aware of Gianluca's investigation?' Sebastiano asks. 'If not, I'll have a word with him.'

'Gianluca assured me your boy knows all about it,' I say. 'Maybe you can find out from him if he has put a tail on the girl?'

'Will do.' Sebastiano nods.

'It's time we went after Barzini ourselves.' Carla's voice is firm. 'I'll never forget what that vile bastard did to me.'

I reach across the table and touch my hand to her arm. For privacy reasons, I left out of my tape recording the conversation she and I had the day of our wedding ceremony. She was ashamed of what had happened with Barzini, worried about how her first night with her new husband would turn out so soon after being raped. I'd reassured her as best I could at the time, and she'd resolved to live life in the moment and make Sebastiano happy. I'd done the same with Paolo, I remember, and my vision blurs with sadness. *Oh, how I wish he were here with me today.*

'Are you suggesting we tail the girl ourselves?' Roberto interrupts my nostalgic thoughts.

I smile at the man who used to be known as Tigre; he's lost none of his old enthusiasm for tackling the tasks at hand. Married with four children, he lives beyond the old city walls in Borgo Panigale not far from the Ducati factory where he works as a foreman. 'Perhaps we should set up a rota and follow her at a discreet distance,' I suggest.

'Maybe I should speak with Sergio first,' Carla cuts in.

Sebastiano puts down his knife and fork. 'My son might have his hands tied by budget constraints. He won't be able to do much unless he has concrete evidence, I think.'

Bruno turns to me. 'Why don't you ask your lodger to find out where the Lebanese girl lives in Bolognina? That wouldn't be dangerous, would it?'

I flinch away from him. 'I want to keep Rhiannon out of this. She's an innocent and I've already warned Gianluca not to involve her in his investigation.'

'I don't think you have much choice, Vittoria.' Carla looks me in the eye. 'What if Barzini is planning something heinous and using the Lebanese girl to achieve his goal? Your exchange student might be the only way to discover what's really going on.'

My breath catches. Barzini is evil and Carla knows that better than anyone. He's also an ideologist. I bought a copy of his tabloid newspaper once, out of curiosity. Then I wished I hadn't. Practically every column propagated the fascist doctrine that liberal democracy is obsolete, rejected assertions that violence is automatically negative in nature, and reiterated a belief in Italian racial purity. *Absolutely disgusting.*

If Barzini is up to something, he needs to be stopped. But how can I take advantage of Rhiannon? I shouldn't even consider it. 'There has to be another solution,' I say to my comrades.

'What other solution could there be?' Bruno leans towards me. 'Unless you find a way of meeting the girl yourself...'

'I suppose I could ask Rhiannon to invite her for supper one evening. A friendly invitation to a foreign student wouldn't be seen as anything suspicious.'

'Sounds like a good plan.' Sebastiano's face crinkles in a smile. 'In the meantime I'll find out what Sergio knows.'

'Perfect!' Bruno gives a thumbs up and everyone joins in.

A strange feeling takes hold of me. It's as if time has slipped backwards and I've returned to 1944 planning a partisan action. I give a little shiver of anticipation. Barzini will get his comeuppance if it's the last thing I do.

24

RHIANNON

Rhiannon spots Gianluca waiting in the piazza as she bustles through the door with a group of students. She goes up to him. 'Ciao. I'm happy to see you.'

'I'm happy to see you too.' He bends and kisses her on the lips. 'Where would you like to go?'

'Somewhere quiet would be nice...'

He rubs his chin. 'How about my place?'

'Okay...' She finds herself assuming her habitual rabbit caught in the headlights expression and wishes she sounded more confident.

'I won't do anything you don't want me to do, Rhiannon.'

'I know you won't. It's me I'm worried about, not you.'

'You're so funny.' He laughs. 'Funny and adorable.'

She laughs with him to dispel her disquiet. What on earth made her say that? She can be such an idiot.

He takes her hand, and they stroll towards the two towers. 'How was school?' he asks.

'We had a lecture on the Byzantine art in Ravenna. It was amazing. But I'm glad it's Friday and the weekend has started...'

'How about I take you and my aunt to Ravenna tomorrow or on Sunday? It's not far from Bologna and worth a visit.'

'Wow! That would be wonderful,' Rhiannon says. 'Leila loved our trip to Ferrara last Sunday.'

'We can ask her later.' He pauses. 'Did you go for lunch with Marie as usual?'

'She skipped class again today.' Rhiannon frowns. 'At this rate she won't qualify for a certificate of attendance.'

'I doubt that's of much concern to her.'

'Do you think her being a student is an act? That it's a cover for whatever she's involved in with Barzini?'

'I've been asking myself the same question. Until I can pin her down and get some answers, all I have is guesswork.'

Rhiannon opens and closes her mouth as she struggles to find the right words. She wants to help but she knows Gianluca will voice his opposition to any attempt she might make to get closer to Marie. Rhiannon keeps quiet for the rest of the walk and soon they arrive at the palazzo in Zamboni Street.

'This is such a beautiful place,' she says after Gianluca has taken her coat and offered to pour them both a glass of San Giovese.

'I'm very lucky.' He pours the wine into two chalices. 'It's been in my mother's family for generations.'

'Oh, I didn't realise the palazzo belonged to you. Shame your mum no longer lives here...'

'Let's sit on the sofa and I'll tell you a very sad story.' He lowers himself next to her, hands her a glass of wine, then recounts what happened to Rebecca and her parents during the war.

His words bring tears to Rhiannon's eyes and her chest fills with sadness. 'I'm so sorry. I had no idea. It seems such a platitude to come out with that statement. But I'm truly, sincerely, heartbroken for your mother.'

Gianluca wraps his arms around her and holds her close. 'You're so sweet. I'd like you to meet my parents, but don't want you to think I'm rushing you.'

Rhiannon leans back and gazes at him. 'Let's take things slowly, Gianluca. I'm only just getting comfortable with you.'

'Only comfortable?' He winks.

'It's a big step for me. I've never felt this comfortable with a man before.'

'Not even your ex?'

'Nope. He called me the ice maiden.'

Gianluca kisses the top of her head. 'You're gorgeous, *bambina*. There's nothing icy about you. You're kind and warm and totally enticing. I must exercise my self-control every second I'm with you.'

She giggles. 'You have excellent self-control, Gianluca.'

'Can I kiss you properly? I promise to be a gentleman.'

She nods, not trusting herself to speak. If she did, she might beg him not to be a gentleman and that would be stupid because she'd find herself pushing him away and, God forbid, he'd call her a prick tease like Owen used to do and she wouldn't be able to bear that.

'Are you sure?' he asks, holding her in his gaze. 'Only you look a little... taken aback.'

'No – I mean, yes. Please...'

He takes her wine glass, places it on the table, and...

When Gianluca kisses her, she starts to melt. The ice in her veins doesn't just dissolve, it heats up until she's burning for him. He kisses her so thoroughly, every nerve in her body tingles and desire courses through her. They fall back on the sofa, and he lifts her jumper and kisses his way up her stomach to the top of her breasts. It feels incredible. She wants him more than she's ever wanted anyone in her life.

Except, without warning, he stops what he's doing and shifts away from her. 'I'd better get you back to my aunt's, or she'll worry.'

Rhiannon sits up, straightens her jumper. 'We could always phone her and let her know I'm safe.'

'Let's take things slowly like you asked me to do, Rhiannon,' he says. 'Besides, Auntie has probably made supper for us. We should get going.'

Back at Leila's, Rhiannon listens to Gianluca and his aunt discuss the proposed trip to Ravenna while they enjoy the traditional lasagne *al ragù* she has made for them. They decide they will go on Sunday, and Rhiannon tells them she can't wait to see the famous mosaics in the buildings created at the time when the ancient world was on the brink of transforming into the Middle Ages.

'It's an incredible place.' A smile crinkles the corners of Gianluca's eyes. 'You'll love it.'

Leila glances at him, then at Rhiannon. 'Are you two sure you want me to tag along?'

'Of course,' Rhiannon says, and Gianluca echoes her.

'*Grazie.*' Leila reaches across the table to take their plates.

After all three of them make short work of the washing up, they go through to the sitting room with their coffees.

Leila glances at them. 'There's something I must discuss with you both...'

'Oh?' Gianluca quirks a brow.

'I met with my ex-partisan comrades at lunchtime and told

them about Barzini, the Lebanese girl and her Palestinian friends.'

'Why did you do that?' Gianluca's tone is sharp.

'Several reasons. One, I was worried you'd taken a step longer than the length of your leg allows as far as Barzini is concerned. Two, because of what happened at the railway station we need to take preventative measures. And, three, Carla has unfinished business with that bastard.'

'Auntie,' Gianluca groans. 'This isn't your fight.'

'You're wrong, my dear. You've listened to my tapes...'

'You haven't given me the last part yet.'

'Take the final cassettes home with you tonight and you'll know why I can't let this matter rest.'

'I'd like to listen to your story too,' Rhiannon interrupts. 'I mean to say Marie is my classmate, and I'd really like to help Gianluca with his investigation.' She glances at him. 'But he doesn't want me to be involved.'

'Neither do I, dear girl. It's far too dangerous.' Leila clasps her hands together in her lap. 'There is one thing you can do, however. We need to know where Marie lives. So I was thinking you could invite her to have supper here one evening, and during polite conversation, I'll ask her.'

'Better still, I could ask her myself,' Rhiannon offers.

'She'll want to know why you're so curious, the two of you.' Gianluca leans forward in his chair. 'Did you tell Carla that Sergio knows about this, Aunt Leila?'

'Yes. She and Sebastiano will find out if he can put a tail on Marie. If he can do so, then we can leave the matter to the *carabinieri*.'

'I've already asked him,' Gianluca says. 'But his hands are tied. Not enough evidence, apparently.'

'I thought as much,' Leila huffs. 'We'll just have to get that evidence for them...'

'Oh, God, Auntie. You're impossible,' Gianluca snaps. 'What if anything happens to you?'

'You forget I was a partisan.' She gives him a determined look. 'I know how to take care of myself.'

'But, Auntie, it was not so long ago that you were passing out on the floor. You're not as young and as fighting fit as you used to be.'

'Maybe not,' Leila says, holding her chin up. 'But the fight in me will never die.'

He shakes his head, plainly at a loss for words.

And Rhiannon doesn't know what to say either. The argument is between Gianluca and his aunt. But Rhiannon is involved as well because it's through her that he has met Marie, she thinks.

Leila takes Gianluca through to his study to give him the cassettes, and Rhiannon carries their empty coffee cups to the kitchen. She washes and dries them, then puts them away, her mind in a whirl. Something has happened to her here in Bologna. She's not the same girl who arrived in the red city a month ago. She can't stand by and do nothing. She must take her courage in both hands despite the risks. Gianluca and Leila need her help and she'll do all that she can to support them.

25

RHIANNON

After breakfast the next day, Leila suggests a stroll to Piazza del Nettuno. 'I want to show you Paolo's photo,' she says. 'Then we can go for a coffee in the main square.'

'That would be lovely, *grazie*.' Rhiannon eyes the raindrops splattering the kitchen window. 'Shame about the weather.'

'It's only a passing shower, but we'd better take an umbrella just in case. The square is open to the elements.'

Leila's prediction turns out to be correct. By the time Rhiannon has stepped outside with her, the sun has broken through the clouds and she lifts her face to feel its warmth.

They walk arm in arm down Oberdan Street, turn into Rizzoli and, before too long, arrive at the piazza with Neptune's fountain. Water gushes noisily from the urns held by the four marble cherubs who perch at the top of each corner of the sea god's pedestal. Rhiannon stares at the sprays squirting from the sculpted breasts of the four kneeling river nymphs, bent back upon their fleshy tail fins. It strikes her that the women have a seductive yet vulnerable air about them. She peers at Neptune – his muscular buttocks, well defined and taut, appear to hold centuries of unspent energy.

Leila tugs her away from the statue's cheeky charm. 'Come, Rhiannon. I want to show you my Paolo.' There's pride in Leila's tone, tinged with sadness.

'He's so young,' Rhiannon exclaims as she takes in the shiny black and white ceramic image of Leila's beloved, his prominent Adam's apple, long thin face, and dark brown hair.

'This was taken before the German occupation when I was about to turn nineteen and Paolo twenty-one. We grew up a lot in the following year. Especially Paolo...'

Rhiannon's heart aches for her. 'I'd really like to listen to your story, Leila.'

'Gianluca said he would stop by with the cassettes later this afternoon. Your Italian has improved so much I'm sure you'll have no difficulty understanding.'

'I hope so.'

Leila kisses the tips of her fingers, touches them to Paolo's photo. 'Let's go for that coffee,' she suggests, linking her arm with Rhiannon's again.

On the way to the café at the corner of the square, Rhiannon stops at a kiosk to buy some postcards. 'For Mum, my sister Lowri and best friend Nia,' she explains.

'And your father?'

'I'm not in touch with him.'

'No possibility of a reconciliation?' Leila squeezes her arm.

'He's made a new life for himself and that doesn't include my sister and me.'

'I'm sorry,' Leila says.

'Thanks, so am I, but there's nothing I can do about it I'm afraid. He didn't even respond to the Christmas card Lowri and I sent him last year...'

Leila leads Rhiannon to an outside table, and they pull out chairs. A waiter takes their order of cappuccinos, and Leila shades her eyes from the sun. 'This square used to be called Piazza Vittorio Emanuele II until 1943. The equestrian monument of the king, who took part in the unification of Italy, was transferred to the Margherita gardens. That's when the name changed to Piazza della Repubblica. In June 1945 it became known as Piazza Maggiore, or Piâza Mażaur in Bolognese.'

'How interesting! I'm fascinated by your dialect, by the way, ' Rhiannon says. 'I might write my dissertation on it back in Cardiff.'

'I will miss you when you go home,' Leila says.

'Likewise. It's not for a few months, but I'm already wishing there was some way I could stay.'

'You can always come back, you know.'

'I know, except I'll need to finish my studies in Cardiff first.'

Leila reaches across the table and pats her hand. 'Flights between Italy and the UK are getting cheaper, from what I've heard. You could visit quite often and you'll always have a room at my place.'

'That's so kind of you, Leila.' Warmth spreads through Rhiannon. 'I'd love you to visit me in Wales one day.'

'Just me?' Leila tilts her head.

'Gianluca too, if he'd like that.'

'Ah, I'm sure he would,' Leila chuckles.

Rhiannon's cheeks burn. Time to change the subject, she thinks, as their cappuccinos arrive.

'Gianluca is not that keen on us getting involved in the Barzini investigation, is he?'

'Us? What do you mean?'

Rhiannon leans forward. 'You and me. I want to help. Inviting

Marie to supper might not be a good idea, though. You don't want Barzini to discover where you live.'

'Oh, he knows.' Leila takes a sip of her coffee. 'You'll find out when you listen to my story. Gianluca's father took part in an action known as 'Operation Radium' and Barzini came with an SS officer to search our cellar.'

'How terrifying!'

'I called Barzini my nemesis. I thought I'd killed him in 1944, but it looks like he's returned to haunt me.'

'You're incredibly brave. But maybe Gianluca is right? You need to be careful of your health...'

'I'm perfectly fine now I'm on the right medication. I haven't felt light-headed in weeks.'

Rhiannon scoops froth from the top of her cappuccino and licks her spoon. 'Even so, you should take care.' She fixes Leila with what she hopes is a sincere look. 'I've said it before and I'll say it again. I want to help.'

'*Grazie*, dear. I expect you'll change your mind about helping after you've listened to my recordings and discover the truth about Barzini, however.'

Gianluca drops off the cassettes in the early afternoon on his way to a meeting with Sergio, his *carabiniere* friend. After Gianluca has spoken at length with Leila, in the privacy of her study, he says he'll probably stay and have dinner with Sergio and his wife, if that's okay with Rhiannon. She's touched he feels the need to run it by her first, even though they aren't exactly a 'couple', and responds that she doesn't mind at all. In fact, it will give her time to get her homework done, have a quiet supper with Leila, then focus on the tape recordings. Later, after she has eaten and helped Leila clear up, Rhiannon leaves Leila absorbed in reading Umberto Eco's *Name of the Rose*, then goes to her room.

She slots a cassette into her Walkman, a present from Mum before she left for Italy, plugs in the earphones and stretches out on her bed, her tummy tingling in anticipation.

25 September 1943

Keeping my head down so as not to draw attention to myself, I made my way past the German tank stationed next to the Basilica of San Petronio. I was in a hurry to get home after spending the morning at the library and didn't want to waste time having my identity documents checked. I stopped. Listened. A distant rumble followed by the ominous drone of aircraft engines echoed in my ears. The terrifying noise grew louder, and I imagined a swarm of giant angry hornets hellbent on destruction. Dread squeezing my chest, I risked a quick glance upwards. Heavy cloud cover billowed over Bologna; there was no sign of any planes.

Rhiannon listens late into the night. She's fully immersed in Leila's story from the first words, transported to wartime Bologna and a period in the history of Italy of which she only has a sketchy knowledge. The more she hears, the more she admires Leila for her courage and determination. Tears spill from her eyes as she learns about Rebecca and her parents' arrest. When Barzini makes his odious appearance in the account – described as the man with the pockmarked face at first – Rhiannon's skin prickles with dislike. Hearing about Paolo and Leila's relationship fills her with sadness. She's riveted by the account of Operation Radium. Leila's encounter with Barzini searching for the stolen chemical element has her gasping, and the reprisals make her tremble. When she discovers what happened at the Baglioni, her admiration for Leila intensifies. The university battle, the execu-

tion of Leila's comrades, hers and Carla's subsequent imprisonment and torture, not to mention Carla's rape, bring so many
tears to Rhiannon's eyes, she needs to go to the basin and wash
her face.

She carries on listening well into the early hours. Leila, Paolo,
Carla, and Sebastiano's 'partisan weddings' warms Rhiannon's
heart. But she also experiences a deep sadness, knowing that
Paolo lost his life. Leila's description of the Porta Lame battle is so
exciting, Rhiannon's spirits lift. However, when Leila moves on to
the siege in Piazza dell'Unità Rhiannon hugs her knees to her
chest and weeps hot tears of grief for Leila's husband who lost his
life in his prime. She wishes it were Paolo not Barzini who'd
survived, oh how she wishes it, and she feels a rush of sympathy
for poor Leila. No wonder she wants 'Pockface' to be brought to
justice...

When she's listened to the final instalment, Rhiannon
switches off her Walkman and sighs heavily. She should sleep or
she'll be in no fit state for the trip to Ravenna tomorrow.

She goes to the washbasin, cleans her teeth then puts on her
pyjamas. Once back in bed, she tosses and turns. Leila's story has
brought home to her so clearly the tragedy of war. She can't
imagine the fear and devastation felt by northern Italians when
their region was occupied by the Germans. Young people fired by
patriotic feelings, paid the ultimate sacrifice. What would she
have done in the same circumstances? Would she have taken up
arms like Leila? She doesn't know, can't know as she hasn't experienced what Leila and her comrades experienced.

All she does know is that she needs to get involved with Gianluca in finding out what Barzini is planning. From what she's
learnt of the man with the pockmarked face, Rhiannon is certain
he's up to something evil. A leopard doesn't change its spots.
Barzini has a hidden agenda, and he's obviously using Marie for

his vile purposes. Rhiannon blows out a long, slow breath. *Oh, how she wants to help.*

The minutes tick by and eventually she falls asleep. Her dreams are disturbed by images of Bologna being bombed to bits, of Wehrmacht soldiers goosestepping through the city, of black-shirted fascists hunting down the partisans. Leila floats above the piazzas like an avenging angel and Rhiannon floats with her. Suddenly she falls to earth with a bump. Jolted out of her nightmare by the dream-fall, she turns over in bed and succumbs to sleep once more.

26

RHIANNON

Rhiannon's eyes widen at the sight of Marie as she comes into the classroom on Monday morning. The Lebanese girl has a purplish bruise down the left side of her face and she winces when she sits at her desk. 'Are you all right?' Rhiannon whispers.

'I fell down some steps,' Marie says. 'Looks worse than it feels. I'm fine.'

A memory of Mum's bruised face after her final fight with Dad springs to Rhiannon's mind, and it makes her heart ache. It was the only time he hit her, as far as she knows, but it was the straw that broke the camel's back, together with discovering he'd fathered a child, and it prompted Mum to kick him out once and for all. Mum had also made the excuse she'd tripped down the stairs, then confessed to Lowri and Rhiannon after Dad had left.

The arrival of Signora Mutti, their teacher, distracts Rhiannon from her thoughts. She focuses on the lesson and completes the grammar test quickly. With time to kill, she reflects on her visit to Ravenna yesterday with Gianluca and Leila.

They set off soon after breakfast and, during the drive, Rhiannon told them how moved she'd been by Leila's cassettes, and how she wanted to help them discover what Barzini could be up to.

'I've told you before. That man is very dangerous,' Gianluca muttered. 'Please, Rhiannon, don't go anywhere near him.'

'I won't,' she promised. 'I just want to get closer to Marie.'

Gianluca lapsed into silence, and Rhiannon hoped he wasn't annoyed. She wouldn't back down, though. She was their only link to the Lebanese girl and, through her, hopefully to Barzini and his almost certainly nefarious intentions.

After about an hour on the road, they arrived at the picturesque town on the Adriatic coast. 'Let's show Rhiannon everything,' Leila suggested, striding at a fast pace with Rhiannon and Gianluca in tow.

They kicked off with the Arian Baptistry, built between the end of the fifth and beginning of the sixth centuries. Rhiannon gazed, awestruck, at the domed ceiling, which was covered in beautiful shining golden mosaics depicting a procession of the twelve apostles with Jesus being baptised at the centre.

Next, they went to the Basilica di San Vitale, unquestionably the crown jewel of Ravenna, Leila said, one of the most important monuments of paleo Christian art in Italy and in the world, with a dizzying array of mosaics and murals on the walls and ceilings. Walking into the church felt like entering a legendary temple. Just enough light came through the windows to illuminate the scenes covering almost every available surface. Rhiannon stared, transfixed, at depictions of episodes from the Old and New Testaments, colourful animals, plants, and fruits alongside angels and other biblical figures and even the Emperor Justinian and his Empress, Theodora.

Gianluca then took them to visit the tomb of Dante Alighieri, known as the father of the Italian language, in a simple-looking domed building off the Basilica di San Francesco. Out front, they strolled through a small garden with a stone monument describing the supreme poet's life. Rhiannon had read *The Divine Comedy* in her first year at Cardiff, and she felt a little thrill at seeing his final resting place.

Afterwards, they went into the basilica itself. Rhiannon looked around in confusion, thinking there wasn't much to see. The simple white walls and stone floor were pretty enough, but a far cry from the dazzling mosaics she'd viewed that morning. 'Just wait,' Gianluca laughed, clearly sensing her disappointment. 'This building has a fun surprise.' He took her hand and led her to the back of the church. A crypt lay submerged in several feet of blue-green seawater. Rhiannon gave a start at the sight of the mosaic patterned floor underneath and several fish swimming around. 'Wow! That's magical,' she exclaimed, taking her insta-matic camera from her handbag, and framing a shot, one of many she'd taken that day. Relief spread over her that Gianluca's apparent annoyance at her defiance with respect to Marie seemed to have passed.

They had a quick *piadina* lunch before continuing with their sightseeing. She loved the blue and gold ceiling mosaic in the Neon baptistry, showing Jesus' baptism by John the Baptist in the Jordan river. The Basilica of Sant'Apollinare Nuovo was next on their itinerary. Rhiannon decided it had a vastly different atmosphere from Ravenna's other mosaic sites as it was flooded with natural light and painted in pastel colours, giving it an open, airy feel which she thought resembled a medieval great hall. Mosaics lined the upper walls of the church's apse, depicting dozens of near-identical figures draped in Roman robes. 'I've seen so many pictures of this, but the reality is amazing,' she said in awe.

They finished the visit by taking a stroll through the Rocca Brancaleone public gardens to view the mausoleum of Theodoric the Great, who'd ruled a vast area of Italy in the late fifth and early sixth centuries. There wasn't a lot to view inside the tomb, so they simply walked around the ancient monument before heading to the car park and then back to Bologna.

Gianluca dropped them off in Marsala Street. Leila went up to the apartment, but Rhiannon stayed back to have a quiet word with him. 'I'm sorry if I made you angry about Marie this morning,' she said.

He gave her a hug. 'I'm sorry for being such a shithead. I'd never forgive myself if anything happened to you, Rhiannon.'

'Nothing will happen to me. I'll make sure that I'm never alone with her and I won't go anywhere near Barzini.'

She lifted her face and Gianluca kissed her. He wrapped his arms around her, rocking her gently. 'Stay safe, *bambina*.'

She nodded. 'I will.'

He stroked her back, her shoulders, her head. '*Ti...*' he bit back whatever he was going to say next and kissed her again. 'I need to go to Florence tomorrow and will be away for a couple of days. That's where Licio Gelli hangs out and a contact of mine has an important lead on him.'

'I'll miss you,' she sighed.

And she would. She'd got used to seeing him every day.

The school bell rings, jolting her back to the present, and Signora Mutti asks everyone to hand in their work. Rhiannon walks to the front of the class and places her paper on the teacher's desk. She glances at Marie, standing next to her. 'Would you like to grab a bite to eat with me?' she suggests.

'*Grazie.* Yes.' Marie shuffles her feet and stares at the floor. 'The same place?'

'Piazza Santo Stefano. Of course.' Rhiannon shoulders her rucksack. 'Let's go.'

They sit at their usual café, pulling out chairs at a metal table under the portico after ordering panini and glasses of sparkling water from the bar. Marie rubs at her forehead and breathes a sigh. 'That lesson this morning was so boring. I thought it would never end. The test was so easy I felt patronised.'

'Don't you like studying grammar?'

'Been there. Done that. Bought the T-shirt,' Marie huffs.

'I know what you mean, but I'm intrigued by the patterns of language learning. I like seeing how it all works. And I find doing the tests afterwards so satisfying.' She gives Marie a sideways glance. 'How does studying Arabic compare to Italian?' Rhiannon remembers Marie telling her about her studies at the Sorbonne.

'Italian is much easier and smoother. But hand gestures are common to both. Except they can have different meanings.' Marie makes the finger purse motion, pressing her thumb against the other fingers and holding her hand upwards. 'Italians use it as an exclamation of annoyance, exasperation, or confusion. But they also add it to questions like, 'But what do you want?', 'What are you doing?', 'What are you saying?' She pauses. 'If you made that gesture to an Arab, you'd put the fear of God into him.'

'Oh? Why's that?'

'It usually signals a sinister threat that basically translates into 'just wait and see what'll happen to you'.' Marie giggles.

Rhiannon giggles with her, then decides to change the subject. 'Did you have a good weekend?' She eyes Marie's bruised face.

'It was okay...' Marie glances away. 'How about you?'

'I went to Ravenna with my landlady.' She doesn't mention Gianluca, given Marie's admitted dislike of journalists. 'Have you ever been there? It was amazing...'

'No, I haven't.' Marie shrugs.

Rhiannon fixes her with a steady gaze. Now or never, she thinks. 'Would you like to come for supper at my place one evening? I've told Leila Venturi, my landlady, about you and she said she'd love to meet you.' Rhiannon pauses, hoping she hasn't sounded too abrupt.

'What have you said?' Marie's tone is sharp.

'Only that you're my classmate. Leila is lovely. So kind and caring. You'll like her a lot.'

A fleeting expression akin to longing passes across Marie's bruised face. 'That would be great. How about tonight? Ugo is out of town and I haven't got anything on...'

Strike while the iron is hot, Rhiannon tells herself. She doesn't want to give Marie time to change her mind. 'Perfect,' she responds. 'I'll just go to that call box over there.' She points across the square. 'I'll check with Leila but I'm sure it will be fine.'

* * *

'So, how do you like Bologna?' Leila asks Marie as she fills her glass with red wine. They're eating in the dining room instead of the kitchen, and Leila has made tagliatelle *al ragù*. She agreed to the dinner as soon as Rhiannon phoned, and they came to the table straight after Marie arrived.

'Bologna is so small compared with Paris, but easier to get around.' She sips her wine.

'Have you always lived in Paris?' Rhiannon enquires.

Marie sips her wine again. 'I grew up in Beirut. But Ugo sent me to France for my education.'

'That's interesting,' Leila says. 'How did you meet him? I mean, he's a famous newspaper proprietor, slightly older than me and therefore so much older than you...'

Marie's face assumes a flustered expression. She glances from Leila to Rhiannon and back to Leila again. 'He found me on the streets of Beirut. My parents had died in the bombing. I was homeless and destitute. Of course, he took advantage of me, but he also made sure I got an education.' She knocks back the rest of her wine and holds out her glass for a refill.

'How old were you then?' Rhiannon asks, shocked.

'Thirteen. I'd never been to school, but he sent me to a convent and the nuns taught me well. So well, I was able to get into the Sorbonne.' She glugs down more wine.

So, that much was true.

'Eat up, dear,' Leila says. 'Or the wine will go to your head.'

'It's delicious.' Marie licks her lips. 'Ugo doesn't let me drink. He says I can't hold my wine.'

'Then maybe you should slow down?' Rhiannon can't help suggesting.

'I'm perfectly fine. Ugo is just a fusspot.' Marie's words slur, but she glugs down half her glass then gives a little burp.

Leila fills the glass again. Rhiannon shoots her a look. Leila gives her a surreptitious wink. Is she deliberately trying to get the girl drunk? That seems to be the case as the glass is filled time and again while they finish the tagliatelle and move on to cold meats and salad.

Without warning, Marie starts to sob. 'Ugo hits me. Practically every day. I want to get away from him, but I can't. He pays for everything...'

Rhiannon jumps up from her seat, puts her arm around the girl. 'Do you live with him?'

'Oh, no. He can't be seen to be living with the likes of me. He rents a basement apartment for me in Rizzoli Street.'

'You told me you lived in Bolognina,' Rhiannon blurts before she can stop herself.

'Did I?' Marie shrugs. 'I can't remember. Maybe I got confused. That's where Bakir, Feraz, and Roshid live.'

'Your Palestinian friends?'

'I'm Ugo's go-between. The poor boys. He's manipulating them.' Marie's voice has gone up a pitch and she's crying openly now. 'They're young and filled with ideals…'

'Whatever do you mean?' Leila creases her brow.

'Ugo is in touch with an arms dealer. He wants the boys to do something terrible,' Marie wails. 'I tried to tell him I wanted no part of it, but he wouldn't listen.' Marie touches her hand to the bruise on her cheek.

'What is it that he wants them to do?' Leila leans in towards the girl.

'I don't know. I only take them messages written in code.' Her face turns pale and a sheen of sweat covers her forehead. 'Oh, God, I think I'm gonna throw up.'

Rhiannon and I half carry Marie to the bathroom, where she vomits the entire contents of her stomach into the toilet. I fetch her a glass of water, which she drinks down and promptly spews up again.

'Let's take her to the spare room,' I suggest. 'She can sleep it off in there.'

And that's what we do, placing her in the recovery position and tucking a blanket around her. 'I feel a bit ashamed of myself for encouraging her to drink,' I whisper to Rhiannon as we return to the dining room to clear up. 'But it certainly loosened her tongue.'

'It sure did.' Rhiannon stacks the plates and heads for the kitchen.

I join her and we make a start on the washing up. 'Marie is a victim of Barzini, like so many others. I feel sorry for her and for those Palestinian boys if they've been duped.'

Rhiannon stops scrubbing at a plate and says, 'I remember Gianluca telling me about some sort of agreement between your government and the PLO...'

'Oh, what kind of agreement?'

'Apparently they're allowed to carry out undercover para-military activities here, offering Italy, in exchange, their promise never to perpetrate terrorist attacks on Italian soil.'

'It's the first I've heard of it,' I gasp, surprised.

'Gianluca said he only just found out that Aldo Moro had made the pact with them in 1970. I hope Barzini isn't encouraging Bakir, Feraz, and Roshid to break that pact.' Rhiannon visibly shivers.

'If, indeed, they are members of the PLO. Didn't you say they were students?' I pick up a tea towel and join Rhiannon at the sink.

She hands me a rinsed plate. 'They seem to be so. I met them after they'd had lunch in the university canteen. They looked the part, the right age and all that.'

I frown. 'I should tell my comrades about this.'

'And Gianluca. He needs to know what we've discovered. And the police.' Rhiannon passes me another plate.

'I'll try and get hold of Gianluca in the morning. He left me a phone number in Florence, thankfully. I'll also arrange a meeting with my partisan friends. Oh, and I'll ask Carla to inform her son, Sergio the *carabiniere*.'

'I feel as if I know your comrades already, having listened to your story.' Rhiannon smiles. 'You're so brave, Leila. I'm in complete awe of you.'

'I was young and fired up with the spirit of insurrection. And, after what happened to Rebecca, I couldn't stand by and do nothing.' I blow out a breath, debating whether to confess my thoughts. 'I often wonder, if I hadn't been fighting alongside Paolo, would he have stayed in our base to draw fire? He could have ordered a retreat in time for him and the others to get out.'

'He probably thought he could take down the Germans and live to fight another day.'

'Yes, that's what I tell myself. But I still feel guilty.'

'Survivor's guilt.' Rhiannon touches her hand to my arm. 'I read about it once...'

'Ah. Could be. Anyway, I'd better go and check on Marie. Don't want her choking on vomit in her sleep.' I hang up the tea towel.

'I'll come with you.' Rhiannon pulls out the plug in the sink. 'Although I expect she's *fuori gioco*.'

'Out for the count.' I laugh wryly. 'Your Italian has improved so much, my dear.'

Her eyes glow at my praise. '*Grazie*.'

* * *

'Marie is having a shower,' Rhiannon announces the next morning, coming through the kitchen door. We set up a rota and checked on the Lebanese girl through the night. She snored terribly but wasn't sick again.

'How is she?' I enquire.

'Doesn't remember anything. She was quite confused when I woke her. Also, she seemed scared.'

'Probably because of Barzini.' I lift the coffee pot off the stove and place it on the table.

Rhiannon slices into the loaf of bread I bought earlier. 'I hope I never meet that man.'

'Promise me that you'll stay away from him, Rhiannon!'

'I promise.'

The door swings open and Marie steps gingerly into the room. 'I've got a really bad headache,' she moans.

I retrieve a packet of paracetamol from the cupboard and

extract two tablets. 'Take these.' I hand them to her with a glass of water.

'You should eat something,' Rhiannon advises, pulling out a chair.

'I couldn't. My stomach feels queasy.' Marie gives me an accusing look. 'It must have been something I ate.'

I don't want to contradict her so I leave it at that. I pour her a cup of coffee, which she accepts. 'I'm too ill for school. I'm going to take the day off,' she groans.

Rhiannon pats her hand. 'Let me walk you to your apartment, make sure you get home safely, before I head for class.'

Marie thanks her and, once the girls have left, I pick up the phone and dial Carla's number. 'I need to organise a meeting straight away,' I say.

* * *

Carla, Sebastiano, and Bruno come to my place in the early evening. Roberto will join us later, after he's finished work.

I offer everyone a glass of wine and tell them about the Lebanese girl's revelations.

Bruno's nostrils flare. 'So, she's confirmed what we suspected. Barzini is up to no good.'

'We should have gone after him when the war ended,' Sebastiano growls. 'After what he did to Carla I wanted to cut off his balls and stuff them down his throat.'

'Me too,' Carla agrees. 'If only we hadn't handed in our weapons to the Americans. It infuriated me when those *partigiani* who kept their guns started getting bad press because of surreptitious vengeance killings.'

'People today have no idea what those *fascisti* did to us partisans. The tortures, executions, turning brother against brother,' I mutter. 'If they knew the half of it they wouldn't be so hard on our comrades for perpetuating reprisals.'

'I heard that even the German Command was revolted by the violence of the *repubblichini*,' Bruno adds. 'But violence breeds violence, I suppose.'

'And now we have the *neofascisti* perpetrating yet more violence. God forbid they assume power one day.' I check my watch and a prickle of unease creeps up my spine. 'Rhiannon should be home by now.'

'Oh?' Carla gives me a worried look.

I run an unsteady hand through my hair. 'If she's going to be late she always rings me.'

Oh, dear Lord. Could something have happened to her?

Suddenly, the phone shrills. I leap from my seat and hurry to answer.

'Ciao, Auntie,' Gianluca's voice comes down the line. 'I just got a message you've been trying to contact me.'

'Yes, I rang the number you left me earlier.' My heart beats an uneasy rhythm against my ribs. Gianluca isn't going to like what I'm about to tell him, and there's no easy way of breaking it to him. Without preamble, I tell him about last night and, my voice trembling, add that Rhiannon hasn't come home yet.

'*Porco cane*,' he swears. 'I'll get on the next train to Bologna. Have you called Sergio?'

'Carla is about to do that now.'

'Ask her to tell him I'm on my way. Oh, and, Auntie, don't do anything rash, okay?'

'I won't,' I promise.

I disconnect the call and Carla phones Sergio.

Her face falls. 'He's out of town on a mission,' she says. 'He won't be back until later. I left a message for him to come straight here.'

Abruptly the bell to the entrance downstairs rings. I press the buzzer, thinking it must be Roberto. 'Come in,' I shout. 'The door is unlocked.'

'Most considerate of you.'

My blood freezes. I instantly recognise Barzini's voice echoing from the stairwell. 'Why are you here?'

I remember the loaded Beretta in the hall cabinet, the one I bought after the bombing of the station last year. I fling open the cupboard and grab the weapon.

Sebastiano, Carla, and Bruno rush forward, but I signal them to stay still.

I stand with the gun behind my back.

Barzini barges through the door. 'What have you done with my bitch, partisan whore?' he snarls.

For a second, I have no idea what he's talking about. 'You mean Marie?'

'Yes, her. She's gone.'

'Nothing to do with me,' I spit.

Rhiannon and she must have gone straight to school. Why would Barzini think that she's here?

'Give me my bitch and I'll leave you in peace,' he snarls.

The man whose voice can freeze my blood now has my blood boiling.

'Leave me in peace,' I repeat his words, 'I have never been in peace, not since...' My hand holding the gun is shaking. I want to shoot the bastard right now and be done with it.

'Tell me where my bitch is or I'll shoot,' Barzini barks, drawing his gun on me.

'Never!'

I spiral back in time, and he's interrogating me in the prison, but this time it's different.

This time I have my Beretta.

I pull it from behind my back, take aim in one swift movement, and squeeze the trigger.

Bang goes my pistol.

Bang goes Barzini's gun.

Our bullets pass each other in their trajectory.

Sharp pain pierces my chest, and I stagger.

Barzini yelps, sinks to his knees and falls sideways to the floor.

He gives a shiver, as if a jolt of electricity just passed through him. Then he goes still.

I manage to take a step forward and look down at his corpse, at the blood bubbling through the neat hole in the centre of his forehead. *Got you at last, you bastard.*

Then I, too, sink to the floor.

Carla and Sebastiano kneel next to me, staunching my bleeding with a tea towel.

Bruno is phoning for an ambulance.

Flashes of light pinprick behind my eyelids and I feel myself becoming floppy.

I open my mouth to speak, but no sound comes out.

Instead my eyes flutter shut.

And something pulls me backwards though a long tunnel into nothingness.

28

RHIANNON – EIGHT HOURS EARLIER

Rhiannon linked arms with Marie as she walked the girl all the way down Oberdan Street, and it was a good thing Rhiannon was there or Marie would almost certainly have fallen she was so hungover.

At the palazzo on the corner of Rizzoli, Marie handed Rhiannon her keys to unlock the street entrance. 'Can you help me?' she begged Rhiannon. 'My legs are shaking and the stairs are quite steep.'

'Of course.'

The studio must have been converted from part of the building's basement, Rhiannon thought as they descended to the depths. She helped Marie once more with the keys, opened the door, and linked arms with her again to guide her into the flat.

Marie switched on the light.

A man was sitting on a sofa in the centre of the room.

Rhiannon's heart pounded.

Barzini. She recognised him from when she'd seen him with Marie in the Baglioni and there was no mistaking his pock-marked face.

Marie stumbled forward. 'What are you doing here, Ugo?'

'I've been waiting for you all night, bitch.' He got to his feet and turned his cold gaze to Rhiannon. 'And who is this girl?'

'My classmate.'

'You spent the night with her?' He looked Rhiannon up and down.

'Yes. She invited me for dinner at her landlady's.'

'And who is her landlady?'

'Leila Venturi.'

'Oh really? The partisan whore? I'll never forget that name.' He shoved his thumb towards his shoulder. 'That whore shot me and left me for dead.'

Rhiannon took a step backwards, ready to make a run for it.

Barzini pulled a pistol from under his jacket. 'Not so fast, signorina. Give me that key.'

He snatched the key from her hand then went and closed the door.

Marie cowered as he made his way back to the sofa, and he slapped her full on the face. 'I've warned you before not to mix with strangers. How dare you disobey me!?'

She fell to the floor and he aimed a kick at her upper thigh.

'I'm sorry, Ugo. I didn't think you'd mind...'

'You'd better not have been blabbing my business to them,' he snarled, pulling her up by her hair.

'Of course not. I felt unwell after supper. Rhiannon and Leila put me to bed.'

'Were you drinking?'

'I don't remember.'

'Lying bitch! I've told you time and again not to drink. You can't hold your liquor and alcohol loosens your stupid tongue.'

'No, Ugo. I swear I didn't touch a drop.'

He slapped her again.

'Don't be so horrible,' Rhiannon cried out, moving forward.

Barzini raised his gun, aimed it at her. 'Stand still or I'll shoot.'

Rhiannon broke out in a cold sweat, stopping dead in her tracks.

'There's some business I need to attend to. But I'll be back soon to deal with you.' Barzini went to the door and stepped outside.

Rhiannon's stomach clenched in disbelief. Barzini was leaving the studio, locking the door behind him.

'Are you all right?' She helped Marie to her feet.

'That was nothing,' she said, 'I'm used to it.'

Rhiannon went to the door and rattled the lock, but it held firm. '*Aiuto!*' she shouted. Help!

Marie added her voice to Rhiannon's.

No one came.

They yelled until they were hoarse.

Still no one came.

Hours passed. Marie lay on her bed, claiming exhaustion. She slept deeply, her snores reverberating. But Rhiannon paced the apartment, searching for a way out. She was worried that Barzini's business entailed going after Leila, and she said as much to Marie when she woke at last.

'I think you might be right,' Marie said, rubbing her eyes. 'He was so angry.'

'Could he have gone to see your Palestinian friends?'

'He's never had any contact with them, to cover himself. I've always been his go-between.' Marie massaged her thigh where Barzini had kicked her. 'You must think me so weak for staying with him and letting him treat me like that...'

'It's your choice, Marie. But if that choice harms others, then you should have nothing more to do with him.'

'But where would I go if I left him? What would I do?'

'I'll try and help you, but first we must get out of here.'

Rhiannon tilted her head to the side. In the silence, a sound filtered up through the floor tiles.

Running water.

She suddenly remembered going under Rizzoli Street when she'd explored the underground Aposa channel with Gianluca and Angelo.

Rhiannon glanced around. Pine planks cladded the kitchen area at the far end of the studio. Could there be a door behind them?

'Have you got any tools, Marie?' It was unlikely, but worth asking.

She shook her head.

'Kitchen utensils?'

Marie went to open a drawer.

Rhiannon extracted a long, pronged fork. She inserted it between the planks and started prising them apart.

Marie stared at her. 'What are you doing?'

'Looking for a way out of here.'

Rhiannon carried on stripping the cladding until an old wooden door emerged behind it.

'Give me a hand,' she said to Marie after pushing the door and getting nowhere. 'It seems to be stuck.'

Together, they put their shoulders to the wood and, with a loud creak, the door swung open.

'God, what a foul smell,' Marie exclaimed, gagging. 'You don't seriously expect me to go down there with you?'

'Again it's your choice. Stay here and face Barzini. Or come with me. ' She paused. 'It's one of Bologna's underground canals. I visited it a while ago, and I know where it leads.'

'I'm claustrophobic and I hate the dark. I'd only hold you back...'

'Do you really want to stay here? Barzini will be furious when he returns and finds I've gone. He could really hurt you...'

'Are you sure you know the way?'

Rhiannon wasn't one hundred per cent certain, but she kept that fact to herself. 'There are stairs leading up to Piazza Minghetti,' she said in a confident tone of voice.

Marie shrugged. 'Okay, I'll come with you.'

With Marie following close behind, Rhiannon felt her way down slippery stone steps which led to the ledge running along-side the canal. It wasn't totally dark. Some light filtered through ventilation shafts in the brickwork. She got her bearings and led Marie in what she hoped was the right direction.

Rats scuttled in front of them and the stench was disgusting. Marie complained constantly that the stream stank, the tunnel was too dark, and she was terrified of rodents.

Eventually, they came to the cast iron stairs Rhiannon remembered and she guided Marie up them. At the top, she found the switch on the wall that Angelo had pressed to open the covering. Would it work? She was worried they'd be trapped down there. But it slid back and they emerged into the fresh air of Piazza Minghetti.

Rhiannon turned to Marie. 'I'm going to Leila's,' she said. 'To tell her about Barzini.'

Marie stiffened. 'I'm scared he'll already be there.'

'You and me both. But I must take that chance and warn Leila.'

'I'll go to my friends in Bolognina,' Marie said. 'I want to persuade them not to do whatever it is that Ugo has manipulated them into doing.'

'Where is their student accommodation, exactly?'

'Piazza dell'Unità.'

Of all the places, it had to be there, Rhiannon thought. She kissed Marie on both cheeks, and Marie kissed her in return. 'Do what you can to stop them,' Rhiannon said. 'I just hope I'll be in time to warn Leila.'

She waved Marie off, and then she set off running as if the hounds of hell were snapping at her heels until she arrived at Leila's apartment.

* * *

Rhiannon is greeted by a scene of such horror she almost can't believe her eyes. She kneels and clasps Leila's hand. Her dear friend is lying so still, blood oozing from the wound in her chest. A woman with silver blonde hair is crouching over her, attempting to staunch the bleeding with a tea towel. A man is kneeling, holding Leila's other hand, and an older man is on the phone.

'I'm Rhiannon.' Heart thudding, she averts her gaze from Barzini, nausea rising from her stomach. 'Is Leila going to be all right?'

'There's a pulse,' the kneeling man says. 'But I'm afraid she's bleeding out.'

The man who was on the telephone fixes Rhiannon with a despairing look. 'The ambulance is on its way. Barzini came here looking for the Lebanese girl...'

'I'm so sorry about that.' Rhiannon gives a little sob. 'I came here as soon as I could, to warn Leila.'

'She was very worried about you.' The blonde woman's eyes well with tears. 'I'm Carla, by the way.'

Bruno and Sebastiano introduce themselves, although Rhiannon has already worked out in her head who they are.

The sound of feet pounding on marble echoes from the stairwell. Two paramedics rush in. One of them checks Barzini and the other, Leila. 'This is a crime scene,' the shorter of the two men mutters. 'Have you called the police?'

'It was self-defence and we are all witnesses,' Bruno clarifies.

'Still needs to be reported immediately,' the taller paramedic says.

Carla fixes both men with a steely stare. 'I've left a message for my son. He's a *carabiniere* and will deal with the matter.'

'We'll call it in on our way to the hospital.' The short paramedic takes Leila's pulse, then staunches her wound. 'What is the victim's name?'

'Leila Venturi,' Bruno answers.

'Leila, can you hear me?'

No response.

'Is anyone here Leila's next of kin?' the tall paramedic enquires.

'Her nephew, Gianluca Venturi, is on his way home from Florence.' Sebastiano glances at his watch. 'Due to arrive any minute now.'

'We're taking Leila to Sant'Orsola.' The tall paramedic peers at Carla. 'You can ride in the ambulance. Keep talking to her.'

Rhiannon feels torn. She wants to go with Leila too, but someone should stay here and wait for Gianluca. She offers to do so, and Carla gratefully accepts.

Out of the blue, another man appears in the doorway. 'What's happened?'

'Ciao, Roberto.' Bruno goes on to give a brief explanation of the shooting.

'*Caspita*,' Roberto exclaims. *Whoa.* 'My car is parked in Piazza San Martino.' He glances at Sebastiano and Bruno. 'I'll drive you to the ER.'

Rhiannon's vision blurs and a tear trickles down her cheek.

Carla gives her a look of sympathy. 'Will you be all right here on your own?'

'I'll lock the door. Gianluca has his own key.' It occurs to Rhiannon that Barzini might have told someone where he was headed and they'd come looking for him.

'I'll stay with you,' Bruno offers.

'*Grazie*.' Rhiannon eyes Barzini's body. She wishes the paramedics would take him with them but knows that will be a job for the police.

'Come through to the kitchen, Bruno,' she suggests after the paramedics have strapped Leila onto a stretcher, carried her down to the ambulance, and Carla, Sebastiano and Roberto have left. 'I'll make us a cup of coffee.'

'I'd prefer a glass of wine.'

'*Certo*.' Of course.

* * *

Gianluca arrives at the same time as the *carabinieri* and a forensics team. 'Sergio filled me in downstairs.' Gianluca wraps his arms around Rhiannon. 'How are you, *bambina*?'

'I'm okay.' Her voice chokes. 'But Leila isn't...'

Gianluca holds Rhiannon in his gaze. 'You, Bruno, and I will go to the hospital. Sergio and his guys will clean up here. We'll all need to give formal statements, but they can wait until we go to the police station tomorrow.'

'I'm so sorry, Gianluca.'

'My aunt will be fine. She's a fighter.'

'I hope you are right.'

'I know I am right.'

'I agree with Gianluca,' Bruno says. 'Leila is the best fighter I know.'

Gianluca introduces Rhiannon to Sergio, who is blond and slim like his mother. '*Piacere.*' Pleased to meet you. Sergio shakes her hand. 'Although I'd have preferred to have met you in different circumstances.'

'Let's get going,' Gianluca says from where he is already making his way to the door. 'I left my car double-parked.'

They hurry downstairs. Rhiannon rides shotgun and Bruno gets into the back of the Lancia.

The drive to Sant'Orsola will take about ten minutes, Gianluca informs Rhiannon as they set off. Fear for Leila gnaws at her gut. 'This is all my fault,' she says. 'I went against your wishes and asked Marie to come for dinner. If I hadn't done that, this would never have happened.'

He removes his hand from the steering wheel, takes hers and gives it a squeeze. 'I imagine my aunt wanted you to invite her, so please don't blame yourself.'

'Barzini was waiting for Marie in her apartment. Such a vile man...'

Gianluca rolls his Lancia to a stop in the hospital car park. 'You can tell us precisely what happened later.'

'Okay.' She gets out of the car.

Hand in hand with Gianluca, Bruno walking the other side of him, she makes her way to the hospital entrance.

'They've taken Leila in for surgery,' Carla informs them as they step into the waiting room.

Gianluca sinks to a chair. 'Did the doctors say anything?'

Sebastiano, sitting beside Carla, spreads his hands wide. 'They need to open your aunt up and remove the bullet, then check if any vital organs have been affected.'

Bruno lowers himself to the right of Sebastiano and Roberto. Gianluca indicates to Rhiannon that she should sit next to him.

They make a forlorn group, surrounded by sterile white walls and the odour of disinfectant.

Gianluca puts his arm around Rhiannon. 'Tell us what happened at Marie's place.'

And so, she tells them, stopping every now and then to clarify. They listen attentively, prompting her when she struggles with getting the words out in Italian. It occurs to her that it's as if she were an actress in a television drama, the events seem so unreal. *Unreal and utterly terrifying.*

* * *

'So Marie should be in Piazza dell'Unità?' Gianluca inclines his head towards Rhiannon after she has told them everything.

'Yes, and we left the entrance to the Aposa uncovered.'

'I'll let Sergio know about that and about Marie,' Carla reassures.

The door to the waiting room swings open and a middle-aged male doctor appears.

'Leila has come through the procedure without any complications.' The doctor smiles reassuringly. 'Fortunately, the bullet lodged in her chest cavity, missing her heart, lungs, and liver. She lost a lot of blood, however. The trauma surgeon has decided to keep her sedated so she can rest.'

'Can we see her?' Gianluca asks.

'Come with me.' The doctor turns towards the door.

They follow him down the corridor to a two-bedded room. Leila is hooked up to machines and drips, her face almost as white as the hospital sheets.

Gianluca bends and presses a kiss to her pale forehead. 'Stay strong, Auntie. We all love you so much.'

Leila's eyelashes flutter, but she doesn't open her eyes.

A dark-haired female nurse approaches. 'Who is Leila's next of kin?'

'I'm her nephew,' Gianluca says.

'You have permission to remain with your aunt through the rest of the night.'

'*Grazie.*' He glances at Rhiannon. 'Please, stay with me. Leila's apartment will be a crime scene for at least the next twenty-four hours. Also, I think you will be safer here...'

Tears of relief well behind Rhiannon's eyelids. She was dreading having to find somewhere to go and doesn't want to be on her own.

Sebastiano offers to phone Leila's brother, Daniele, and Carla confirms she'll get in touch with her son. 'He'll know what to do about those Palestinian lads and Marie.'

'I hope she won't get into too much trouble,' Rhiannon says. 'She was coerced by Barzini...'

Sebastiano shrugs. 'That depends on what the Carabinieri discover...'

'Knowing how Barzini operates, I can't help fearing the worst,' Bruno mutters.

'Me too,' Roberto says. 'But there's nothing we can do about it now. Who'd like a lift home? It's past midnight. My wife will be worrying and I'm ready for my bed.'

Rhiannon and Gianluca wish the others goodnight, then Gianluca lowers his frame onto the chaise longue by Leila's bed. He pats the space next to him. 'Sit with me, *bambina.*'

She does as he suggests, leaning into him as he puts his arm around her. She likes being called bambina, baby, by him. Her heart beats loudly. She cares deeply for Gianluca, she realises.

It's the first time she's ever felt this way about a man.

29

LEILA

Everything is a blur. I don't know if I'm awake or dreaming. Gianluca and Rhiannon are talking to each other by my ear, and then they're gone. Carla's shadowy presence is close by. After that, she too disappears.

It's as if I'm struggling through a thick fog. There's also a smell of antiseptic and I'm aware I'm lying in a hospital bed, machines beeping behind my head.

My eyes flutter open. A hazy figure occupies the periphery of my vision. I focus my gaze. It's my brother, Daniele.

My mouth feels dry and I whisper, 'Water.'

'Here you are, little sister.' He places a sponge between my lips. 'Suck on that.'

'Wh-wh-what happened?' I screw up my face, try to remember.

'You've had an operation to remove a bullet from your chest.'

Operation? Bullet in the chest? My head feels as if it has been stuffed full of cotton wool.

'How did you get here, Dani? Where are Gianluca and Rhiannon?'

'Sebastiano phoned me and I caught the first train from Vicenza. Gianluca and Rhiannon are safe at the Zamboni palazzo. You need to rest now and get over the effects of the anaesthetic. I'll tell you everything when you wake up again.'

I'm so terribly tired I gratefully fall back into oblivion.

Minutes or maybe hours later, I can't be sure, I'm aware that a white-coated doctor is checking me over. 'You've had a lucky escape, Leila. The bullet grazed a rib and lodged itself less than an inch from your heart. Your lung partially collapsed.'

'What?!' I release a breath. Even breathing is too much effort, so I let sleep overtake me again.

The third time I wake, my gaze lands on Dani sitting in an armchair, reading a newspaper. I whisper that I'm thirsty again and he pours some water into a plastic cup, holds a straw to my lips. 'Just a couple of sips or you'll feel nauseous.'

'What day is it?'

'It's Tuesday night. You were shot in the chest by Barzini twenty-four hours ago.'

A picture comes into my mind of a gun in my hand. Bang. Two bullets passing in their trajectory. Barzini toppling over, a neat hole in the middle of his forehead.

'Is he dead?'

'Oh, yes. Very dead.'

'Good.' I feel no remorse. 'Is Rhiannon all right?'

'Yes, she's fine. Gianluca seems to be extremely fond of her.'

'I know. She's a lovely girl.'

'He wants to introduce her to Rebecca, so it must be serious.'

I smile, but then a chill goes through me as I remember the events that led to the shooting, and the smile is wiped from my face. 'Do you know what happened to Marie and the Palestinians?'

'They seem to have disappeared. Sergio is out looking for them.'

'Oh God.' Fear freezes my blood. 'I hope they aren't about to do something terrible.'

Dani reaches across the bed and takes my hand. 'Isn't it time you stopped taking the burdens of the world onto your shoulders, Leila? You're no longer a young partisan. I was shocked when I met Gianluca earlier, and he told me what had happened. You're lucky you weren't killed.' He exhales a breath. 'We'd all have been devastated to have lost you.'

'I couldn't stand by and do nothing when I found out Gianluca was digging into Ugo Barzini's background. I was worried he'd try to take a bigger step than the length of his leg would allow.'

'You should have more faith in him, darling.'

'Aren't you concerned for his safety?'

'Of course. He's my son. But he's also a grown man.'

My head sinks back on the pillow and I nod, too exhausted to continue this conversation. I close my eyes and drift off once more.

Morning has come. A tube remains in my arm and one in my chest that's acting like a drain. They've given me painkillers and I even managed to eat a little breakfast before doing the breathing exercises they taught me.

After tossing and turning all night in the hospital chaise longue, Daniele has already left to return to Vicenza. He promised he'd be back on the weekend, and that he'd bring Rebecca with him. I told him I'd hold him to that promise. It has been so long since I've seen my best friend.

I hate lying here, in physical pain and feeling as helpless as a new-born baby. But, before he set off, Dani told me that Gianluca and Rhiannon will visit momentarily. I can't wait to see them.

I fall asleep again. An echo of their voices drifts towards me and I think I am dreaming. I blink my eyes open. They're approaching my bed, looking so beautiful, the pair of them, they gladden my heart.

Gianluca kisses me then asks, 'How are you feeling, Auntie?'

My mouth twists. 'Happy to be alive.'

Rhiannon brushes the hair back from my forehead and plants a kiss there. 'I was so scared. I thought we were going to lose you.'

'It would take more than a bullet in the chest,' I joke.

She pulls up a chair, sits and takes my hand. 'It was all my stupid fault.'

'How can it have been your fault?'

She gives a brief account of how she'd gone into Marie's apartment. Barzini was there and he found out that the Lebanese girl had been to dinner at my place.

I squeeze Rhiannon's fingers. 'None of this is your fault. If anything, it's mine for drawing you into the whole situation.'

'I wanted to help,' she says. 'And now I'm devastated Marie and her Palestinian friends have gone missing. She said she was going to try and persuade them not to do whatever it was that Barzini had manipulated them into doing...'

'Have you given statements to the *carabinieri*?'

'We both have,' Gianluca confirms. 'Sergio said to tell you he'll visit this afternoon, by the way. You need to give a statement too.'

I nod. 'Is everything all right back at my apartment?'

'The crime scene has been cleared.' Gianluca looks me in the eye. 'But Rhiannon is staying with me until we know what has become of Marie, Bakir, Feraz, and Roshid.'

I glance at Rhiannon. She's blushing, not meeting my gaze. Ah, young love, I think to myself. I just hope Rhiannon and Gianluca find the happiness that eluded me all those years ago.

30

RHIANNON

Rhiannon tries to gauge Leila's reaction to Gianluca telling her that she's staying with him. It's all perfectly above board, she wants to tell her. But she's forestalled by the arrival of Carla, who has come to keep Leila company for the rest of the day.

Rhiannon squeezes Leila's hand. 'I'll be back to visit tomorrow.'

'I will too,' Gianluca promises.

'Can you go to my apartment and feed Romeo?' Leila asks.

'I'll check on him every day,' Gianluca promises.

Leila and Carla wave them off and they make a quick detour to Leila's apartment, where they top up the cat's bowl of kibble. Rhiannon changes into clean clothes and packs a bag with her personal belongings. The floor has been wiped of all traces of blood, but in her mind's eye she can still see Barzini lying there, his pockmarked face waxy in death. She gives a shudder, and Gianluca holds her close. 'Come, *bambina*. Let's go grab a snack lunch, then head back to my place.'

He takes her to a bar in Via dell'Indipendenza, where they are served mini pizzas oozing with mozzarella cheese and sundried tomatoes.

The food lifts Rhiannon's spirits. 'I'm so relieved your aunt will be okay.'

'She's tough.' Gianluca smiles. 'After God made her *He* threw away the mould.'

'She's certainly a one-off.' Rhiannon smiles back at Gianluca, and a flush heats her skin. She spent the entire day and night with him yesterday. He gave her his bed up in the loft while he slept below on the sofa. She woke in the early hours and contemplated joining him. But she was too reticent.

'How did your investigation of Licio Gelli in Florence go?' she asks to distract herself from thinking about getting into bed with Gianluca.

'I met with my journalist friend and discovered Gelli runs a Masonic lodge, the P2. He holds clandestine meetings in his Arezzo villa. Journalists, financiers, representatives of the armed forces, the secret police and the government are members.' Gianluca shakes his head. 'My associate has evidence they're trying to misdirect the investigation into the Bologna station bombing by sowing the poisonous seeds of uncertainty through an orgy of fake information. I suspected as much.' Gianluca blows out a breath. 'My buddy is about to break the story.'

'I'm sorry, Gianluca. I know how much you wanted to be the one to crack it. Do you think Barzini was a member of Gelli's lodge?'

'Undoubtedly.'

'I wonder what he wanted Marie's Palestinian friends to do...'

'My gut feeling is he has set them up to perpetrate an act which will make the investigators think it was the Palestinians and not the neo-fascists who exploded the bomb at the station.'

Rhiannon's stomach rolls with dread. 'I'm concerned they've gone AWOL.'

'Sergio will find Marie and her friends. His boss has allocated men and resources to the mission. Oh, and the press have been informed of Barzini's death. It's been reported as a shooting accident in today's papers. Thankfully, we've managed to keep my aunt out of it.'

'That's good.' Rhiannon plays with the mini pizza on her plate; she's lost her appetite.

'Let's go back to my place,' Gianluca suggests, eyeing her untouched food. 'We can relax and listen to some music. It's been a tough couple of days.'

* * *

They stroll hand in hand along Rizzoli Street and, at the two towers, turn down Zamboni. Within minutes, they're riding up the lift to Gianluca's apartment. Rhiannon slips off her coat and hangs it by the door. 'Shall I make us both a coffee?'

'Grazie.' He goes to his stereo and puts on a record. Steely Dan's *Aja*.

'Oh, I love this album.' She adds ground coffee to the filter, fills the boiler with water, and places the pot on the gas cooker.

Gianluca takes a step towards her. 'Would you like to dance?' He gives a little bow. 'It will cheer you up.'

She giggles. 'Okay...'

He twirls her around the room and she breathes in his masculine scent, enjoying the feel of his body pressed to hers.

She could stay like this for hours, but the Bialetti emits a burst of steam, and the aroma of freshly percolated coffee infuses the air.

She slips from Gianluca's arms and goes to pour their espressos, which they drink standing at the kitchen counter.

'Another dance or shall we just sit and relax?' he asks.

'Let's just sit...'

She perches next to Gianluca and stares down at her lap.

'Are you okay, *bambina*?'

'I'm concerned about Marie and those boys.'

'I am too, but there's nothing we can do about it.' He lifts her chin and kisses the tip of her nose. 'Try not to worry, darling.'

She nods and he draws her into his arms.

Her heartbeat echoes in her ears.

She clings to him, and he runs his hands down her sides, presses his fingers along the tops of her shoulders, traces them down to the curve of her hips.

'Mm, that feels nice.' Boldly, she rubs herself against him. 'Please, Gianluca, make love to me.' The words spill from her mouth before she can even think about them. Has she been too blatant? She gazes at him, her heart pounding.

A tentative smile spreads across his face. 'Are you sure?'

'I am.' She touches her fingers to his chest, feels the beating of *his* heart.

'I love you, Rhiannon. I've wanted to say this for days. I want a future for us.'

Her skin tingles with sudden happiness. 'I want that too, Gianluca. I love you so much.'

With deft movements, he undresses her and then himself. He rests her back down on the sofa and kisses her without stopping.

She gives a whimper of pleasure and arches her back.

He tears his mouth away from hers. 'You're so beautiful, *bambina*.'

She threads her fingers into his hair, then holds his face close. 'So are you.'

'Just a second, my love.' He gets to his feet, turns away.

She feels the heat of a flush, realising that he's sheathing himself. Her gaze rests on his fine physique, his muscular shoulders, and firm buttocks. A quiver of worry tickles her tummy. What if she reverts to being an ice maiden? But no. This time it will be different.

She hopes.

Back on the sofa, he kisses her again and she becomes like molten lava, burning with need.

He eases himself into her, his eyes fixed on hers.

She tenses; she can't help it.

'Tell me to stop and I will, *amore*.'

'Don't stop.' She takes in a long, slow breath.

She clutches at his shoulders as they rock to the same rhythm, and she loses all sense of time, of space, of good and bad. She forgets about her dad's treatment of her mum, and her disastrous relationship with Owen, even about what happened with Marie. All she knows, all she cares about, is the gorgeous man in her arms and his ability to make her feel so wonderfully loved.

She looks deep into his eyes, and he looks deep into hers. '*Ti amo*, Rhiannon,' he says.

Her soul opens to him, welcoming him like a long-lost part of itself.

He kisses her deeply. 'I love you. I can't stop saying it.'

'Me too.' She smiles. 'I love you. I love you. I love you.'

31

RHIANNON

Rhiannon wakes up the following morning next to Gianluca in his double bed. She stretches and turns to face him, memories of the wonderful night of lovemaking giving her a warm, fuzzy feeling inside. He's sleeping soundly, his long dark eyelashes fanning the tops of his stubbled cheeks. She's tempted to wake him so they can make love again. She can't quite believe she's even thinking these thoughts, but she is and it's all thanks to him.

Suddenly, the telephone on the bedside table shrills. With a groan, Gianluca stirs and reaches for the receiver. '*Pronto.*' Hello.

He listens to the caller, then sits bolt upright. '*Arriviamo subito.*' We'll be there straight away.

'That was Sergio. Marie is at the *carabinieri* station.' Gianluca leaps out of bed and pulls on his boxer shorts. 'She went back to Auntie's, probably looking for you. One of Sergio's men was on patrol in the vicinity. He saw her and brought her in. Hurry and get dressed, *bambina*. She won't talk unless you are there.'

'Oh God.' Rhiannon hurries to the en suite bathroom, throws on the jeans and jumper she changed into yesterday.

They rush down to Gianluca's Lancia, parked in the courtyard below, and, within minutes, he's found a spot in front of the police HQ in Galliera Street.

A uniformed officer in black jacket and trousers, with red stripes down the outside of the legs, is waiting for them under the portico at the entrance. Rhiannon eyes the pistol on the left-hand side of his white cross belt. Policemen aren't normally armed in the UK, and seeing the gun gives her a shock.

'Follow me.' The *carabiniere* takes her and Gianluca to an interview room, where Sergio is sitting opposite Marie.

'Your friend has declined to have a lawyer with her and has refused to talk unless you are present, Rhiannon,' Sergio says.

Rhiannon peers at her friend. She looks terrible. Her clothes are dirty and her hair hangs lank and greasy. 'Are you all right, Marie?'

'I'm okay.'

'Ask her about the Palestinians,' Sergio barks.

Marie straightens her spine. 'If I tell you, Rhiannon, will you help me? You promised...'

She appears so pathetic, Rhiannon's heart goes out to her. But how can she fulfil the rash promise she made back at Marie's apartment? Rhiannon sighs. She's only a student – she doesn't have the resources.

'I'll help you,' Gianluca cuts in. 'But I'm not being entirely altruistic. I want your story in exchange.'

'Typical journalist,' Marie mutters.

He holds up his hands. 'Guilty as charged.'

Marie glances from Gianluca to Rhiannon, to Sergio, and back to Gianluca. 'I'll need somewhere to live and a job.'

'That can be arranged,' Gianluca says. 'Where are your friends?'

'How can I trust you?' Marie glances at him sideways.

'You can trust him.' Rhiannon gives her what she hopes is a sincere look. 'Of that I am certain.'

Sergio bangs his hand impatiently down on the desk. 'If you don't tell us where your friends have gone and what they are up to, I'm going to have to arrest you for perverting the course of justice.'

'They're hiding.' Marie voice's has gone quiet. 'I tried to persuade them to hand themselves in after we heard that Ugo had died. But they're too scared the police will shoot first and ask questions later.'

Sergio glares at her. 'What did Barzini involve them in?'

'I only just found out. The boys wouldn't tell me anything before. Ugo arranged for Strela surface-to-air missiles to be delivered to them. They're lightweight and can be fired from the shoulder. He said they would be heroes in Palestine if they shot down a passenger plane taking off or landing at the airport. But now that Ugo is dead, they've got cold feet.'

'Thank God,' Gianluca exclaims. 'Where are they?'

'Via Bovi Campeggi. By the open stretch of the Navile Canal.'

Sergio stands, his chair scraping the tiled floor. 'Come with me, Marie.'

Marie folds her arms. 'I'm not going anywhere without Rhiannon.'

'And I'm not going anywhere without Gianluca,' Rhiannon adds.

'It goes against protocol, but time is of the essence,' Sergio huffs. 'We need to stop those guys.'

They follow Sergio outside. There, they wait until a police van pulls up. Two sharpshooters with rifles join them. Rhiannon trembles at the sight of them and Marie's face turns white. They get into the van and set off at full speed, passing the freight yard with its high fences, stationary railroad cars, and piles of tracks. Marie gives directions, and they come to a concrete barrier running along the edge of a canal. Electric wires criss-cross above them, the connecting towers straddling overgrown shrubs and weeds.

'Stop!' Marie yells.

With a screech of tyres, the van abruptly halts.

Sergio jumps out, followed by Marie, Rhiannon, Gianluca and the two riflemen.

Rhiannon inhales the musty smell of brackish water and peers at the small river meandering slowly under an arched stone overpass below to the left.

'They're down there.' Marie indicates towards a cement island in the middle of the waterway.

'What the hell are they doing there?' Sergio shades his eyes.

'After I told them about how I got out of my apartment with Rhiannon, they thought the canal would be a good escape route, that they could go underground and stash the missiles. But there's a mesh wire fence across the water, blocking it.'

'Do your friends know you've come to fetch us?'

'I said I would bring someone who could guarantee they wouldn't be harmed.' She glances at Rhiannon. 'So it's better if just the two of us go down there first.'

Rhiannon is touched that Marie has such faith in her abilities, but she knows that faith is unfounded. 'I want Gianluca with me. He'll say the right things to your friends and win their confidence.'

'If they don't hand themselves in.' Sergio peers at his sharp-shooters. 'We'll have to force the issue.'

'Are the boys armed?' Gianluca asks Marie.

'I don't think so. They just have the Strela missiles.'

Once again, Rhiannon feels as if she's taking part in a TV melodrama. This kind of thing doesn't happen in real life. Except, it is happening and she can't help wishing she were anywhere else but here.

Marie leads them across a rickety metal-plate bridge.

Bakir, Feraz, and Roshid step out from behind a shrub.

Rhiannon gasps.

The boys have the green missile launch tubes on their shoulders, pointing up at the sky.

The rumble of an aircraft engine reverberates above and Rhiannon lifts her gaze.

A plane is coming in low overhead.

Oh, my God, they must be directly under the flight path for the airport.

Everything seems to happen in slow motion.

Marie rushes forwards. 'No!' she screams.

With a burst of fire, the sharpshooters let rip from the bank of the canal.

A bullet catches Marie in the back and she falls to the ground.

Bakir, Feraz, and Roshid drop the missile launchers, raise their hands.

Rhiannon goes to Marie and kneels next to her, turns her gently on her side.

Blood and froth are bubbling from Marie's mouth. Her perplexed eyes meet Rhiannon's and then glaze over.

Rhiannon cradles her head. 'You'll be okay,' she soothes.

But she can see that it's hopeless and she exhales a sorrowful breath.

Gianluca takes up position on the other side of Marie. He feels for a pulse, then shakes his head. 'She's gone, my love...'

Rhiannon stares at the lifeless face she's still holding in her hands. Her heart aches for Marie. *What a tragedy*. Rhiannon bends and presses a kiss to the cold forehead. 'I'm so sorry, dear friend,' she sobs.

32

LEILA –SIX WEEKS LATER

I smile at Rebecca, sitting across from me at the glass-topped kitchen table in her elegant Vicenza apartment. Her hair is streaked with grey, like mine; we are both in our late fifties now. But it took years for the spark to return to her eyes after the horrors of the Shoah. Daniele's love, together with the arrival of her children and then grandchildren, have brought her much joy. She shares that happiness with me and I love her dearly for it.

She glances at me. 'How are you feeling, my dear?'

'So much better and looking forward to going home.' Two weeks after I was shot, I was pronounced out of danger and discharged from Sant'Orsola. Dani came to collect me and brought me here so I could recuperate under his watchful eye.

'Are you sure you're well enough to go back to Bologna?' Rebecca reaches across the table and pats my hand.

'Of course. Besides, I don't want to miss the Liberation Day celebrations.'

Her shoulders droop. She has never returned to Auschwitz; she doesn't even like to talk about the war. So, I change the subject. 'I can't wait to see Rhiannon and Gianluca,' I say. They are due to pick me up shortly in his Lancia and drive me home.

'Will Rhiannon return to live with you in Marsala Street?'

Rebecca knows that Gianluca took her in after that dreadful evening when Barzini turned up. Rhiannon was terrified of being in my apartment on her own, apparently, and then suffered from grief after Marie was killed. *The poor Lebanese girl.* I'll never forget the evening I learnt of her tragic death. Rhiannon and Gianluca came to see me in the hospital, their faces ashen. We wept hot tears of regret together. 'She was a victim of Barzini,' I sobbed. 'What a waste of a young life...'

After we'd dried our eyes, Gianluca went on to tell me about the arrest of the Palestinian boys. They would face trial in due course. But Bakir, Feraz and Roshid had been adamant they'd had no intention of shooting down a plane that fateful day. They were simply holding the missile launchers, they said, and were ready to hand them over to the police. Gianluca is trying to get to the bottom of the matter, thanks to Sergio giving him access to classified information. He is also investigating the source of the Strelas, which he told me are of Soviet make.

'Rhiannon will be moving back in with me as soon as I get home,' I confirm to Rebecca. 'We get on so well together...'

'She's been good company for you.' Rebecca looks me in the eye. 'You'll miss her when she goes back to Wales.'

'I'm hoping it won't be forever.'

'I hope so too.' Rebecca's expression turns dreamy. 'I'd give anything to see Gianluca settled...'

We're interrupted by the loud ring of the doorbell. 'I'll get it,' Dani calls from the living room.

The sound of Rhiannon and Gianluca's voices brings a thrill to my heart. Although they've visited every Sunday since I came to stay in Vicenza, Gianluca has taken advantage of their visits to show Rhiannon around the city of his birth and to introduce her to his brother, sister, and their families. I miss spending time with my favourite nephew and his girlfriend and I'm looking forward to getting back to our old routine.

'*Ciao*, Auntie.' Gianluca breezes into the kitchen, hand in hand with Rhiannon. 'How are you?'

'Fine, thanks. All the better for seeing you two.'

He pecks me and his mother on the cheek, and Rhiannon does likewise.

'Lunch is nearly ready,' Rebecca says. 'Risotto with wild herbs.'

Gianluca rubs his belly. '*Grazie*, Mamma,' he says.

Next morning, I wake up in my own bed with Romeo sleeping by my feet. The bells of San Petronio echo across the city, heralding the thirty-sixth anniversary of the liberation of Italy from the *nazifasciti*. My breathing slows as I remember the Germans and *repubblichini* marching out of Bologna and the jubilation of the *bolognesi* when the Allies arrived. We were filled with such hope for the future. But social and political turmoil seem to have reigned supreme in Italy for years, since the late sixties in fact, and I ask myself when will we finally have true peace.

Romeo settles onto my chest. I stroke his soft fur, the vibration of his purr tickling the palm of my hand. 'Sorry, my boy,' I tell him. 'But I must get up now. Today is all about Paolo.'

Rhiannon and Gianluca greet me in the kitchen. I guess he has spent the night here with her, but I don't ask. Young people conduct themselves differently these days and I don't begrudge them one little bit. I wonder if they have made plans for when she returns to Wales, but again I don't ask. They will tell me when they are ready, I expect.

We walk to Piazza del Nettuno, which is already heaving with people. Soon, the celebrations begin. It isn't as lavish an event as the thirtieth anniversary, which we celebrated in 1975. On that occasion, I marched with my *partigiani* comrades along Via Rizzoli together with other partisan brigades and army units. There were massive crowds cheering us, many making the communist raised fist salute of political solidarity.

Standing with Gianluca and Rhiannon today in Neptune's square, my vision blurs while I watch the raising of the Italian flag by a military guard of honour. Wreaths are laid at the Memorial to the Fallen Partisans. The mayor, the representative of the Region and the president of the National Association of the Partisans of Italy make speeches. The ceremony ends with a rendition of our song, 'Bella Ciao'. Tears trickle down my cheeks and my heart aches.

> *This is the flower of the partisan*
> *Bella ciao, bella ciao, bella ciao, ciao, ciao*
> *This is the flower of the partisan*
> *Who died for our freedom*

I inhale the sweet scent of the red azalea blooms I'm holding before placing them below Paolo's photo. 'Let your death not be in vain, my love,' I whisper.

Bruno and his wife, Giovanna, approach, and we hug and kiss. We form a huddle with Roberto and *his* wife, Irene. Carla and Sebastiano arrive and there's more hugging and kissing. My comrades' children and grandchildren join us, followed by Diego and Mafalda, who attend the event every year from their retirement home in Rimini. We all go for coffee together in Piazza Maggiore, our hearts heavy with remembrance.

* * *

In the afternoon, Gianluca drives me and Rhiannon to the Monumental Certosa cemetery. I have more flowers – a pot of spring daisies – which I will place by my husband's tomb. Rhiannon holds a bunch of tulips in her hand, but they are not for Paolo.

We exit the city centre through Porta Sant'Isaia and soon Gianluca is parking in front of the red-brick walls surrounding the cemetery.

'This is such a stunning place,' Rhiannon says in an admiring tone after we've stepped through the archway at the entrance. 'It's like a mini-Bologna.' And it is. Cream-coloured porticoes have been built to recreate the city walkways the deceased once strolled when they were alive.

Rhiannon has been here before, when Marie was laid to rest, but evidently the beauty of Bologna's cemetery, set in the grounds of a fourteenth century monastery, impresses her still.

Gianluca takes the pot of daisies and he and Rhiannon link arms with me, encouraging me to lean on them. We stroll past the family crypts of wealthy Bolognese of yore. The colossal mausoleums give the impression of attempting to outdo each other with their opulence and piety, one great avenue after another, filled with competing baroque memorials.

Nowadays our dead are obliged to occupy the ubiquitous galleries of burial chambers set into marble walls, and this is where we head to find Paolo. The Certosa seems to go on forever, but eventually we make our way down a narrow cloister with ranks of little photographs featuring the images of those who are entombed behind them. I breathe in the heady scent of various fresh flowers, placed in vases attached to the vaults. Even though their occupants might have passed away decades before, like my husband, their memory is kept alive.

We stop in front of Paolo, who is on the 'ground floor', and I place the pot of daisies before him. Gianluca and Rhiannon give me a moment of privacy while I talk to my beloved, tell him I'll always love him and there will never be anyone else. I bend and press a kiss to his ceramic photo. 'Goodbye for now, my darling. I will be back to visit you again soon.'

Gianluca and Rhiannon rejoin me, and we walk towards the patch of land surrounding the former Carthusian charterhouse where the medieval monks used to grow vines. It is here where Marie rests in a burial plot I have paid for. It's still a mound of earth – I have ordered a tombstone for her, but it has yet to arrive. Permission for her to be buried in Italy involved a lot of paperwork. It was especially difficult as it was impossible to locate a next-of-kin. But after I assumed responsibility for the upkeep of her grave, and Gianluca pulled a few strings, she was laid to rest at last.

Rhiannon kneels and empties the jar containing old flowers, replaces them with the tulips. She wipes a tear from her cheek. 'Sleep in peace, dear friend,' she says. 'I'm so sorry for what happened.'

'We are all sorry,' I add. It occurs to me that Marie might have made the ultimate sacrifice. No one can be sure if her Palestinian friends were about to perpetrate an act of terror or not. I keep my thoughts to myself, though. 'Let's go home,' I say instead, glancing up at the dark clouds billowing above. 'Looks like it's going to rain.'

33

RHIANNON – TWO MONTHS LATER

Rhiannon meets Gianluca for a drink after her last day at the university. They are due at Leila's for a farewell dinner, then Rhiannon will spend the night with Gianluca before he drives her to the airport in the morning.

He takes her hand and they walk to Piazza Santo Stefano, heading for their usual café. 'I'm going to miss this so much,' she sighs. 'And you too, of course.'

'Good thing you qualified that statement.' He laughs, pulling out a chair for her. 'Or I'd have been worried...'

'You know I love you unconditionally, *amore mio*.'

'I know.' He bends and presses a kiss to her cheek. 'Love you too, *bambina*.'

A waiter arrives to take their order of prosecco. It's a warm June evening and sunshine bathes the beautiful russet-coloured buildings opposite in a golden glow.

Rhiannon thinks about her first conversation with Marie here, back in February, when they chatted about their studies. Marie said her ambition was to become an interpreter at the United Nations. Would Barzini have allowed that? Rhiannon has her doubts. She remembers telling Marie how she might take a law conversion course after she'd graduated in Italian, but that won't happen now. Instead, she'll return to Bologna next year and enrol at Unibo to study for a master's in social work. After what happened with Marie, Rhiannon has developed an interest in working with abused women. And, with Gianluca's help, she has researched becoming a social worker in Bologna. She'll be able to apply for a job in the city once she has the appropriate qualification and gained experience by doing voluntary work. It has sweetened her imminent departure from Bologna somewhat to have a concrete plan.

Their drinks arrive and they clink glasses. 'Promise you'll visit me in Wales before the end of the summer, Gianluca.'

'I can't wait.' He takes a sip of wine.

Her heart pangs. How will she manage without him? You'll just have to, she tells herself. She'll keep her head down, focus on her studies, and a year will have gone by before she realises.

She hopes.

She finishes her prosecco and goes to settle the bill. 'My treat.'

'*Grazie.*'

She returns to the table and he gets to his feet. 'Time to go to Auntie's,' he says.

'I've decided to let you edit my memoirs and then find a publisher,' Leila announces after a delicious dinner of Parma ham and melon, followed by seabass baked with cherry tomatoes and olives.

'Wow,' Gianluca exclaims. 'Why the change of heart?'

'I didn't want to draw attention to myself before. But, now

Barzini is no longer an issue, I think it will be a good moment to remind people about the sacrifices made by our *partigiani*.'

'I think you are right, Auntie. We could call the book *The Girl From Bologna*, what do you think?'

'Oh, yes. I do like that...'

'I do too,' Rhiannon chips in. 'It should be all about you, Leila.'

'And Paolo, too, of course.' Leila gives a deep sigh. 'How are your investigations coming along, Gianluca? Are you any closer to discovering what Barzini was up to?'

'Only that his name was on the list of members of the clandestine P2 lodge.'

Rhiannon recalls Gianluca telling her that the police had raided Licio Gelli's villa in Arezzo and that he'd gone on the run. 'Have they found Gelli yet?' she asks.

Gianluca shakes his head. 'I forgot to tell you, *bambina*. He's gone into hiding in Switzerland, apparently. It will take years for the extradition process.'

'That's a shame...'

'What about the Palestinian boys?' Leila enquires.

'Their trial will take place in the autumn, by all accounts.'

'I hope you get to the truth behind all of this, Gianluca.'

'I'm doing my best, Auntie.'

Rhiannon makes a move to start clearing the dishes. Gianluca helps her and they tackle the washing-up together. 'Do you think Leila would enjoy a trip to Wales?' Rhiannon wipes at a plate and puts it in the cupboard.

'Why don't you ask her?' He hands her another plate.

They finish the task at hand, then go to the sitting room, where Rhiannon proposes the visit to Leila. 'I'd love that.' A smile spreads over her face.

Rhiannon hugs her. 'Brilliant. I can't wait for you to meet Mum and Lowri.'

Leila returns the hug. 'Well, my dear. I suppose you should be off now.' A sigh escapes her. 'Your flight tomorrow morning is quite early, isn't it?'

'It is,' Rhiannon confirms. '*Arrivederci*, Leila. *Ci vediamo in Galles.*' Goodbye, Leila. We'll see each other in Wales.

Leila kisses her fondly on the cheek. '*A presto, mia cara.*' See you soon, my dear.

Next morning, Gianluca rolls his Lancia to a stop in Guglielmo Marconi airport's parking lot. Rhiannon sucks in a shaky breath and gets out of the car as Gianluca retrieves her suitcase from the boot. 'We've time for a coffee after you've checked in,' he says, his voice gravelly.

She squares her shoulders. 'If you don't mind, Gianluca, I'd rather go straight through.' She doesn't trust herself not to break down in front of him. After they'd made love in his bed last night, she'd wept so much her eyes had turned puffy.

They say goodbye, repeating the promises they've already made to phone and write regularly. He turns away and she joins the line for passport control and security. Suddenly her tummy clenches. What is she doing? This is tearing her apart, and, by the look on Gianluca's face, it's tearing him apart too. No way can she get on that plane without spending as much time with him as she can before her flight is called.

She spins around and pushes her way back down the line, hoping against hope he hasn't left the terminal yet. She's crying and laughing at the same time when she spots him by the sliding doors. 'Gianluca!' she calls out.

'Darling, what's wrong?' He holds out his arms.

She goes to him, wraps *her* arms around his waist and peppers his chest with desperate kisses.

He bends and kisses her, then he traces his finger down her cheek. 'Let's go get that coffee.'

The airport bar is crowded, but Gianluca manages to find them a table. A waiter arrives to take their order of cappuccinos.

Gianluca reaches for Rhiannon's hand and squeezes her fingers. '*Coraggio, bambina.*' Cheer up, baby!

'I'm okay, Gianluca.' She tucks a strand of hair behind her ear. 'I was just being silly.'

He lifts her hand to his lips and kisses her wrist. 'You weren't being silly at all.'

Their coffees arrive. There isn't much to say for fear of bursting into tears. Gianluca too. He looks so miserable. Rhiannon glances nervously at her watch. 'Maybe I should go through...'

Holding her hand, he walks her to the departure gate. '*Buon viaggio*, have a good journey, darling. Call me as soon as you get home.'

'I'll do that.' She smiles a sad smile.

She lifts her face to his, and he kisses her. He kisses her so thoroughly she's in no doubt that he loves her as much as she loves him.

She stands back and gazes into his eyes. 'Goodbye, Gianluca.'

'*Arrivederci, amore mio.*' Until we meet again.

EPILOGUE

I'm sitting by Leila's bed in the old people's home where she has been living the past four years, since she reached the grand old age of ninety. She's taking an afternoon nap after we had lunch together in the dining room and I read her a chapter from Gian-luca's latest book. Leila's eyesight is poor these days and she likes it when I read to her, especially stories written by her favourite nephew. He has become a successful thriller author since he retired from investigative journalism when his first novel was a bestseller eight years ago. The plethora of political scandals he helped bring to light in his award-winning career have been a springboard for his creativity, he maintains, but he also claims that the truth is much more unbelievable than his fiction.

I recall the time when I was a student. It was a tumultuous period in the history of Italy which came to be known as 'the years of lead'. The unprecedented acts of terrorism, carried out by both far-right and far-left groups, left the country reeling. It pains me every day that Marie, Bakir, Feraz, and Roshid were caught up in Barzini's attempt to divert attention from the fascist Licio Gelli. Marie was an enigma to me at first, but when I found out how badly Barzini treated her, I felt sorry for her. I believe she desperately wanted to protect the Palestinian boys. I sigh to myself. They were eventually condemned to seven years' imprisonment, reduced to five on appeal, after which they left Italy.

Gelli was ninety-six when he died in Arezzo three years ago. The more I learn about him, the more I come to realise how evil he was. Not only did he interfere with and possibly order the bombing of the Bologna railway station, but it is thought he was involved in the murder of the Milanese banker Roberto Calvi, found hanged under Blackfriars Bridge in London a year later.

When I returned to Wales after I'd finished my Italian studies in Bologna and told Mum about what had happened with Marie, initially she tried to persuade me to give up my plans to go back to Italy. But, once she'd met Gianluca and Leila she changed her mind. 'I understand completely,' she said. 'You're in love and are deeply loved in return.'

Not long afterwards, Mum joined the women at the Greenham Common Women's Peace Camp. She was there, on and off, for the next ten years. Mum formed a partnership with Megan, whom she met at Greenham, and they lived blissfully together running a bed and breakfast in Swansea until they retired. I visited them last year, during the same trip when I went to stay with Lowri. My sister has never married, claims to be perfectly happy on her own. She's still working in London, but visits Mum and Megan regularly, as well as me, Gianluca, and our two sons, Paolo and Filippo.

Gianluca is a wonderful father to our boys. We waited until my career as a social worker, helping abused women, had been established before we started a family. Paolo, a doctor, is twenty-seven and Filippo, who is with the *carabinieri*, is twenty-three. Paolo and his wife, Alice, are expecting a baby next month. Gianluca and I are thrilled we'll soon be grandparents and Leila is over the moon about becoming the infant's great-grand-aunt. Unfortunately, Daniele and Rebecca won't get to meet their new great-grandchild. Daniele passed away seven years ago at the great age of ninety-seven closely followed by Rebecca – the starvation she experienced in Auschwitz had weakened her heart. Gianluca was distraught, of course, and me too. Daniele had become the father I'd never had, and Rebecca the most wonderful mother-in-law.

I'll never forget the misery I felt when I returned to Cardiff in 1981. I lived for Gianluca's visits, which he managed to squeeze in whenever he'd finish a work assignment. True to his word, he brought Leila with him on one occasion. Unfortunately, it rained every day she was in Wales. She didn't seem to mind, though; she was just happy to see me, she said, and to meet Mum and Lowri. We took her sightseeing to Caerphilly Castle, the Roman amphitheatre in Caerleon, and to the Wye Valley. But what she loved most, she kept repeating, was the beautiful green countryside and the lovely gardens.

She visited Wales on another occasion, when Gianluca and I held our wedding in a country house hotel near Cardiff thirty years ago. Nia was my maid of honour and her little girls my bridesmaids. (She and her long-time boyfriend tied the knot after I returned to Bologna and they started a family immediately.) Dad was conspicuous by his absence at my wedding, even though Gianluca and I sent an invitation.

I glance up as the door to Leila's room swings open and Gianluca steps inside. I place my finger to my lips, indicating that he should try not to wake his aunt. Quietly, he lowers himself to the armchair by the window and takes out his mobile phone. Soon he's tapping away on it, and I marvel at how much life has changed since we first met. I have never regretted meeting and marrying Gianluca. Never regretted moving to Italy. We've had our ups and downs like many couples. And Italy continues to evolve politically. But at least the years of lead are past. *I hope.* I give a little shiver as something Leila has often repeated comes into my mind. 'The past is never past.' Gianluca used the words as the strapline to her memoirs. She was concerned about the future, and, for a while, I shared her concerns. Then my days became filled with Gianluca, work and our kids and I stopped worrying, stopped having nightmares reliving what had happened with Marie. Life has been good to me, and I relish every minute, knowing how tenuous those minutes can be.

Leila stirs in her bed and slowly wakens. 'Ciao,' she says, noticing Gianluca. 'Have you come to pick up Rhiannon?'

'Yes, Auntie. How are you today?'

'I'm well, *grazie.* Just wish I could walk better. Otherwise I can't complain.'

We help her out of bed and I accompany her to her luxurious en suite bathroom. The old people's home is the best available. Gianluca is covering the cost by using the proceeds from the sales of Leila's memoirs.

The girl from Bologna – Leila the *partigiana* – returns to her room and we hug her gently, her old bones so fragile they might break. 'See you tomorrow, Auntie,' I say to her.

'I'll look forward to it, my dear.' She smiles.

AUTHOR'S NOTE

I decided to write *The Girl From Bologna* after I visited Bologna with my husband and saw the monument to the partisans in Piazza del Nettuno. The photos of the young men and women who'd died for freedom touched me to the depths of my soul. The more I read about what happened in the red city after the Allies stalled their advance, the more my heart broke for those brave *partigiani*. I hope I've managed to convey the magnitude of their sacrifice adequately to my readers. War returned to Europe while I was writing this novel and many of the feelings expressed by Leila are shared by me. 'The past is never past' is so true.

Although *The Girl From Bologna* is based on real events, it is a work of fiction and therefore all my characters, except for those in the public domain, are fictional. Messenzio Masia was one of the top leaders of the resistance in Emilia Romagna, a leading exponent of the Action Party and anti-fascism, who was executed in September 1944 and posthumously decorated with the gold medal for military valour. Marroni was the battle name of Mario Bastia, who led a group of partisans in the Battle of the University and was shot by a fascist firing squad. He was also awarded the gold medal for military valour. The other partisans in my novel are inspired by stories of the youth of Bologna who took up arms to fight for their beliefs during that dark period in the history of Italy.

Alongside the monument to the partisans in Piazza del Nettuno there is another monument, listing the names and ages of those killed by the terrorist bomb on 2 August 1980. The fact that Bologna had chosen, some years later, to honour the victims in the same location where so many partisans had given their lives, made me decide to construct the 1981 narrative around that heinous event. There are many articles about Licio Gelli online. It is now almost certain that he paid neo-fascists to carry out the bombing of the station and that he bought the collusion of security officials. However, it took years for the tangled web of deceit to be unravelled. Only in April 2022 was the man who left a rucksack filled with explosives in the first-class waiting room finally sent to jail for the attack.

I have read the following books for inspiration and information:

Luciano Bergonzini, *La Svastica a Bologna*

Giuseppe Capriz, *Pensavamo Fosse Un Gioco, Voci di Guerra a Bologna*

Valerio Cutonilli and Rosario Priore, *I Segreti di Bologna – La verità sull'atto terroristico più grave della storia italiana*

Renato Sasdelli, *Fascismo e Tortura a Bologna*

ACKNOWLEDGMENTS

I would like to thank the entire team at Boldwood Books for their help and encouragement in the publication of *The Girl From Bologna*, in particular my lovely editor Emily Yau who has been instrumental in bringing this book to a wider audience.

MORE FROM SIOBHAN DAIKO

We hope you enjoyed reading *The Girl From Bologna*. If you did, please leave a review.

If you'd like to gift a copy, this book is also available as an ebook, hardback, large print, digital audio download and audiobook CD.

Sign up to Siobhan Daiko's mailing list for news, competitions and updates on future books:

https://bit.ly/SiobhanDaikoNews

Explore more hauntingly epic historical fiction from Siobhan Daiko...

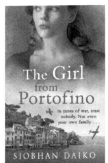

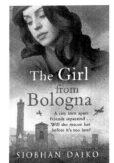

ABOUT THE AUTHOR

Siobhan Daiko is a British historical fiction author. A lover of all things Italian, she lives in the Veneto region of northern Italy with her husband, a Havanese dog and a rescued cat. After a life of romance and adventure in Hong Kong, Australia and the UK, Siobhan now spends her time, when she isn't writing, enjoying her life near Venice.

Visit Siobhan's website: https://siobhandaiko.org/

Siobhan loves to connect with her readers and would be thrilled if you followed her on social media:

Boldw⚭d

Boldwood Books is an award-winning fiction publishing company seeking out the best stories from around the world.

Find out more at www.boldwoodbooks.com

Join our reader community for brilliant books, competitions and offers!

Follow us
@BoldwoodBooks
@BookandTonic

Sign up to our weekly deals newsletter

https://bit.ly/BoldwoodBNewsletter

Printed in Great Britain
by Amazon

37527606R00152